INNOCENCE

KRISTIN MAYER

OTHER BOOKS BY KRISTIN MAYER

AVAILABLE NOW
THE TRUST SERIES
Trust Me
Love Me
Promise Me
Full-length novels in the TRUST series
are also available in audio from Tantor Media.

TWISTED FATE SERIES
White Lies
Black Truth

THE EFFECT SERIES
Ripple Effect
Domino Effect

STAND ALONE NOVELS
Whispered Promises
Bane (Trust Series Spinoff)

JOINT COLLABORATIONS
Finding Forever
(Co-written with Kelly Elliott)

COMING SOON
Untouched Perfection
Flawless Perfection

To my dad, I'll always be your punkin' . . . forever and always.

INNOCENCE

ONE

T HE CLANKING NOISE OF THE cell door signified it was opening. "London, are you ready?"

With shaking hands, I grabbed my bag. One last glance in the mirror showed my caramel eyes were wide and scared. I tucked a strand of chestnut hair behind my ear before turning toward the sweet face of Deborah, the on-duty woman guard. "Yes, I'm ready." My voice was shaky.

I was about to be free.

Free.

The word felt like a vice in my chest. A bittersweet moment. One I longed for, but at the same time didn't deserve for what I was told I had done. Part of me thought I should never be free again if it was true.

"We have your new ID ready as well as some new clothes." Her sweet voice brought me out of my negative thoughts.

Forcing a small smile, I nodded and followed the auburn-haired guard out into the main block. Deborah was kind and always looked out for the best interest of the inmates—unlike others who worked there. Some prison guards were downright terrifying. I learned as long as I minded my own business, didn't complain, and stayed off their radar . . . they ignored me.

An involuntary shiver ran through me as I thought about the more unpleasant memories from my four years in prison. Once I'd been transferred from a medium to minimum-security prison, two and a half years ago, life became easier.

The screams.

The fights.

The having to be on your guard every second.

Closing my eyes, I pushed the memories aside.

It was a small penance to pay in comparison. Four years ago, I'd been sentenced to prison for involuntary manslaughter. Though I have no recollection of the events from the night that changed my life, I served my time.

Doctors believed my lack of memory was due to the impact of the collision. In their terms, I had localized amnesia due to brain swelling. From the photos I saw afterward, the indention of the windshield told the story of how hard I hit. *I flinch at the thought.*

The events of what happened that fateful night were erased. The fog never lifted in the four years I'd been in Aliceville Alabama Federal Prison. From all the evidence presented, there was no doubt I'd been responsible for hitting the boy with my car. My lawyer expressed that, in his opinion, I was lucky to have only gotten four years.

Lucky.

There was nothing *lucky* about what happened.

Taking a deep breath, the bleach smell from cleaning time permeated my nose. For the last time, I cast my eyes over the chow hall as we passed through. Every surface was hard, cold, and a dingy white that never looked clean.

Sterile.

Unfriendly.

Unyielding.

Deborah glanced over her shoulder. "I'm glad you're getting out, London. I know what happened, but you have an innocence about you. You're young and still have your life ahead of you."

I was twenty-four years old. At times, I felt as if I was older and other times younger—not sure where my place was in this world but I desperately wanted to find it . . . feel like I belonged. The problem was, I wasn't sure where to begin. Baby steps. My life was ahead of me, but I'd already served time in prison. That in itself altered me.

The familiar clawing at my chest started. "Thank you. I appreciate how kind you were." Goodbyes were hard for me. Most goodbyes had a finality to them—or at least the ones I'd experienced.

Three days ago, I'd been informed I would be getting out a week early due to a space issue. Only Dad and my best friend knew. They were the only two people I still kept in touch with. Everyone else faded from my life.

I glanced out the window to see the women outside in the yard. *Were any of them my friends?* I hoped so, but the truth hurt. In prison, friends meant survival. We played our part to stay out of the spotlight—to keep any targets off our backs. I never heard from anyone once they were released, which spoke volumes to the depth of friendship.

No one here knew the true me. I wasn't sure I knew who the true me was anymore.

Leaving quietly was for the best.

As I saw a group of ladies at the table I normally sat at, the goodbyes I'd endured four years ago came rushing back. Each one was acutely felt.

Goodbye to my family.

Goodbye to my dance scholarship at Juilliard.

Goodbye to the love of my life.

Goodbye to my friends.

Goodbye to all I knew.

All because of an event I couldn't remember. The night of the accident, while home for the summer from college, I'd been three times over the legal limit for alcohol. It was amazing I was alive. Sometimes I wished the alcohol had finished me off. None of it made sense. I didn't drink because it was too hard on my body for dancing. Occasionally, I had a glass of wine. A bottle of tequila, nearly drained, was on my bed when officers investigated my room. Another bottle found in my car.

I hated tequila.

There was something more to that night—I knew it in the depths of my soul, but there was no proof. My parents and lawyers left no stone unturned. None. At some point, acceptance of my transgressions became eminent in order to try and gain some semblance of myself back.

Focusing on the tile floor, I reined in my emotions. It had been a while since I thought about it all. But, in the scheme of things, I deserved every goodbye I'd been dealt. A boy lost his life because of me. My four-year sentence was nothing compared to the life sentence I'd given him and his family.

The guilt never left me. Slowly, over the years, it chipped away at my soul.

I followed Deborah into the light-blue walled office to complete the next step for my release. The rooms at the front of the prison were the only ones with any color. A pair of jeans and a gray sweatshirt lay on the table along with my new ID and a manila envelope.

Another female guard, Cassie, who was less than friendly through the years, stood in the corner with a scowl on her face. The spiky haircut and stocky stature only added to the apprehension when paired with her body language. On purpose, she would spill her coffee over a place that was recently cleaned or make unneeded noise while we slept.

Needless to say, I was leery of her and she was not pleased I was released early. After the warden gave me the news, I overheard her saying, *"She's a murderer and should not be getting out early."* This guard believed the justice system was too lenient and my sentence was too light. *Murderer* . . . the name would be forever associated with me.

I hated it.

Behind me, Deborah lingered and I was thankful. Cassie stepped forward. "London McNally, please sign your name on the line. Within the manila envelope is your discharge certificate." Cassie huffed and rolled her eyes. "You'll need the certificate to vote again. You'll also find gate money in the amount of fifty dollars. There's a transport waiting outside the gate which will take you to the bus station unless you've made other arrangements."

"My dad, Ken McNally, should be here to take me home." I tucked the escaped hair behind my ear again and looked down.

"Very well. Once you change, Deborah will take you to the gate."

The envelope was shoved in my direction along with the piece of paper. Scribbling my name across the line, I took a deep breath. Cassie snatched up the paperwork and stomped out of the room.

Deborah gestured in my direction. "Go ahead and change. I'll be waiting."

I nodded and the door closed behind me. With shaking hands, I removed my orange scrubs with my inmate number on them. The jeans and sweatshirt were loose fitting as I'd lost weight since coming here. Being a dancer, I had been thin before but could notice a difference. I finger-combed my hair, hoping I looked somewhat presentable.

I gathered the manila envelope. Waiting patiently, Deborah pushed off the wall as I came into the hallway. Silently, I followed her through several doors while feeling perspiration form on my brow. I kept my head down until the sunlight hit my face.

A new life. Everything familiar before would be different now.

I felt as if I was starting over without any sort of guide.

My dad's old red pickup sat in front of the prison. I cleared my dry throat. "That's my dad."

Nervously, Dad got out of his truck. A sense of comfort came over me seeing him in his standard jeans and flannel shirt. He waved, which brought the first genuine smile from me. I raised my hand back. It seemed off to me to wave in front of a prison where I had been incarcerated. All I wanted to do was run into his safe arms, but I refrained, not sure if Deborah needed to tell me anything else.

Deborah held out her hand which I shook. "Good luck, London. I wish you the best."

I looked down and barely said above a whisper, "Thank you."

After Deborah stepped out of the way, I walked toward my dad. There was something about a dad's embrace that made everything better. I couldn't wait to be safe in his arms.

"Hey, London." I paused and turned back Deborah's way. "Don't let the past dictate your future. Rise above it and be better."

"I'll try." Her words warmed me.

Deborah nodded and a tear formed in my eye. Turning, I focused on my dad standing beside his vehicle. My dad was here supporting me—like always. This morning I remembered packing up a picture we took as a family a few weeks before the accident. In the four years since I'd gone to prison, Dad's chestnut hair became speckled with gray. His once carefree face was laced with four years of stress as I thought back to how he looked prior to me being sentenced. Time had taken its toll.

Shortly after coming to Aliceville Alabama Federal Prison, Mom was unable to visit me when she was diagnosed with Dementia. Three and a half years ago was the last time I saw Mom. She'd come with Dad for one of the monthly visitations and hadn't remembered who I was. When I tried to explain, she broke down and screamed things I knew she never meant. *My daughter is at home. My daughter would never end up in prison. My daughter is a good person.*

I never got to say goodbye to her. It happened quickly and we weren't prepared. Doctors said her case was rare with the rate of progression. Normally, the disease moved slower. Part of me wondered if the stress of the trial and my incarceration brought it on. Dad assured me it wasn't the case. I wasn't sure.

Mom now lived in a nursing home. Dad said Mom hardly recognized him anymore. I missed my mom. Over and over again, I wished I said more the last time she'd been coherent—told her how much I loved her, how much she meant to me, how much I wished I could get a redo at life.

Warm arms engulfed me. "I'm glad to have you back, punkin'."

"I missed you too, Dad."

I felt safe, secure, and loved. The familiar scent of wood shavings eased the tenseness in my shoulders.

"Let's get you home and settled. We're having your favorite for dinner."

Giddiness came over me. "Lasagna?"

Dad gave me a wink. "You'll have to wait and see."

As we eased out onto the road, the inner lightness I'd felt ebbed. My gut churned, wondering what it would be like being out of prison.

Taking a deep breath, I tried to embrace what was to come . . . going home.

Home.

TWO

THE OLDIES STATION PLAYED LOW in the background as we drove the hour and a half to my hometown of Guin, Alabama. Air whooshed through the cab with the windows halfway rolled down. It felt like our trips we took to the wood mills for Dad's furniture business. As the miles passed us by, Dad told me about the happenings for nearly everyone and everything in our small town. Guin was a population of less than fifteen hundred people.

Everyone knew everything about anything of interest.

The only subject not discussed—my ex-boyfriend, Charles. Four months after incarceration, he broke up with me.

The memory assailed me as we passed a lake where we spent our summers swimming.

Charles sat across from me with the plexi-glass divider between us. I missed his embrace. We loved each other and knew we'd see each other through the storm.

A storm I caused.

We were the real thing happily-ever-after's were made of. Eagerly I picked up the two-way phone. "I miss you. They say in a little over a year,

I'll be eligible for minimum security. We won't have to deal with this glass."

Charles gave me a bittersweet look. "That's good news, London."

There was something off in his tone. I knew Charles as well as I knew myself. "What's wrong?" My brows scrunched in concern. Was his mom, Caroline, okay? Had something happened to my best friend, Millie?

Thrusting his hand through his blond hair, Charles looked torn, upset maybe. "Baby, I mean, London." This was bad. My heart felt like it was stuck in my throat. "We need to break up while you're in here."

I gasped. "Why? Charles, I love you."

"I love you, too. It's re-election year for Dad. Our relationship is causing issues. Attention is coming back to your parents again." The words seemed hard for him to speak as his eyes cast down.

Charles' dad was a senator. I knew this would be a problem, though everyone assured me it wouldn't.

My lip trembled. "Is this permanent?"

Charles eyes shot to mine. The warm chocolate seemed dulled. "No. I'll wait for you. I'll figure this out. After this is over, we'll be together. We'll get through this."

There seemed more to his promise than he was telling me.

"Okay. Promise me if something changes, you'll tell me."

"I promise."

Charles put his hand to the window. "Together, baby. You and me, like we've always talked about. You'll be the only girl I'll ever love."

"You and me. I love you, too."

I bit my lip to the point of pain as I cleared the memory. It was supposed to only be for show until I got out. At the time, I understood and wanted to make his life easier regardless of how much it hurt. Nothing had been farther from the truth.

Lies.

All lies.

One month after things ended, I asked Dad if Charles was seeing anyone. By the way the blood drained from his face I knew the answer, but insisted on him telling me. Charles started dating Rachel Graves right after we broke up. Her family was well connected. We'd gone to school together. The news stung, and from that point forward, I never asked about Charles again. The loss of the love of my life was an ache that could not be soothed. Some things were better off locked away than dealt with when nothing could be done.

Now, it was time to hear what I had avoided after all this time.

"Does Charles still live in Guin?" I needed to be prepared if there was a chance I'd run into him.

Dad winced. That wasn't good. Taking a deep breath, he ran a hand through his hair. "Punkin' . . ."

"I know, Dad. Shoot me straight. I need to know."

He glanced my way for a second. "He's still seeing Rachel. They've been dating all this time. From what folks say, it's pretty serious."

I dug my fingernails into my right palm. The last time I saw Charles he said he would wait for me forever—he loved me. He promised to tell me himself if something ever changed. Maybe he was cheating on me all along. Buried anger bubbled to the surface and I pushed it away.

"Punkin'—"

"It's okay, Dad. I promise. I needed to know."

Dad squeezed my knee. "Four years doesn't change how your mom and I feel about you. Nothing could." I gave him a weak smile. "London, your mom loves you. She may not remember who we are, but she loves us."

"I know, Dad. I know."

We lapsed into silence. The city seemed untouched as we drove through. Tears burned my eyes as I focused on anything but memories of the laughs, the dreams, the friendships. There was so much promise back in those days.

Dancing had been my future.

The world had made sense.

Before I was able to shake it away, another memory assaulted me. One I hadn't thought about since it happened.

Charles was having a party at the lake. I was late since I was just getting back into town after a dance competition. Since Charles wasn't able to leave while the party was in full swing, Millie picked me up.

"Girl, you kicked ass. First place. I bet Juilliard is pleased since you just accepted the scholarship."

"They are. The head instructor was at the competition. She said she looked forward to instructing me this fall and I had beautiful lines."

Millie danced in her seat. "I'm so proud of you! We're going to have so much fun living together during college. Except I'll be getting fat while I'm sitting at a desk studying."

"I'll drag you out for runs."

"Deal!"

Millie was headed to nursing school near Juilliard. Healing people was Millie's passion. Selfless to the core. It was beyond lucky we both got into our first school of choice and they were so close. Charles was attending school about an hour away which was good. We wouldn't be far apart. We chatted about our new place we were renting. Mom was making curtains to spruce it up. The whole apartment was about the size of two medium-sized bedrooms. It was perfect.

The car pulled up. Charles stood on the front porch with Rachel Price watching him. She was never too far away from whatever we were doing. Always present. I hardly knew her.

"There's my beautiful girl." Charles walked to me. I could tell he had been drinking. "Want something to celebrate?"

He gave me a kiss. Hard liquor was the dominant smell and taste. "Just you."

"Good answer." Turning to the crowd on the porch, he announced, "Isn't my girl the most beautiful girl ever?" Charles was drunker than I thought. Nuzzling my ear, he said, "You'll be forever mine, London."

Forever turned out to be not long at all.

I shook my head to clear all the negativity from it as we left town. Millie and I rode our bikes all through here growing up. Charles and I were Homecoming Queen and King in the parade. In our senior class, we'd been voted most likely to succeed. Looking back, I thought we were happy. I still couldn't see any warnings that there was something wrong with us.

Nothing made sense.

The city gave way to our dirt road. We lived on a small farm just outside of town. Dad made furniture and boarded horses. He'd grown up in Montana on a horse ranch with his parents who had passed when I was a child. I don't remember much of them since I was five when they died in a car accident.

The truck shifted to park and I looked at our white farmhouse with the silver tin roof. The memories were filled with love. The swing blew in the wind on the wraparound porch. Mom would tell me stories under the night sky out here while fireflies danced about.

Charles—I refused to think of him right now and any memories of him here.

The barn became my sole focus. "Is Sparkles in her stall?"

"She's waiting for you. Last weekend she practiced all her tricks for you." My father gave me a warm look as I bounded out of the truck and made a beeline for the redwood barn. In the first stall stood my majestic black Quarter Horse. She was a gift from Mom and Dad for my tenth birthday.

Sparkles stopped eating and looked at me. I closed the gap. "Hey, girl. I'm back." Tossing her head, Sparkles whinnied. I touched her jaw and leaned my face against hers, the familiar soft fur a soothing balm. "I know I've been gone. I'm so sorry. I'm sorry for everything." Tears rolled down my face. Sparkles nuzzled me. "I know, girl. I know. I missed you too."

"Well, isn't this a sight for sore eyes."

I whipped around at the familiar voice of my best friend, Millie Craig. She was five feet, four inches of blonde hair, blue-eyed sass. Millie was the only friend who hadn't abandoned me. When Charles left me, so did the majority of my friends. No one wanted to cross paths with the Graves'.

Because of nursing school in New York, Millie was only able to see me when she came home which was for a couple of weeks in the summer. We wrote letters to each other every week to stay in touch.

Millie walked up to me and engulfed me in a hug. "It's good to have you back, London. It's so good. I missed you."

"Missed you too—so much. What are you doing here?" I pulled back. Millie worked in New York City at a local hospital.

She wagged her eyebrows. "In three days you are looking at the newest nurse at Northwest Medical in Winfield."

Excitement bubbled through me. *My best friend was here. Close to me.* "What? Are you serious?" Winfield was only about fifteen minutes from Guin and a smaller hospital. Millie had graduated early and then worked her way up at an exponential pace. "You loved New York City. Why didn't you tell me?"

"I didn't want to jinx anything. With Momma being sick, it was time." Recently Dorothy Craig was diagnosed with stage-two breast cancer. The chemo treatments were intense.

I gave my friend another hug. "Let me know if you guys need anything. I'm here for you."

Dad walked in the barn with a grin on his face as Millie pulled back. Being home for only a few minutes showed me how much I isolated myself in prison. It hurt knowing what I caused myself to miss out on all this time. He put his arms around each of our shoulders. "Why don't we go in the house? Verna made some of her famous lasagna for us."

An unladylike sniffle escaped. "I knew you made lasagna. Best welcome home meal a daughter could ask for."

Verna was a friend of the family who helped Dad out a lot since Mom was sick.

Thinking of all the changes, I hoped I still fit in. Guilt assuaged me at the selfish thought. The Dorsey family no longer had a son because of me. My thoughts and emotions felt like a pendulum moving from one extreme to the other.

Millie leaned forward. "I brought cookie ice cream for dessert."

"My favorite. You guys are spoiling me."

Millie and Dad chuckled.

Shards of happiness beamed through the dark skies of my soul. A sickening feeling came over me. *Did I deserve to be happy?* I wasn't sure.

Prison, in some ways, was easier than being free. At least I knew I was paying for what I had done and not enjoying life. Four years for someone's life seemed trivial.

THREE

"THANKS FOR COMING, MILLIE."

We stood on the front porch, hugging as the stars lit up the night sky. "Of course, I'd be here, London. How are you doing?"

Zipping her lightweight blue jacket, Millie watched me closely.

I glanced back toward the kitchen where Dad insisted on cleaning up. "I'm okay. I feel out of place, but I'm trying. My feelings are all over the place. Feeling guilty and happy. I don't know what I'm feeling."

"It takes time. I'm here for you. Did your dad tell you about Charles?"

That was why I loved Millie. She always had my back. Though the news hurt, Millie knew it would be worse if I was told when I couldn't process everything first. "Yeah, can we talk about that later? I'm exhausted."

Millie gave me an understanding look before gazing back out into the sky. I kicked at a board on the front porch. "I was thinking about visiting Alec's grave tomorrow. To say I'm sorry." Millie was quiet . . . too quiet. Doubt crept into my mind about going. "Do you think that's a bad idea?"

Millie leaned against the porch. "No, sweetie, I don't. I can't imagine what you're going through. The adjustment. The guilt. It's a lot."

I nodded, at a loss for words.

"London, try to forgive yourself."

"I'm trying."

We stood there a few minutes when a yawn escaped. "We have forever now to catch up. I'll let you rest and stop by tomorrow."

"Night, Millie."

Giving me a quick hug, Millie headed to her car. I watched the taillights disappear and then was bathed in the starry night sky. A shooting star swept across the sky as the wind rustled my hair. I refused to think of a wish. It was something my mother and I always did and hurt too much to do it without her.

Maybe one day.

Clattering from the house brought my attention back to Dad. So much had changed. Dad was now self-sufficient. Before, Mom took care of everything.

I walked to the door and leaned against it as Dad put the last of the dishes in the dishwasher. The house still looked the same. He hummed to himself. The white daisy curtains brought the corners of my mouth up. Mom and I picked the fabric out one Saturday afternoon when we'd gone to town. The sewing lessons which followed weren't so successful. Mom stayed patient with me the entire time. I missed those moments.

Turning my way, Dad gave me a loving smile. "I can't believe you're here."

"Me either."

Another yawn slipped from me.

"Let's get some sleep. I'll lock up." Dad gave me a quick kiss. "Night, punkin'."

"Night, Dad."

I trudged up the stairs to my old bedroom. Nudging the door open, I peered inside after flipping on the light. The corkboard across the room was filled with pictures of my old life—mainly Charles and Millie.

Dance trophies lined the shelf which ran a few feet under the ceiling. Dance shoes were neatly lined up in the closet.

I walked farther into the room.

The scarf Charles bought me from Italy lay on the back of the chair. The stuffed animal he'd given me was on the bed where I left it.

My reflection caught in the mirror of my white-wood vanity. Dark hair like my father's spilled over my shoulders. Haunted chestnut eyes watched me through my thin frame. A picture of me laughing with Charles' hands wrapped my waist was a stark difference from what I saw now.

The room was like a tomb.

A stack of papers caught my attention. I swallowed hard and took a steadying breath as I recognized them as my scholarship renewal at Juilliard. Everywhere I looked, I couldn't escape my past.

I ran my fingers over a picture of the dance studio at Juilliard on the mirror. When the accident happened, it was my college summer break. As soon as my conviction was announced, my scholarship was pulled. The papers caught my attention again and I shoved them in a drawer. Quickly I changed into my soft, pink pajamas. Tomorrow, I'd box all the memories up. Start fresh. For now, the closet would keep everything out of sight—out of mind.

The teddy bear Charles gave me for our one-month anniversary was the first to claim a spot in the closet. Dad knocked at the door as I pulled the covers over me. "Are you getting settled okay?"

"I am. Thanks, Dad." The familiar goodnight routine soothed the anxiety my walk down memory lane caused.

Dad looked around the room and then back to me. "I wasn't

sure what you'd want to keep. We can box up some stuff tomorrow if you want."

"That sounds great. Love you." Dad got me, he always had.

"Love you, too."

As I closed my eyes, I took a deep breath. I survived my first partial day out. Sleep claimed me before long.

"London, wakeup, sweetheart. London, I'm here."

Charles' warm voice was like a caress. My eyes fluttered open, met by warm loving eyes.

He sighed and released the tension in his shoulders. "Thank God, you pulled through."

"Pulled through what?" My voice came out hoarse. There was something under my nose. I touched the obstruction, wanting it removed. Charles stopped me. Was it an oxygen line? Was I in a hospital?

Charles pressed his lips to mine. A sneer formed on his face as his eyes became evil. "You pulled through so you can pay for all you've done."

"What?" My heartbeat thudded in my ears. I tried to move. Concrete filled my limbs, keeping me immobile.

Charles held a photo in front of my face. His breath smelled of alcohol. A boy lying unnatural-like underneath my left front car tire. It was terrible. My stomach lurched.

He tossed it aside revealing a new image.

A picture of me bloody from the crash. A bottle of alcohol in the passenger seat. Bile rose in my throat.

A new image appeared.

The mother of the boy knelt down at his body, crying. Make it stop! Make it stop!

The images were gruesome. Uncontrollable sobs left my body. I never wanted this to happen. I was so sorry. So so sorry. I never meant for someone to get hurt.

"This is all because of you, London. All your fault." Charles spit in my face.

I sat up gasping for air. My skin clammy. *My room.* I was in my room. A dream. It was just a dream. Desperate for light to banish the darkness, I searched for the lamp switch. A soft glow bathed the room as I heaved oxygen into my lungs.

A dream. Only a dream.

Pulling my knees to my chest, I worked on calming myself. Every time I had the dream, it always affected me like that.

Through the court hearing, I had seen the images of the crime scene repeatedly. They would be forever burned into my mind. They lingered not far from my thoughts, waiting to torture me. It had been a while since a nightmare showcased them.

Would I ever be free?

I laid back down and pulled the covers over my head. Slowly, I counted each deep breath. My mind filled with soft grass swaying, the clouds moving, anything peaceful to erase the images.

I'm so sorry, Alec. I'm so sorry. Please forgive me.

FOUR

STANDING AT THE GATE, A sea of gravestones spread before me. My hands shook. At the burial, the Dorsey family demanded I not be there. I understood and respected their wishes, but always felt the need to give my last respects.

A car drove by, slowing down and then speeding up, causing my stomach to turn at the nasty look I received. I'm sure people already knew I was back. Guin was a small town. Everyone knew everything. It was almost an archaic feeling at times. Growing up, Mom and Dad instilled in me to stay out of rumors. If I was supposed to know, the person involved would let me know. How true those words were. Hopefully in the time I was gone the town became more open-minded, so I could integrate myself back into society with minimal blow back.

Part of me wished we had moved, but Mom loved the land and made us promise to never take her from it. Dad still held hope Mom would be able to come back to the farm eventually. I knew that was a pipe dream, but Dad stayed in Guin just in case.

I forced myself to push open the gate while my stomach knotted again. Dad offered to come with me, but it was something I needed to do on my own. I chose to walk to the cemetery in order to get my thoughts in order since we only lived two miles away. Of course, he understood. Part of me wanted Dad to come with me. However, these were my transgressions to bear, not his. Alec deserved my undivided attention.

The morning still held on to a slight chill from the colder than normal summer Alabama was experiencing. It wouldn't matter if it was one-hundred degrees; I would be cold being at the gravesite. Guilt assuaged me. Carefully, I wound through the graves. Dad told me where Alec was laid to rest.

An eerie calm came over the place. A hundred feet from my destination, I stopped to gather myself. My trial had been expedient and I was sentenced by the end of June. The lawyers were shocked at how quickly everything happened.

I can do this. Alec deserves to hear how sorry I am.

Unbidden, my feet unwillingly moved closer. My stomach knotted. Because of me, a boy was here. The horridness of the situation still had a hard time connecting with my brain—that I actually was responsible.

I stopped in front of the tombstone belonging to the nine-year-old boy who had died a little over four years ago.

My hand drifted to my mouth as a sob broke free. I couldn't stand, I collapsed at the foot of the grave. *This was my fault.* All my fault. Laying my hand at the foot of the grave, where the gravel outlined the perimeter, I poured my heart out. "I'm so sorry, Alec. I'm so sorry for the choices I made. I know sorry doesn't bring you back, but I am. There's not a day that goes by I don't think of you. I wish I could change it all. I—I—I can't remember what happened." Another sob erupted. My eyes clenched tight. "I wish I could take it back." More sobs. "Trade my life for yours."

He had been a boy full of life. A person with his whole future ahead of him. During the summers, I babysat him a few times. We would play fort in the backyard. Soldiers on the coffee table. Undercover spies in the house.

And because of a choice I don't remember . . . I took it all.

Tears flowed freely. "I'm so sorry, Alec. So so sorry."

"What are you doing here?" I jerked around at the menacing voice. Alec's mom, Farrah, stood there. The loss had aged the once vibrant woman. "You murderer! What are you doing here?"

"I-I-I came to g-g-give my r-r-respects."

"Get out of here! You killed my son! You killed my son! MUR-DERER!" Farrah waved her hands, stomping toward me. "You don't deserve to be here. Someone told me you were here. Get away from my boy! Stay away!"

Abruptly, I stood not knowing what do. The anguish on Farrah's face ripped through me. "I'm so sorry, Farrah. I wish it had been me."

"MURDERER!" Farrah marched up and slapped me. The sting lit the side of my face on fire. I stepped back, distancing myself as I cradled my cheek. "Don't come back here! Never come back here! You don't deserve to be okay after all you did."

"I won't. I didn't mean to upset you."

I stumbled out of the cemetery while Farrah screamed more. I'd never meant for any of this to happen. My pace picked up to a jog, then a run. All I wanted was the pain to go away. For Alec to be here. Mom to be okay. To dance at Juilliard. Have the love of my life by my side.

For June third to have never happened.

All of it to go away.

I slowed at the gate when I realized where I'd run to. *The Paddington's*. I was at Charles' childhood home. My home away from home. Sweat poured off my brow after running the four miles. In prison, I'd managed to stay somewhat in shape, but nothing like I used to be. Leaning over, I eased the burning in my lungs.

Why was I here? I needed to leave. Showing up here would only cause me more heartache, especially if Charles was home. Where was he living? Was he living with Rachel? I stared at the gate wondering why our love wasn't enough.

You're the only girl for me, London.

On countless occasions, Charles whispered those exact words to me. What else had been lies between us? There was no way our love was as strong as I thought with how fast he moved on.

Wanting to leave before I was seen, I turned just as a car pulled up. I jumped, not expecting anyone. I stopped breathing, praying it wasn't Charles. When the face became visible, I released the air I'd held. Caroline, Charles' mom, eased up in her Lexus as I moved out of the way.

"London?"

Would she want me here? This had to be strange with me showing up unannounced to my ex's house. The stress affected me. I started to back away. "I'm so sorry. I was at the cemetery. Then, I ran and I wasn't thinking. I'll leave now. I didn't mean to show up uninvited."

I turned to start jogging when Caroline called after me. "London, please wait." Stopping, I closed my eyes ready for anything. A car door opened. Caroline was always kind to me, but being convicted of murder could change how a person looked at someone. All of the loss proved that.

A hand gently pressed on my shoulder and I turned around to face her. "Come up to the house. Charles is gone until tomorrow. I thought your letter said you were getting released next week? I planned to come by your dad's place to welcome you home."

Letting out a sigh of relief, I watched her tentatively. Caroline and I were close and maybe somewhat of a relationship with her could be salvaged between us. I missed our long talks. She had been like a second mom to me.

Caroline looked me over and a loving smile graced her lips. Her crisp pink suit reminded me of something Jackie Kennedy would wear. Not a blonde hair out of place. Caroline was the picture-perfect image of a senator's wife.

"Can you come up to the house, London? I would love to catch up." I'm sure I looked half-crazy in my jeans and light jacket, sweating and all my makeup cried away.

I took a deep breath. "I can only stay for a few minutes before I need to head back to Dad's. I told him I'd only be gone for a few hours."

"Of course, dear. Would you like for me to drive you back?"

"I appreciate it, but I think I'll walk back. I like the exercise. It feels good to be outside."

She gave me a tender look as she slid into the driver's seat of her silver car. "Of course, London."

After getting in, we drove up to the large estate as Caroline talked about various changes. The three-story home always reminded me of a fairytale with the large white columns and black shutters. The water fountain in the middle of the circle drive only added to the magnificence.

Getting out of the car, Caroline waited for me at the bottom of the steps. "Can I give you a hug, London? I've missed you."

Maybe there was hope for me to stay in touch with Caroline.

My smile was genuine. "Yes, of course."

Caroline wrapped me in a hug. "Welcome home, London."

"Thank you, Caroline. I mean Mrs. Paddington." Charles and I weren't together anymore. I had to remind myself. I looked around for her husband, Charles Senior. Since Charles was named after his father, this was how Caroline differentiated between the two.

Pulling back, Caroline looked at me. "It's still Caroline. I know things got difficult between you and Charles, but I never stopped thinking of you as one of my own. And I know Charles Senior feels the same way."

Tears welled in my eyes. Charles left me. I thought it had been because of his family, but maybe it was his choice after all. I wasn't as close with Charles' dad, but no one really was.

"You and Charles Senior will always have a special place in my heart."

"Let's go have some hot tea and catch up."

I followed Caroline into the pristinely designed home. It felt as though I stepped back into the Civil War times with the ornate furniture and lavish fixtures. Fresh flowers could always be found strategically placed throughout the home, giving off a divine smell. Not much had changed since I left.

We entered the study done in rustic wood walls. Charles and I did our homework together in this room. A few times we'd made out in here, but never anything more. That was always saved for the bedroom.

I pushed the thoughts aside as I sat on the floral loveseat with Caroline. The aroma of hot jasmine tea filled the air as she poured us a cup from the sterling silver teapot.

At first Caroline visited every once in a while, but it brought too much unwanted attention to me at the prison—making me more of a target. I'd suggested the visits be limited. Instead they'd sent me things to make my life easier. "Thank you for all the care packages you sent. I know you received my thank you letters, but I wanted to tell you in person."

Caroline took a sip of tea. "I know, dear. I wish we could have done more, but didn't want to overstep my bounds and bring you more heartache. When Charles told us of his decision to end things, it broke my heart. Charles Senior and I weren't expecting the break-up. I asked if it was because of the election, but Charles assured us it wasn't. I still wish things had gone differently."

I worked on schooling my shock at this news. All of this was drastically different from what Charles told me, but now made sense. He needed a scapegoat and his parents fit the bill. Charles knew I loved his family and wouldn't want them hurting. With me behind bars, what could I do once he broke ties and dated the town's debutant? If I said anything, I would be the scorned murderer behind bars.

The illusion of love I'd known began to dissolve.

I steadied myself. "Me, too. But we can't change the past. If only my memory would come back."

Caroline scrunched her eyebrows. "Have you thought about hypnosis?"

"No. Maybe I'll look into it. I've tried to remember something . . . anything from that night, but it's a black swirl. The doctors don't believe it will ever come back." I looked down at the steam as it rose from the cup. "I wish I could remember. I've seen all the photos, but without the memories, it's hard to feel like it was me."

"I know. I can't imagine."

The silence lingered. "Dad told me Charles has been seeing Rachel. I hope me being here won't cause issues."

Caroline grimaced and I felt sick as the knots in my stomach tightened. "Of course, it won't. Charles has decided to pursue politics. He's running for mayor next fall and seeing where it takes him from there. His father thinks he can do it. Charles and Rachel have been quite involved in the community."

Hearing their names together was hard. *Charles and Rachel.* It used to be Charles and London. A criminal background didn't lend too well on the campaign trail. More and more made sense as the pieces of the puzzle fell into place. *Maybe fate brought me here to give me closure on something.*

I needed to respond and thought of something politically correct. "Charles was always brilliant at anything he set his mind to. I'm glad things are working out for him."

"What are your plans?"

Thankful for the change in subject, I sipped my tea. "Tomorrow, I'm looking for a job. Help Dad out on the farm and start over—or at least as much as I can, considering."

"Let me know if there's something I can help you with. I'm heading out of town early in the morning tomorrow to meet Charles Senior in DC. I can't wait to tell him you're out. He'll want to see you next time he's in town." The sincerity of Caroline's voice confirmed why I'd subconsciously run here. They were my second home . . . they still felt like family.

Commotion came from the hallway. "Mom! I have news! We came back early!" Excitement filled his voice.

His voice.

The voice I knew better than my own.

I froze.

This wasn't happening.

Female giggles followed and then another woman's voice I hadn't recognized. A sickness flooded over me as I placed my teacup on the table then tightly gripped my kneecaps to stay focused on the pain lacerating into my skin versus the red-hot poker barreling through my heart.

Everything happened in slow motion. A shocked look crossed Caroline's face as she looked at me with concern. The doors burst open before I had a chance to make an escape. In unison, two people said, "WE'RE ENGAGED!"

The bile rose in my throat. I was going to be sick. *Keep it together. Escape as soon as possible.*

Charles and Rachel walked in the room looking at each other . . . in love. A fresh wave of nausea hit me. Her parents followed shortly after. It was impossible not to stare at him. Charles was always good looking. His blond hair was shorter, clean cut versus the slightly more tumbled look he used to wear.

Engaged.

They were engaged.

Look away, London. Look away. I wasn't able to listen to the voice in my head as I saw the moment meant for us.

Charles threw it all away for the political life.

You're the only girl for me, London.

In the moment I was witnessing, nothing could be further from the truth.

Caroline rose and walked in front of me, hiding me from their sight. They were so wrapped up in each other, I'd gone unnoticed thankfully. She spoke with modest excitement. "That's wonderful news. Congratulations. Let's celebrate in the atrium with some champagne."

Thank you, Caroline. Hopefully, I'd be able to slip out. Hearing Charles' warm voice shot daggers to my heart.

"Isn't it wonderful, Caroline? Oh, we've been waiting for this moment for so long." Rachel's mom paused. "You have company? Oh . . . I heard you were released."

It was obvious Rachel's mom, Agatha, recognized me. The snarl on her lip obvious evidence of her feelings for me. Caroline protectively stood in front of me.

My hands shook. Charles stepped around Caroline. "London? You're out?"

On shaky legs, I stood and forced a calm façade. "Charles. Rachel. Congratulations. I ran into Caroline on a run. Mr. and Mrs. Price, it's nice to see you."

Agatha peered at me with her steely-gray eyes. Why I felt the need to explain myself, I wasn't sure. Caroline invited me up to the house after she found me at the gate. Charles was supposed to be gone. Rachel looked at me with a masked hatred, a trace of indignation on her face.

Stay pleasant.

This isn't your life anymore, London.

Rachel hung on Charles more possessively, her long black hair looking bouncy like a shampoo commercial. Rachel was always a pretty girl in school who wanted to be known and adored by the masses. Charles' career ambitions, which no doubt included more than the mayor's office, would accomplish that for her.

Charles' warm chocolate eyes melted and his features were soft—like he used to look at me, only sending the knife deeper into me. A stark contrast to the dream that still lingered.

An awkward silence fell on us. Caroline cleared her throat, but I spoke first. "I need to be leaving to get home to Dad. I was released early and wanted to thank Caroline, but don't want to intrude on this happy occasion. Again, congratulations."

"Let me see you out, London." Caroline's calming nature kept the situation from spiraling out of control.

I followed her to the front, ready to be out of this awkward situation. I never wanted to be in the same room as them again if at all possible. There was too much history there. Maybe someday I wouldn't feel the hurt. Until my heart mended some, it was best to stay away. Nerves overtook me as I heard my heartbeat pounding in my ears.

Emotionally, I was done for the day.

We reached the door and Caroline gave me a quick hug. "Call me and we can do lunch. I'm sorry about that. They weren't supposed to be back until tomorrow. I know it's hard."

Hard was an understatement, but she wasn't the person to share my sorrows with. This was supposed to be a happy occasion for the Paddington's. "It's okay. I need to get going. Thank you, Caroline."

"Anytime, London."

I jogged down the driveway, needing away from this place. Seeing Rachel and Charles happy made everything real. Charles moved on. He chose someone else to be his wife . . . have his children . . . share his life with.

It was time for me to move on.

Nearly making it to the gate, Charles called, "London, wait! Please!" I stopped and closed my eyes, slowly turning around. When was this day going to be over? There was nothing left for me to give.

"I had no idea you were out." I wasn't sure how to respond. "You look beautiful." I blanched at his comment, eyes going wide. "London, hell, I'm sorry. I shouldn't have said that. I saw you and it was like four years ago. It's hard not feeling . . . something."

He left me. He chose to leave me. I only nodded instead of saying those things which would expose me and further my humiliation. We needed a subject change. "Caroline says you're running for mayor. Congratulations."

An indiscernible look crossed his face. "I am."

He took a step closer and the familiar pull to be near to him coursed through my body. It was the ingrained natural reaction since Charles was all I knew. We'd been each other's first kiss, lost our virginity to each other, experienced everything . . . together. I wanted to take a step closer, but that was wrong. He'd left me. He was engaged. Charles pledged his undying love to someone else.

"London, we weren't supposed to be home until tomorrow. I would have never come here if I'd known. London, I want—"

I raised my hand and talked over him. This wasn't healthy. He had a fiancée. "This is your parents' home. I won't stop by anymore and make it awkward for you and Rachel. I'm okay, Charles. Now that I'm out, I can start over. I'm starting over."

"London—"

I took a step back and Charles took a step forward. This needed to stop before my heart was totally obliterated in the emotional blender. "No, I get it, I do. Charles . . ." I paused. "I thought at one point our love would be enough, but sometimes it's not."

"London—"

I held up my hands. "Please, Charles. Nothing else needs to be said. I won't be a problem for you or Rachel. Regardless of what happened that night, I'm still me."

"I didn't think that, London. I never thought that."

For some reason, after all this time, it helped seeing the sincerity on Charles' face. "Thanks for that. Congrats, Charles. You deserve to be happy." I turned and jogged away. Forcing the tears to say at bay, I quickened my gate.

He called after me, but I pressed forward. There was nothing left to be said. Charles was my past. As I drew closer to home, I focused on tomorrow. I'd find a job, focus on helping at the farm, and try to live.

FIVE

"**D**ID YOU STILL WANT TO go into town today?" Dad's voice interrupted the packing binge of my room. So far, five boxes were filled of memories I hoped faded. I was nearly done.

I taped the last full box before stopping. Dad was freshly dressed for the day in his normal attire. "Yes, I wanted to look for a job, if that's okay."

"Punkin', you know you don't have to work."

"I know, but I need to work. It will help me move forward and be productive with my time."

He nodded his head. That was another thing we had in common; neither of us could remain idle. In prison, I volunteered for anything that wouldn't bring attention to me. It kept me busy and in the good graces of the warden.

Dad lifted the box. "Let's take these to the barn and then we can head in."

"Sounds perfect."

I glanced around my nearly-bare room. A fresh start. Everything felt lighter, cleaner and I knew I would survive.

Picking up one of the boxes, we headed down to the barn. Sparkles whinnied at us as we passed her. "Hey, girl, I'll bring you a treat on my way out."

We placed the first load of boxes in the back of the tack room. *Out of sight. Out of mind.* I grabbed a handful of oats and brought them to Sparkles. She eagerly ate them. "Tomorrow, we'll go for a ride. You and me. How does that sound?"

She moved her head in acknowledgment and I laughed. Dad always thought Sparkles understood what I said. We had a connection. She had learned her tricks at incredible speed. We were bonded for life.

After finishing with the boxes, we drove into town. A slight unease came over me as I thought about facing all the people . . . knowing they would be judging me somehow someway. Alec was like a grandchild to so many. *I was too for that matter.*

Dad updated me on the furniture he was building and the different horses he boarded. My mind went on autopilot. Things felt normal, but I wondered if it was an illusion.

Dad and I never talked about his thoughts on the accident. I knew he loved me and stood by me. The thought of what the answer could be scared me to death. Every time I got the courage to ask, I let it die on my tongue. Sometimes knowledge wasn't power. Sometimes it did irreparable damage.

Shifting the truck to park, Dad gave me a wink. "What time do you want me to pick you up? I plan on heading back home to work after I pick up supplies unless you want me to hang around."

"I'm good. Millie's picking me up at three to bring me back if that works for you."

"Sounds perfect. I got you something." It had been a while since I'd gotten a gift. We were limited in prison and only the necessities were allowed. He pulled out a phone from the glove compartment. "I got you a new cell phone. Just call if you need anything.

I programmed Millie's and my numbers in. I'm only a phone call away."

"Thanks, Dad." I clutched the cell phone. "This means a lot."

To be cared for by someone else wasn't a feeling I was accustomed to after four years of looking out for myself.

Dad patted my knee. "You're home now, London. You're home. That's all that matters."

"Love you, Dad."

"Love you too, punkin'."

Giving Dad a kiss on the cheek I got out of the truck. I needed a few minutes to collect my thoughts before I spoke to anyone. After keeping my emotions at bay, now that I let them out, they hit me like a storm.

I needed a game plan.

On a nearby bench, I sat on the outskirts and took everything in. Tried to familiarize myself with a place I once called home. So many things were the same. Mrs. Patterson was walking her dog. As she passed the bench in front of the old-fashioned barbershop where Mr. Stewart and Mr. Lambert sat, Mrs. Patterson handed them a donut she bought from the bakery. I smiled thinking about the times I sat on the bench with the men. They talked about all the city's happenings and how whippersnappers today weren't appreciative for the things they had.

Taking a deep breath in, I saw the owner of the Gazette, Mr. Harvey, sweeping his portion of the sidewalk. After that, I knew he would start polishing the window letters for the Guin Gazette.

The comforting familiarity brought a genuine smile to my face. Life was going to be okay. Everything was going to work out. These people were like my family too.

Standing, I got my thoughts together as coffee aromas wafted through the air. First, I'd wander the town and see who was hiring. From there, I'd decide where to go first. Seeing all the familiar stores brought a smile to my face.

I was home. And with any luck, I would be employed.

"I'M SORRY, LONDON, but we're not hiring," Marion Fisk said as she gave me a sympathetic look and patted her flour-coated apron.

This was the third rejection I'd gotten. I glanced over to the *Help Wanted* sign. The sign clearly indicated she was hiring, like the other two jobs I inquired about.

Marion owned the bakery. She'd known my family forever . . . so had Bob at the lumber store and Gwinnett at the doctor's office.

"Mrs. Fisk, can you be honest with me?" Marion wasn't correcting me. Before I left, she always insisted I called her by Marion not Mrs. Fisk.

Something was wrong. No one asked the normal conversational questions. The town may have been physically familiar, but the residents were different. Or maybe different only toward me. Deep down I knew what was happening. I'd feared it with Guin being a small town.

"I'll try, London."

I sat at the nearby table as Marion walked around the counter. "Why can't you hire me? Is something going on that I don't know about? Please tell me."

I figured I would be somewhat estranged from the community as I proved myself, but this was more extreme than I was expecting.

Marion looked at the door nervously before sitting in the chair opposite me. We were alone in the shop. No one could see us from this table with the huge display of cakes behind us. "London, I can't hire you. And I doubt anyone will in this town. Someone is doing a damn good job of making sure that happens. It's like you've been blacklisted."

Blacklisting me? The blood drained from my face. I rubbed my sweaty palms on my jeans. "Who? Is it the Graves?"

The Graves owned most of the town buildings that people rented. They were powerful and well connected.

"The note didn't specify. I'll lose my lease—my income. Your family means the world to me, but I can't risk my business." Marion looked around again and lowered her voice. "London, please be careful."

Be careful? A sour taste entered my mouth. Barely above a whisper, I asked, "What do you mean?"

"Is there anywhere else you can go, away from Guin?" Her hand touched mine.

The words spun in my head.

Leave?

Now?

After all this time?

"I don't understand." The words were sandpaper in my mouth.

"Someone or maybe it's more than one. I don't know. I had a note under my door. The note stated I had to destroy it after I read it or they would take everything from me. I know the right thing to do is go to the authorities, but I can't take the risk. I'm so sorry. I shredded the letter as soon as I read it." There was pure terror in her voice. Bob and Gwinnett were nervous while I was in their shop this morning too.

I grabbed her hand. "Don't take a risk because of me. You have your granddaughter to think about. She still lives with you, right?"

Marion's daughter died of cancer seven years ago. She was the sole provider to her grandchild, Ingrid.

"You have always been a special girl. I'm so sorry."

I stood, having a feeling I shouldn't linger. "Thank you for telling me. Tell Ingrid I said hello. I always enjoyed watching her. "

"Thank you, London. I will. I wish you the best."

I left in a daze as she opened the door for me, sending a message for anyone watching. Why hadn't I asked exactly what the letter said? I wanted to go back, but knew I shouldn't.

Marion's warnings. What did they mean? Was someone out to hurt me? People walked past me whispering as they stared. Now that I thought about it, no one said anything to me while I walked through town this morning. I had been lost in my head, not thinking about pleasantries as I searched out jobs.

How had I missed this?

I was a plague to this town.

Quicker, I moved on the sidewalk. Needing somewhere to gather my thoughts I saw the nursing home, A Home Away From Home, where Mom stayed. At the counter, I greeted the receptionist who eyed me with disdain. She was Rachel's cousin, Ashley. Would she give Mom less attention because of me? This had to be corrected. Mom could not suffer because of my sins.

"I wanted to say goodbye to my mom if that's okay. I'm not sure when I'll be back."

The attitude toward me instantly softened at my announcement. "Of course."

Honestly, I wasn't sure what to do, but if I wasn't walking around town it shouldn't be a problem. For now, I'd focus on Mom.

Not a word was spoken as I followed the woman down the long pale-blue painted corridor. The place was cozy giving a home-away-from-home feel which suited the name of the place. During high school, I'd volunteered here two afternoons a month helping with the activities in the communal room.

At room 218, Ashley announced, "Here she is. Your mom is having a good day. We love having her. Your father comes often. You have a great family, London."

There was so much I missed through the years. I wasn't able to be here to help Dad with Mom. I hated it. Hated myself. The actions of my past angered me. All my fault. Emotions tumbled over me. My bottom lip trembled at my thoughts. "Please take good care of her."

"I promise."

The woman left me alone.

Mom sat in a chair starring out into the garden. Her brown hair was cut short, above her ears. I remembered it being long like mine. I traipsed cautiously farther into the room.

"Mom." Hollow eyes looked my way. "Hey, Mom, it's me, London."

She started singing "London Bridge Is Falling Down." Her frail body still had the sing-song voice that sung me to sleep on countless nights. But clearly she wasn't lucid and my chest hurt. Her hand shook as the empty hollows of her eyes looked past me. The vivacious mother who dried my tears when I was upset . . . was gone. When we were together our laughter filled the room and now only an eerie version of a childhood song I always avoided since it had my name echoed against the walls. If only I was able to turn back time to those memories and escape.

So much changed while I'd been in prison. More than I imagined. A place I never wanted to leave was now becoming my nightmare.

Something more was going on.

Mom sung the song again. I sat in the windowsill, hugging my knees to my chest as I looked out into the park, thinking about earlier at the bakery. Marion acted scared. Scared of what? I know what happened was horrible. I lived with it every day. If I could change anything, it would be to give the boy his life back.

Mom stopped singing and I watched her look out into the park.

"I had a girl named, London. She was a dancer." Mom spoke the words with love.

"I know. She loves you a lot."

Mom closed her eyes. "She was taken from me. Someone did something to her."

Oh, how I wish that was true. The tears choked me like a hand grabbing at my throat.

Mom gazed at me. Her eyes squinted as if she was working something out. Just as fast, the cloud returned. "Come here, sweet child, you look sad. A hug helps everything."

I raced into my mother's arms, grateful for the affection. "I love you, Mom. I've missed you."

There was no response for a few minutes. Then quietly Mom said, "I hope someone is giving my London lots of hugs. I miss her so."

"I bet they are."

Squeezing her tighter, I pretended to be back in our farmhouse, in my room, hugging like we had a million times before. Releasing her, I stepped back and sat in the chair while Mom hummed more songs from my childhood while she impassively watched out the window.

After some time, Mom fell asleep. I didn't care. All I wanted was to be near her. I looked back at the park. The last time I'd been there was with Millie.

We laid on the blanket while eating a sandwich Mom had packed us. We were home for summer break. It was the end of May. Life was perfect. The first year at Juilliard had been amazing.

I took another bite as I watched the lazy clouds pass by. "Have you told Charles about your thoughts?"

"No, not yet. I'm trying to decide when." Before we left for summer break, my instructor wanted to offer me a spot in a show on Broadway he was producing. It was an amazing opportunity. The problem was it would keep me from traveling to the different events Charles was expected to attend.

Millie was silent and I glanced over to her. With her raised eyebrow, I knew what she was thinking before she said it. "It's not good to let stuff sit between the two of you. If he loves you, he'll support you."

"I know. It's just I've always been there. He says politics isn't the life

for him. He wants to be a lawyer." I took a breath. "I'm afraid our dreams will eventually tear us apart. I love him, Millie."

"He's all you've ever known."

I let the words linger before responding. "I know. But we're perfect together."

The memory faded as a boy threw a ball to his dad. *Perfect.* Were the signs obvious back then that we were going down separate paths? I'd never told Charles about the offer. The only one who knew was Millie. After the accident, there was no reason to say anything since it wasn't an option.

Time to meet Millie approached. It was time to leave. Not knowing when I would get to see her again, I gently gave her a kiss on the forehead.

"I love you, Mom."

She remained asleep.

Quietly, I left out the side door. The fewer people who saw me the better. A few blocks away from the nursing home a woman saw me with a scowl on her face. It was Alec's mother. I wanted to apologize again. But I put my head down and quickened my pace. It was the chicken way out, but emotionally I wasn't able to handle anything else.

My apologies only fueled the hate.

After my sentencing in court, I read a letter aloud for everyone to hear how truly penitent I was for actions I couldn't remember. My heartfelt words only heightened their animosity as they shouted explicative after explicative at me while I stood at the front of the courtroom taking it.

Running to the outskirts of town, I collapsed against a building and sobbed. I wanted to let go of the past, but the past wouldn't let go of me.

SIX

S UPPER WAS FINISHED. MILLIE AND I sat on the front porch while the creak of the swing sounded. We gently rocked our legs. In the distance, the lights were on in the barn. Dad was probably finishing up the nightstand he was working on earlier today. A few crickets who were out early sung the evening anthem. All of this normalcy helped calm me from the events earlier today in town.

As we sipped our sweet tea, I said, "Thanks for picking me up a little early today, Millie."

I called Millie as soon as I got myself together. Of course, Millie sensed I was upset. Instead of prodding, she knew what I needed and chatted about unimportant events. It helped clear my head.

Bumping my shoulder as the swing moved back, Millie said, "I'm always here for you, London. What happened?"

Where to begin? I rubbed my forehead as I gathered my thoughts. "It's like I can't make any headway at all. Or be given a chance to prove I'm not a terrible person. Marion at the bakery said to be careful. No one would hire me. There was a note left threatening to take everything away if she helped. I assume others got it. I know

Alec is dead, but I loved that boy too."

"Wait, a note? What the hell? Why didn't they go to the cops?"

"Millie, they can't take a chance on their livelihoods. Marian supports her granddaughter. Bob has a special-needs child with steep insurance. Gwinette lost her husband a few years ago and depends solely on herself. This is a really small town, Millie." I took a deep breath trying to not break down. "I wish I could take the accident back. The images haunt me in my sleep and when I'm awake. I don't know why someone would do this unless everyone feels that way about me."

Millie was pensive a few minutes before she spoke. "I've told you this before, but I always thought it was strange that out of the blue you got wasted and decided to go on a joy ride. You barely drank when we went out. I still believe you were setup."

I sighed wishing the words she spoke were true more than anything. We'd been through this a million times with lawyers. At one point, I believed it myself. "Millie, we've tried to figure out who but nothing makes sense. How would they have known Alec would be crossing the street at that time of night? How would they have planned that I would be driving through the neighborhood? There was only alcohol in my system—a lot of it."

We grew quiet. "London, what if someone thought you would crash before you made it that far into town? What if they were trying to get rid of *you*?"

"Me? Why?"

"To become a trophy wife in politics."

I stood, needing to move as thoughts flitted through my mind. "Rachel? Millie, Charles had nothing to do with Rachel back then. They rarely spoke."

Millie shrugged and kept swinging. "I don't know. But the moment you went behind bars, she was around him constantly—consoling him. I thought he was smart enough to see through it, so I minded my own business. He visited you every chance he got. And then, out of the blue he ended it. They became a couple a month later. By the time I shared my thoughts with your mom, she was too far progressed into the disease. Until I had something concrete, I didn't want to give you false hope so I stayed quiet."

Millie stood and I gave her a hug. "I don't deserve a friend like you."

"We're forever friends, London. We took the oath in my backyard when we were six with ice cream." She released me, but held onto my shoulders. "I think we need to dig deeper, London. See if we can find anything new. It was too hard with me in New York, but I can help now."

A tired sigh escaped. "I can't keep going back to that night. A night I don't remember. I'm losing myself to something I don't understand. I have to move forward."

"I know, London. I get it."

There was something brewing in the back of Millie's mind, but I further explained my reasoning. "I can't let Dad lose anything else. It'll get worse if I start poking around in things. Dad and Mom have suffered enough."

"You said Rachel was there and saw how Charles reacted to you yesterday at the Paddington's?" Millie was furious as her jaw set firm.

I exhaled. "Yes. Rachel, her parents, and Caroline were all there. I ran to Caroline's place and she invited me in. She was shocked everyone came home when they did."

None of it made sense. There was no way to plan it since my showing up had been spur of the moment. Plus, I was released early. Millie cocked her head and I knew what she was thinking. "Charles chose her, Millie. He chose to let me go. I don't want him anymore. It's over."

"And he's a bastard for not realizing what he lost." Millie cocked her head and put her hand on her hip. A giggle escaped. "I'm serious,

London. He deserves to have his beans and frank hurt . . . severely."

More laughter escaped. We couldn't stop. It was cathartic. "Charles better avoid you for a while."

"Damn straight."

After our conversation settled, I realized how tired I was. "I'm going to say goodnight to Sparkles and head to bed. Figure this all out tomorrow."

"Want me to stay the night like old times? We could get fat on ice cream and watch reruns of *90210*. Even though you only eat like a quarter of a cup and leave the rest to me." She sighed. "Dylan always gets my blood boiling. Brandon vrooms my engine."

Another laugh escaped. We were obsessed with these men. The show was a staple through high school. Who cared if it was a show from the nineties? It was a classic we happened to find one night on a channel doing reruns.

"Can I get a rain check on Brandon and Dylan?"

"Of course. Love ya, girl. Keep that chin up. I'll stop by tomorrow to check on you."

"Love you, too. I'll be here."

Millie gave me another hug. Her support was something I treasured. Through everything, she was my best friend.

The barn light was still on. Dad probably was working late in the back part of the shop. I'd let him know I was tired while I made sure Sparkles was okay. All of the sudden, Sparkles sounded into distress. I heard her angrily neighing and pounding, like the stall was kicked.

I picked up my pace hoping a snake hadn't gotten in her stall. The door at the end of the barn swung. Nervously, I glanced around making sure I was alone. Sparkles pawed the ground clearly agitated. My eyes drew to an unwelcome note in red ink that was attached to the stall with a serrated hunting knife.

I screamed.

Leave now
or someone
will get hurt

Dad rushed into the barn and stopped at the sign. "What the fuck?" He grabbed my shoulders. "Are you okay?"

I nodded and he took off toward the open door, grabbing a pitchfork. "Dad, be careful!"

He didn't answer. My whole world swayed as I leaned against the stall. Sparkles nuzzled me, helping to ground myself in the present.

How could this be happening?

Was this all because of Alec?

Or did it really have something to do with Charles, like Millie suggested?

Was it all interrelated?

The questions spun out of control. I had no idea. None of it made sense—whatever way I looked at it. Dad came back in the barn, locking the open door. "I can't see anything this late at night. Are you sure you're okay?"

"I'm shaken, but no one was here when I came in."

Bringing me to him, Dad hugged the life out of me and I let him, needing his strength. "Let's check Sparkles out and head to the house. Okay?"

"Okay. She was kicking the stall. I want to make sure she didn't hurt herself."

Dad and I methodically checked Sparkles over. Well, Dad did. Sparkles kept her neck on my shoulder, giving me a horse hug. It was hard to focus, but I used my horse to help center me. "It's okay, girl. We're okay. We're checking you out and then Dad is taking me to the house."

She nickered in response.

Dad stood. "She looks fine. Let's head back to the house. This needs to be reported."

I tried to keep my voice steady and think I succeeded. "Okay, Dad." I kissed the side of Sparkles' face. "Night sweet, girl. I'll check on you in the morning."

I received another loving sound from Sparkles. Dad put his arms around me and walked us back to the house. A terror resonated within me. Whoever wanted me gone was serious. There would be no hiding out until I figured things out. To protect my friends and family, I needed another solution. Fast.

Exhausted from the day's events, we traipsed upstairs. The family pictures hung along the stairwell brought back fond memories.

Dad and I camping in the backyard.

Mom and I cooking for the county fair pie contest.

Riding Sparkles through the field.

Taking the stage as I let the music move me in my last dance recital.

Now, I was facing threats and blacklisting—putting those I loved dear in harm's way. A cold shiver ran down my spine. "Dad, can you call the nursing home and check on Mom?"

A worried look passed over his face. He picked up his cell phone and spoke to them. My mind kept drifting into nothingness, trying to protect itself from all that threatened the ones I loved. I had gotten out early. Whoever was behind this was acting quickly.

"Your mom is fine. Fast asleep."

I breathed a sigh of relief. Thank goodness. I wasn't sure why I thought Mom would be harmed, but I needed the reassurance. We entered my bedroom. Without all of the memories of Charles and me, the room felt cleaner.

Dad wrapped his arm around me and guided me to the bed. "I'll file a report with the police. See if anything can be done. I don't want you involved."

"Dad, I'm so sorry."

He sighed while running his free hand through his hair. "London, this is not your fault. Not at all. You made a mistake that you pay for every day and regret it. I know you." He paused for a second. "I heard you talking to Millie on the porch. I heard all of it when I went to the kitchen to get something to drink."

"Oh, Dad. I-I-I . . ." Not sure what to say, I closed my mouth. I never lied to my parents.

He shook his head. "You know, punkin', I don't care what anyone thinks. I know my girl and I know she has a heart of gold."

"Dad—"

"Let me finish." I nodded. "I don't think it's safe for you here."

Tears pricked my eyes. "Dad, I just got out. I love being home . . . with you. Why are they doing this?"

"I don't know. But I need to keep you safe while I figure it out." He patted my leg with the opposite hand. "I called an old friend, Levi McCole."

"I remember him." Levi had a huge ranch in the heart of Colorado. I'd met him once quite a few years back. Levi and his wife passed through town and came to dinner. From what I remembered of him, he seemed like a good man. Dad and Mom saw them often when they attended different horse conventions when I was a teenager. I never was able to go because of ballet recitals and modern dance competitions.

Dad looked at me. "Let me finish before you saying anything."

"Okay."

He took a deep breath and I wasn't sure how he felt about what he was about to say. "He has a job on the ranch. Working with horses. Says it's yours if you want it."

This was not what I expected. "What? Dad, I can't."

"Before you say no, think about the fresh start you'll have. We'll talk and I'll come to visit. No one will know where you are except me. You'll be safe there. Able to live. I can't keep you safe here if whatever asshole is brave enough to come to my barn when I'm not even fifty feet away."

This was exactly what I wanted earlier. But now that it was within my grasp, I was afraid. *Find the courage, London. Protect your dad. If I am gone, then they'll leave him alone.*

I cradled my head, knowing he was right. "I don't want to lose you again, Dad. Promise, we'll talk and I'll see you as often as possible."

"I promise, punkin'. I wouldn't suggest it if it wasn't to protect you."

"Thank you, Dad."

He squeezed me and I relished the moment. "Get some sleep. We'll head out tomorrow after lunch. Do a father-daughter road trip. I think Sparkles should go with you."

"Really?" Being able to spend more time with Dad prior to staying in Colorado helped ease the guilt of my decision. Having Sparkles with me was even better.

Dad stood, "Really." He kissed my forehead and for the first time in four years, I felt peace. As Dad made it to the doorway, he added, "London, I agree with Millie. There's something more to what happened that night. I don't think you would have deliberately done that. It's never made sense."

"What if it is the truth?"

He took another deep breath. "I still love you. The guilt of what happened will stay with you, regardless. But, I think there's more to the story. Your mom did too. But, we never were able to find anything. All any of us can do is spend the time we have left making the world a better place."

The door closed. Mom believed in me too. Maybe, there was more. The Colorado sky might allow me to think clearly, remember something—anything to piece together the mystery of what happened.

SEVEN

A SIGN FOR THE MCCOLE ranch hung above the entrance after being on the road for two days. A security gate opened as Dad crept forward. The black iron bars reminded me of prison in a sense. Would this be my new prison? I wasn't able to stay at home, forced to leave. My heart ached at the thought.

I kept a pleasant smile on my face. The last thing I wanted was for Dad to feel guilty about me having to leave. It was safer for him.

Driving up a long dirt road, wooden fences framed in the land on each side while horses grazed. I rolled down the window taking in the fresh mountain air. Colorado was beautiful. Majestic mountains stood in the background creating a breathtaking view. For now, I focused on the beauty and not the reason I was here.

No one knew me here. It was a clean slate. That was the positive to all this. *This is good, London. This is what I need.* At least, that was what I willed myself to believe. My mind was a mess with all the change in such a short amount of time.

I took a quiet, deep breath. A large state-of-the-art barn sat off to the left. There was room for over forty stalls judging from the size. It was exciting to get to do one of the things I loved—taking care of horses. The buildings surrounding the main stable were like a miniature city. The place was grander than I'd imagined, even after hearing my parents talk about it.

The McCole's were involved in rehabilitating injured horses. In addition, they hosted the annual McCole Classic—a jumping event which brought riders and horses of the highest caliber. I was in awe of the beauty and operation and I hadn't left the vehicle yet. It was still family-owned even with many offers to buy them out from what Dad mentioned.

"What do you think?"

I glanced over at Dad. "It's amazing. Sparkles is going to think she's at a resort."

Dad chuckled. "She probably will."

A truck met us coming the opposite way. Dad rolled down the window to greet an older man with peppered-color hair and a day's worth of stubble. "Hey, Levi. Good to see you."

"You too, man. Saw you in the camera at the gate. Thought I'd meet you to get your horse settled. Maybe let her run around while we have dinner."

Dad nodded his head. "Sounds good. It's been a while since you've seen her, but this is London."

Levi smiled, no malice in his eyes like I was used to over these past few years. "You've grown up a lot since I've seen you, London. Welcome to our place. Look forward to your help."

"Thank you for having me, sir. I look forward to working here."

"Just Levi will do."

I nodded feeling a bit of the tenseness leave at his laid back manner. Turning into the large open area, Dad parked the truck. The ride had been long, but worth it. Stretching, my limbs popped as I walked to the back of the trailer. Sparkles was restless as I unloaded her. I was glad she was here with me. I looked out onto the green pastures as I led her to the gate Levi gestured toward. She nudged me to go quicker. "I know, girl. It's beautiful. I'll be back after dinner to put you up."

At the gate I released Sparkles and she took off, burning through the pent-up energy. In the middle of the field, she looked directly at me before neighing and taking off again. Sparkles loved it here.

I took a deep breath and gazed out onto the land. Colorado was rejuvenating. Maybe I would finally be able to move forward . . . remember what happened that night.

DAD AND LEVI retired to the front porch to smoke cigars. I was in the kitchen with Pam McCole, Levi's wife, finishing the dishes. Earlier, she'd insisted I call her by her first name. As I'd gathered information on our trip, Dad mentioned they were in their late sixties. The McCole's aged well. Levi had that Robert Redford look.

Folding the dishrag, I asked, "Is there anything else that needs to be done?"

Looking at me, Pam gave a gentle smile. "I think we've got everything done. Thanks for your help."

"Of course. Thank you for letting me work here for the summer." Pam tucked a stray of gray-streaked chestnut hair behind her ear as she put away the last of the leftovers. I continued, "Dad mentioned I would be staying in the bunkhouse? I would like to get situated, if that's okay."

"Why don't we have a glass of wine and talk about it on the back porch?"

I stared at one of the many cedar beams lining the ceiling thinking about how to respond. It was best to address everything straight on. "Water will be fine for me. I don't drink."

Pam watched me. *Was this a test?* I understood if it was since they were opening their home to me and all those who shared their life. It was aggravating to not be able to escape no matter where I went if it was the case.

"I know Dad told you about the accident. I don't remember anything." I took a deep breath as I pushed away the queasiness that came when talking about what happened. "I rarely drank because of dancing. I'm not sure why I turned to alcohol or what happened that made me want to drink it." My lip quivered as I thought about Alec. "I am responsible for killing a boy, which will haunt me for the rest of my life." A tear fell down my face and I quickly wiped it away. "I get you not trusting me for what I've done. But the person from that night of the accident is not me, and I'll live with the regret for the rest of my life."

Laying her hand on my shoulder, Pam responded, "I'm sorry, London. I wasn't thinking when I asked about the wine. I only wanted to chat about the change in plans."

I swallowed feeling foolish for overreacting. "Thanks. I'd like that."

Pouring two glasses of tea, Pam handed me one. "Here's to a fresh start. Levi and I don't judge a book by its cover. We get to know the person and form an opinion for ourselves."

That was more than I could ask for. "I like the sound of that. Thank you."

Pam motioned for me to follow her to the back porch. Across from the pool was a guesthouse. I took a sip and listened to a few horses neigh in the distance. "I have a grandson, Ty, he's five. Well, just turned five last week. He's a handful to say the least."

I chuckled. "Most five-year-old boys are." This was an odd way to start the conversation.

"Yes, they are. My son is a single dad. He needs help though he doesn't think he does. I wanted to know if you would mind working with the horses and helping out with Ty depending on the schedule?"

Swirling my tea, I paused. "Did Dad tell you about the threat? I want to make sure you know anything that could affect your decision."

"Sweetheart, this place is locked up tight. No one knows you're here. Watching him here won't be an issue."

I smiled. "That would be great. I'm here to help however I can. I love watching kids. Even the wilder ones."

Images of Alec and me blowing bubbles in the front yard raced through my mind. His giggle as he chased them around the yard. The ache in my chest returned thinking about that precious boy.

Pam laughed not noticing my change in thoughts. "Thanks, London. Jaxson, Ty's dad, lives up on that hill over yonder." As she pointed, I followed the direction of her finger to see a large house up on the hill in the distance. Maybe a mile away. "I thought it might be easier with you watching Ty if you stayed in the guesthouse versus the bunkhouse. You'll have your own space. Plus, Ty has a play room out there."

"Oh, Pam. I don't mind staying in the bunk house."

"I know, sweetheart. But, it'll make it easier for me too."

My own place. I hadn't had my own space in such a long time. This was perfect. Almost too good to be true. "If it makes it easier for you, I'll gladly stay there. Thank you. When do I get to meet him?"

What I thought to be another prison was looking like one of the best things to happen in a long time.

"He's at my daughter, Sydney's, house tonight while Jaxson is out of town. He'll be here bright and early tomorrow before she has to head out of town."

"I can't wait."

The screen door opened and the men came out on the back porch. Dad looked at me and gave a genuine smile. Levi asked, "What are you ladies discussing?"

Levi put his arm around Pam as she responded. "London watching Ty and us wanting her to take the guesthouse. She'd love to. "

"He's a handful. But I have a feeling you can handle your own."

Levi gave me a wink.

Dad gave me a hug as he stated, "Then, it's all settled. I better get London unloaded, and then go to sleep. I have an early morning on the road since I need to be in Kansas tomorrow evening to pick up the new boarding horse."

As we unloaded the vehicle, there was a suitcase I hadn't packed. "I don't think this is mine, Dad."

"Millie packed it for you. She wanted to send some essentials out here until she could get here herself."

I froze looking at the bag as if it could explode. "I'm afraid to look."

"I would be too."

We laughed as we approached the guesthouse. I hesitantly wheeled Millie's surprise bag into the house. The wood and rock combination from the main house was continued into the guest home. It was stunning with the cedar beams. The rustic feel made me want to curl up with a good book.

Opening the door, the cream-colored theme continued with the dark accented furniture. Class and elegance were my initial thoughts.

"You're going to be spoiled living here." Dad's voice was excited. I raised my eyebrow with apprehension. Before my thoughts could go forward, he voiced, "You deserve a little spoiling, London."

I wasn't sure what to say as I looked down. A hand came on my shoulder. "Let's explore and get you settled. But, I'm not helping with Millie's bag. She told me not to open it."

A giggle escaped helping to abate the earlier dimmer thoughts. As we walked around, the place was larger than it appeared on the outside. It was three-bedroom and two bathrooms. The third bedroom had been converted to a playroom for Ty. I smiled at the dump truck stencils on the walls.

"Do Pam and Levi have any other grandchildren besides Ty?" I yelled back down the hall.

Dad appeared in the hallway coming from the master bedroom where he'd placed my bags. "Yes, one with Sydney. Ty was unexpected from what I understand. The granddaughter, Mallory is older. I think she's thirteen."

I imagined Jaxson and his sister where in their mid to late thirties from the bits and pieces of information I received from Dad on the way up.

"Well, punkin', I need to get some sleep."

A bittersweet feeling came over me. I wasn't ready to say goodbye to him. Time had flown by too fast. But, I had to be strong. Keep him safe. "Dad, I'm going to miss you."

Giving me a squeeze, Dad kissed the top of my head. "I'll miss you too. I can already tell a difference. This place will be good for you. The McCole's are good people."

"I think so too. Make sure to wake me up when you get up. I want to spend as much time with you as possible."

He gave me a kiss on the forehead. "I will. Night, punkin'."

"Night, Dad."

I made my way to the master bedroom. The deep-purple, plum bed called my name. The two days of traveling caught up to me. Up against the right wall, four suitcases stood. I knew what was in three of them. *What had Millie sent?* Curiosity getting the best of me, I laid the red suitcase on the ground. Taking a deep breath, I unzipped it. Whew. It didn't explode. Inside laid a note.

London,

New clothes for a new beginning. Channel your inner 90210 (only more updated.

Millie

Dylan's girl

I laughed. *Dylan's girl.* Millie had been obsessed with Dylan from the moment we'd first seen a rerun. She claimed he was hers. Inside I kept a silent crush on him. As I looked through the bag, there were all sorts of folded clothes—jeans, shirts, swimsuits, pajamas, dresses. Inside I felt like a giddy schoolgirl.

My best friend always knew how to cheer me up. New clothes. New beginning. People were going to get to see the real me and not the shadow cast on me for the last four years.

Quickly I pulled out my phone.

> *Me: THANK YOU! I love the clothes!*

> *Millie: You're so welcome! Did you see the lingerie?*

My mouth dropped open as I dug deeper to see pieces of clothing which covered nothing. I blushed in the privacy of my room.

> *Me: OMG! Millie, what in the world am I going to do with lingerie?*

> *Millie: You never know. I needed my bestie prepared for all circumstances.*

> *Me: Well, I doubt I will need it. But, thank you.*

> *Millie: I packed you a vibrator just in case Colorado doesn't have any hot guys.*

I froze again as I saw a box. Quickly, I shoved the clothes on top of the box that read *Thunder Down Under.* She bought me a vibrator. Oh my gosh. My dad was in the next room and I had a vibrator. I jumped on the bed like the bag would explode. My phone vibrated again.

> *Millie: You'll thank me later. I've put in for some time off at work so you can hug me then for the awesome purchase. I'll let you know when I get approved.*

> *Me: I can't wait to see you. Have a house all to myself. You'll love it.*

Millie: Yes! 90210 marathon, here we come! Got to go. Hot date with a cop.

Me: Cop? What Cop?

Millie: Doorbell is ringing! I'll explain later!

Me: Millie! You did that on purpose! Thank you so much for making my night. Have fun. Be safe.

Millie: You're welcome. How much trouble can I really get in? Love ya, girl.

Me: Love you, too.

After finding some of the short, silk pajama sets, I zipped the red suitcase back up. The bed was soft like a cloud. Sleep found me as soon as I closed my eyes. Dreams filled with laughter and love followed giving me hope for what was to come.

EIGHT

"**B**YE, DAD. I'LL MISS YOU." Tears choked my sentence. Now that the time was here, I wasn't ready to let him go. *Am I making a mistake? Would everything be okay if I stayed?* Doubt filled me.

Dad hugged me. "Don't overthink this. We'll talk each day and I'll be back before you know it. I want you safe."

I wanted him safe. "I'll be okay. I promise."

The tears stayed at bay and I focused on the pain of biting my lower lip. Giving me a kiss on the forehead, Dad whispered, "I love you, punkin'. I'm a phone call away."

"Love you, too."

With his coffee in hand, he turned toward his truck while waving bye to Pam and Levi. I glanced back. They watched me as Levi put his arm around Pam—a gesture Dad did to Mom all the time when I was younger.

For a moment, I glanced up to gather my strength for the last wave. The morning sky cast hues of orange and red. As the truck cranked, I raised my hand. Dad's arm came out of the window. *I can do this. I can survive this.* My heart ached more as the distance grew between the truck and the taillights disappeared.

This was it.

I was on my own.

Again.

Gathering my thoughts, I stood there for a few minutes, grateful for the reprieve the McCole's gave me. An SUV pulled up with whom I assumed was their daughter, Sydney. A woman with strawberry-blonde hair, who resembled Levi, got out. She looked like I had guessed, mid to late thirties.

"Hey Mom, Dad. We're headed to the airport. Ty had breakfast already this morning."

Pam walked down the steps with Levi. The backseat burst open in a flurry of movement. Little limbs came flying out. "Grama and Grampa, Daddy's coming in one more day! Grama, can you believe it? Aunt Sydney said he got me something special!"

Love shone from Pam as she watched her energetic grandson bound to her. Just before he got to her, Sydney picked him up, showering him with kisses. "I'll miss you, squirt. Love you."

He squealed and giggled. "I love you too, Aunt Sydney."

Barely able to hold onto Ty, Sydney let him down as he rushed to Pam who hugged him. All of the love warmed me. Pam gave Ty a hug, responding to his earlier comment. "I know your daddy is ready to see you. He misses you dearly."

A smile spread across his face. "He woke up Aunt Sydney this morning and told me so. Aunt Sydney says Dad sleeps less because he's old." Ty stopped abruptly and looked at me. "I'm Ty McCole. Who are you?"

I crouched. "I'm London McNally. Your grama and grampa are letting me work on the farm. I was wondering if there was anyone big and brave who could show me around?"

Ty's little chest puffed up. "I can! I'm super brave. My dad says I'm getting so big he can barely lift me." Leaning in closer, Ty whispered loudly. "You lose strength when you get old, but don't tell him."

Leaning back, I crossed my heart. "Your secret is safe with me. I promise."

"Good. Want to be my friend?"

I held out my hand for a high-five which he gave me. "I'd love that. I brought my horse with me. Do you want to help me feed her this morning? I need to make sure she's doing okay in this new place."

"I don't ride big horses." His eyes were big as saucers. Almost scared, which surprised me considering he lived on a ranch.

I gave him a wink. "I'm not riding her. I want to introduce her to you. She needs another friend."

"I can be her friend."

Standing, I noticed Sydney watching me with a sweet expression. "I'm Sydney. It's nice to meet you, London. I appreciate you helping out my parents."

"Thanks. I'm excited to be here and have a new friend." I ruffled the hair on Ty's head which caused him to look up at me with a huge grin.

Pam came up beside us. "Ty, why don't you get your muck boots real quick so you can go with London and Grampa to the stable?"

Like the wind, Ty took off racing and calling over his shoulder, "I'll be right back, London. Don't move."

Touching my shoulder, Pam brought my attention back to her. "Jaxson was thrown from a horse a couple of weeks ago. Ty saw it. He refuses to ride now."

That explained the fear in Ty's eyes. "No problem. Was Jaxson hurt?"

"Not really. A little banged up. It looked worse than it was, but scared the hell out of us."

The front door slammed open. "I'm back! Let's go!"

Ty pulled my arm; I lurched forward.

Over my shoulder, I spoke loudly. "It was nice meeting you. Have a great trip, Sydney."

She waved and laughed. "We'll catch up when I get back."

Levi chuckled. "Calm down, Ty. You'll pull her arm out of the socket."

Ty looked back at me, eyeing my shoulder. "It's still attached, Grampa. Don't worry. We don't need no first aid yet."

Yet. A small giggle escaped me. This boy would keep me busy and I loved it. The barn was about a five-minute walk from the house. I enjoyed the feel of the gravel crunching under my feet. It made me think of home and the walk to our barn. Ty babbled excitedly while I only got a few words in here and there. Levi didn't have a chance to say anything.

As the barn came into view, Levi pointed to a larger building off in the distance. The rock cedar-theme from the homestead was replicated on this edifice also. Levi answered one of my internal questions about the large arena-type building behind the stables. "That is where we have events such as the McCole Classic. You saw the barn yesterday. Ty and I will show you the rehab center attached to the side of the stables, as well as the running arena."

"Perfect. Is there anything I need to do today?"

Levi thought for a moment. "We'll wait until Jaxson gets back tomorrow. He's due early afternoon. From there, we'll figure things out. We have a general idea on the schedule, but need to fine tune it since you're helping out with Ty."

Ty grabbed my hand. "That means we get to play all day since Grampa said no chores. Are you excited?"

"No chores for London, but Ty, you still have yours."

His small shoulders slumped. "Oh, man."

I knelt down. "How about we do them together today? You help me take care of Sparkles and I'll help you."

"Deal."

Shaking on it, we solidified the arrangement.

We headed to the stalls where Sparkles stayed the night. Instantly she perked upon hearing our approach. "Hey, girl. I have a new friend for you to meet."

Shaking her head as it came over the stall door. "Sparkles, this is Ty. Ty, this is Sparkles."

Hands grabbed the sides of my legs. "Why is her name Sparkles?"

"Because, when I picked her up she was in a field that looked like it was sparkling as the sun hit the morning dew."

Ty looked at me as if I was crazy and then asked, "Does she buck?" There was trepidation in his voice.

"No, she's gentle. I'll show you." With a scoop of feed in my hands, I held it out for Sparkles to eat. Gently, she consumed the treat. "Good, girl. How are you liking your new home?"

In response, she neighed. I winked at Ty. "I think she likes it." I nuzzled the side of her face and felt Ty's hands grip me tighter. If I remained calm and showed Ty how gentle Sparkles was, maybe he would trust her more. "I'll let you rest one more day, girl. We'll ride tomorrow. Show Ty a couple of your tricks if he wants."

"She can do tricks?"

I knew that might get his interest. "A couple."

"What kind?"

"You'll have to wait and see."

Scrunching his eyebrows he watched me, then Sparkles. "Can I try feeding her?"

"Sure. She'll love it."

Giving Ty some feed, he held his hand out and giggled. "She's nice like you said." Obviously, Ty was used to horses as he stepped out from behind me to touch her muzzle. "You promise you'll show me her tricks?"

"Of course. We'll come here after breakfast, if it's okay with your grama and grampa."

A clanking sound brought our attention to down the way where helpers were feeding other horses. Ty took off to his grampa. Watching him was like seeing a ping pong ball in action. I loved it. At night, I would sleep well after watching Ty. Glancing over my shoulder, I was tickled as Ty energetically talked to Levi. I gave Sparkles a kiss on the cheek. "I'll be back, girl. We'll ride tomorrow. They'll turn you out to pasture in about an hour or so. Okay?"

I got an answering nudge. A few workers entered from the opposite end with supplies for cleaning the stalls. Levi and Ty approached while Ty said, "Tell her, Grampa. Tell her."

"Ty told me about your plans tomorrow. He—"

Too impatient, Ty interrupted. "He said I can come watch the tricks."

"Perfect. Why don't we get your chores done? Then, we can have fun the rest of the day."

Taking my hand, Ty pulled me like before. Levi called after. "Be gentle, Ty."

"I promise, Grampa. We'll feed the chickens. That's it. Do you know how to feed chickens, London?"

"It's been a long time. Do you mind showing me?"

"My dad says I'm the best chicken feeder. I'll show you how."

TY WAS IN the main house finishing up his shower while I dressed in my pajamas. He wanted to stay with me in the guesthouse. I wasn't comfortable with the idea this early on and I was sure Pam agreed. Babbling through an easy let down, Pam saved me when she suggested I could sleep in the main house. The little guy was too adorable to say no to. Apparently Pam had the same problem.

I wasn't sure where his mom was, but she didn't seem to be in the picture at all. In essence, we were both without our moms. Kindred spirits so to say.

With my phone in hand, I made my way back to the main house.

The night air felt refreshing. Glancing up at the sky, the stars shone bright. Sometime soon, I would make time to lie on a blanket and gaze up into the stars.

"London! Hurry! It's time to read!" The tiny body of Ty bounced up and down on the back porch.

Pam chuckled and shook her head beside him. "I told him to be patient, but he was anxious."

"I'm excited too." I bent down. "Why don't you pick out one book for me to read? Then, we'll have to go straight to bed to get our strength. Sparkles likes to perform her tricks in front of well-rested people."

"Yes!" Ty took off upstairs and I followed.

Pam wasn't far behind when I entered his room. On his lap was "Green Eggs and Ham" by Dr. Seuss. "I love this book. My dad read it to me when I was a little girl."

"Mine does too. He said he's going to make me green eggs sometime. Will you help him?"

"I'd love to. I made them as a kid with my dad."

"Yes! You're the best, London! I'm glad we're friends."

Kneeling beside the bed, I read. Not five pages in, Ty was fast asleep. He was either full throttle or dead to the world. I tiptoed quietly out the door where I met Pam. An apprehensive look was apparent on her face. "You're good with him. What do you think?"

"He's adorable. Full of energy."

Pam's brows creased. "Is he too much? You don't have to watch him. I hope you know that's not conditional."

I touched her shoulder. "I love watching him. We had a fun time today. It's therapeutic I think. Ty doesn't let me think too much about what happened."

"Okay. I know how tough it can be with his energy. I wanted to make sure. We love him to death. A true blessing."

Curiosity got the best of me as I asked. "Is his mom around? Ty never mentioned her, but talks about Jaxson all the time."

We moved a few steps down the hallway before stopping. The television in the master bedroom at the far end was on. I assumed Levi was in there. "Ty was unexpected. When he was two months old, the mother dropped him off on the front porch in the middle of the night. Left a note claiming he was Jaxson's. We took him without question. He was in bad shape—malnourished, dirty, and sick."

My hand covered my mouth as I gasped. I couldn't imagine that sweet boy being neglected. Pam continued. "The lawyers suggested a DNA test, but Jaxson knew Ty was his. He was involved exclusively with the mother for a while before things went south. To make it official, Jaxson took the test and now, he has sole custody. Ty doesn't know the specifics yet. Jaxson will figure out when is the right time. We had no idea Ty existed until he was dropped off on our doorstep."

There were so many questions I had, but wasn't comfortable probing further. We took a few more steps down the hallway. "I hate imagining any child being neglected. Ty mentioned earlier today he was ready for a brother or sister."

Stopping, I assumed we were at my room. Pam shook her head. "He'd love a brother or sister. Someday Jaxson will meet the right girl. If it's meant to be, it will happen. Ty was the best thing to happen to Jaxson."

"Kids are balm to the soul. That's what my grandma always said before she passed when there was a rowdy kid anywhere near her."

Chuckling, Pam said, "That they are. Goodnight, London. We're happy you're here."

"Thanks. I'm loving it." Happiness emanated out.

She gave me a hug. "Thanks for taking a chance on us. Here's your room, next to Ty's if that's okay."

"It's perfect. Thank you."

Stepping inside, I closed the door and took a deep breath. Today was a good day. My phone vibrated with a text.

Millie: Did they do a full blood panel on you after the wreck?

That was sudden and unexpected. The clawing sensation I thought I'd overcome quickly returned as old memories dredged to the surface. I had to take a few deep breaths before I responded too harshly to my friend.

> *Me: Why?*

> *Millie: Sorry for asking. I know this brings up bad memories. It's important. I promise.*

There was no telling why she asked about the report. I didn't want to know. The trail would lead nowhere like it always had. After I responded, I would focus on all the wonderful memories made today.

> *Me: Yes, they did. They admitted the records as part of the evidence which I think you can get copies of if you need it. No drugs were found in my system. They believe I lost consciousness from all the alcohol.*

> *Millie: Thanks! Big help. Love ya!*

> *Me: Love ya too!*

There was no doubt in my mind Millie was up to something. Lying in bed, I pulled the cranberry-colored duvet up over my head. The sooner I fell asleep, the quicker I would escape any more thoughts from the accident.

NINE

"LONDON?" GROGGILY, I OPENED MY eyes to find a little boy an inch away from my face. I gasped. "London, I'm thirsty and had a bad dream."

Ty. It was Ty. *Calm down. It was Ty. For a mere moment I thought I was talking to Alec and my nightmares had returned.*

My voice was scratchy as I responded, "Okay, buddy. I'll get you some water."

I had been in a deep sleep and it took me a minute to get my bearings straight. "Let's get you back to bed and I'll be right back."

"Can I sleep in here until you get back? I don't want the bad guys to get me." Tightly Ty clutched his blanket.

"What bad guys, Ty?" After hearing about his mother, I tossed and turned through my dreams, imagining a neglected Ty being dropped on my doorstep.

He crawled up onto the bed. "The green glob monster who wants to take my toys."

I sighed knowing my imagination had gone wild. "I promise the green glob monster won't get your toys. Stay here and I'll be right back."

If Ty wouldn't go back to his bed, I could sleep in his room. He climbed under the sheets and closed his eyes.

The house was eerily quiet except for the ominous ticking of the hallway clock. *Where do they keep the glasses?* One option was to wake Pam, but I hated interrupting their sleep when I could handle something as simple as getting a glass of water. In the morning, I'd inform them of snooping in their kitchen.

Hitting the first floor, I rounded the corner and ran into something hard. *Oh, shit. Oh, shit. It's a person. The one who wants me dealt with.* Scampering back, I screamed, "Stay away! Leave!"

I crashed into a table as I tried to back away. This was the end of my life. At least Pam and Levi would hear me and save Ty. The stranger said something. The panic felt like cotton in my ears. I screamed again. If he was here to kill me, I wouldn't go down without a fight.

A light flipped on. The stranger held up his hands. "I'm Jaxson—this is my parents' house." Stopping, I froze my backward crawl. "You must be London." His voice was smooth as silk. Hands still up, he continued talking to me like was I crazy while he crouched. Yeah, I was crazy. "London, I'm Jaxson McCole. I came home early."

Scampering from upstairs came Levi with Pam close behind. A shotgun cocked. "London, are you okay?"

Frozen, I wasn't able to respond. I followed Levi's glance toward Jaxson and he put the shotgun down. Jaxson stood. "It was my fault. I decided to come home and surprise Ty early."

My face heated. How embarrassing. Everyone looked at me. "I'm okay. I'm so sorry. I thought—" I stopped myself before I rambled too much. There was someone out there who didn't want me out of prison. Levi and Pam knew what was going on, but I wasn't sure how much Jaxson knew.

Jaxson quirked a brow and watched me for a moment. As my heart slowed, I took a second to see him. All this time I'd pictured him in his late thirties versus his twenties. How wrong I had been. His dark hair and emerald-green eyes cut through me. He was gorgeous and his facial scruff only added to his manly presence.

I felt a flush on my face and looked away. "London, do you need help getting up?" Pam walked toward me, a concerned look on her face.

Had Pam been talking to me? Oh, geez. "No, I've got it."

Standing, I knew I'd be sore from where I took a tumble. Oh no. In all the commotion, I'd hit the table and knocked over a lamp. "I'm so sorry. I'll get this cleaned up." I started to kneel then paused, remembering Ty. My head whipped around. "Did I scare Ty? He woke me up because of a nightmare and wanted water."

Pam walked over to me. "He's fast asleep in your bed. I'll worry about the lamp tomorrow. It looks like you cut yourself on the arm." I looked down and saw the trail of blood. This night could not get any worse. "There's a first-aid kit in the bathroom. Let's get you cleaned up."

"Mom, Dad, I'll show her. Go ahead and go back to bed."

Looking to Pam, I nodded. The last thing I wanted was to inconvenience them more than I had. Pam patted my shoulder. "Let me know if you need anything, sweetheart. And don't worry about the old lamp. I would have been half-scared out of my mind too."

"Thanks, Pam. Goodnight." I nervously laughed. Being in someone else's home and messing things up was incredibly awkward. Jaxson traipsed to the kitchen with an unintentional sexy swagger to grab a paper towel for my cut. Our eyes connected and I was frozen in place as Jaxson handed me the paper towel. An electric current connected me to him, rendering me speechless.

In the back of my mind I registered Pam giving Jaxson a kiss on the cheek, but I couldn't break away. It wasn't until she spoke to him it broke the spell. "Welcome home. We missed you."

"Missed you too, Mom."

We were left alone and it was hard to reconcile the man I had in front of me with the man I had imagined. Without thinking, I said, "You're not old."

"What?"

I wanted to slap myself. There was a reason I shouldn't interact with the human race without a certain amount of sleep. "Umm . . . never mind."

Like a gentlemen, he let it slide. Gesturing to my arm, he said, "Let's take a look at your arm. You aren't going to scream at me again, are you? Maybe try to stab me this time?"

Looking at Jaxson, I tried to keep the smile from forming at his obviously teasing comment. "I make no promises. You shouldn't have been lurking."

"Lurking?"

"Yes, lurking." I felt embarrassed for teasing him, bordering on flirting. *I am new here. In the middle of my second night. Stop whatever this is, London.*

The light flipped on in the bathroom. Jaxson motioned for me sit on the counter near the marble sink. Taking the first-aid kit out of the cabinet, Jaxson asked, "How are you liking it here so far?"

"It's beautiful. Ty and I had fun today. I think he showed me every square inch of this place. You have a very sweet boy."

Chuckling, Jaxson opened the kit. "I bet he loved it. Mom said you didn't mind helping out with him. He's a lot for her to handle. I've hired sitters, but so far it hasn't worked out." With a bottle of alcohol, Jaxson gently held my elbow over the sink. "This may sting."

I winced as the liquid initially hit. The cut wasn't bad, but alcohol even in a paper cut wasn't pleasant. "Why haven't the sitters worked?"

"He's active. They have ulterior motives. The hours are hard. It's been several things." I was sure I knew what the ulterior motives were. "So what did you mean by me being old?"

Closing my eyes, I let my head fall. "I think there are only so many times someone should die of embarrassment in one night."

A cloth was put to my elbow. He was making a bigger fuss of the small cut than it was worth. Bending to meet my eyes, Jaxson smiled wide, showing two dimples. He was beyond sexy. *Stop! Stop! Stop!* And that smell. I would die a happy person wrapped in that woodsy manly smell. "You're secret is safe with me."

Before answering, I watched the Band-Aid get applied.

I leaned my head against the mirror. "No judging. Okay. Oh, geez." Taking a steadying breath, I continued. "All day long Ty has been talking about how old you were getting. It sounded more geriatric than . . ." I cut off the sentence, stopping where my thoughts were headed. *Sexy as hell cowboy.* Please let it be bedtime.

"Than . . ."

I hopped off the counter. "No way, lurker. I have had enough humiliation for one night. I need to get some shut-eye out in the guesthouse. Alone. I mean I didn't think you were coming." I paused. "I'm going now. Thanks for the Band-Aid."

Backing out of the bathroom, Jaxson followed me. "I'll get it out of you at some point."

"I'm pretty stubborn."

"I think you just issued a challenge. Consider it accepted."

I was near the back door when his words registered. "No, no, no. No challenge. I'm not stubborn at all. I was going to say it sounded more geriatric than younger."

Jaxson prowled closer to me. The blood heated within my veins. "I don't think that's what you were thinking."

Ducking out the door, I waved. "Night, Jaxson. I'm going to go die of mortification."

He chuckled and followed me. "I'll make sure you make it to the guesthouse okay. It's the middle of the night." The deep timber of his voice had me all kinds of messed up inside. Parts of me felt alive. This was crazy. I needed sleep. A fresh perspective.

I entered the code on the panel. The lock clicked, granting access. As I grabbed the door handle, I glanced back toward Jaxson. "Night. Thanks for seeing me to my door."

"Night, London. It was my pleasure."

Pleasure. Quivers in my stomach danced about as I thought about that word.

Opening the door, I quickly traipsed inside and locked it. I took a deep breath before pushing off the wall and heading to my bedroom. For now, I would pretend this was all a dream. A bad dream. A really bad dream. Except Jaxson was hot. That part wasn't bad. Oh my gosh! I needed sleep stat!

I touched my arm where his firm yet gentle grip sent an electrical charge through my body. It was as if his touch branded me.

This was crazy.

I was crazy.

Before I could delve any further into my chaotic thoughts, I buried myself under the covers, pretending none of it happened.

TEN

"**L**ONDON, ARE YOU AWAKE?"

This felt like déjà vu. Slowly, I peeked an eye open while I got my bearings straight. I was back in the guesthouse. Ty stood there in his super hero pajamas. Memories came back from the night before.

The water. The screaming. Jaxson. The mortification. Jaxson. The bathroom. Jaxson. Sleep hadn't cured my outrageous thoughts.

"Daddy, doesn't know I'm here. Your phone woke us up. Daddy's talking on it."

I shot straight up. Jaxson was on my phone. "Who is your daddy talking to?"

There were only two options and neither one were good. If it was my dad . . . I'd have to explain everything. If it was Millie . . . Lord, help me. It was only six in the morning. Only three hours since I'd had my awkward encounter last night. I was exhausted.

Ty bounded to the door. "Some girl named Millie. She wouldn't stop calling."

"Where's your daddy now?"

"In the kitchen making coffee. I snuck out to tell on him."

I gave Ty a hug. "We'll have a big bowl of ice cream for snack today. Let's go find your dad and get my phone."

Giving a salute, he raced out the front door. Why was Jaxson talking to Millie? What could they be talking about?

We made it into Pam's kitchen in record time since Jaxson and Ty stayed there through the night. I nearly dropped my mouth to the floor as Jaxson stood at the stove in low-slung lounge pants and a T-shirt that hugged his figure. My tongue felt like it turned to cotton. *Please keep it together.*

Jaxson turned as Ty skidded across the floor. "Did he wake you?"

"He came to inform me someone hijacked my phone."

Taking the skillet off the stove, Jaxson talked into the phone. "London's up. It was nice talking to you, Millie." He started to hand me the phone as I outstretched my hand. Right before I had it in my grasp he snatched it back. His eyes watched mine intently. That same electrical charge sparked between us. "Millie, one last thing. Thanks for all the advice. Here's London."

Advice?

I grasped the phone. "Millie."

"Good morning, sunshine. I had a very nice talk with a very sexy sounding Jaxson."

"What advice did you give him?"

"Oh, you know. Just advice. Don't sweat it." This wasn't good. Not good at all.

"I was sleeping in the room and then Jaxson got home—"

Millie giggled, interrupting. "Oh, he told me about it all . . . including the challenge."

Kill. Me. Now. I took a deep breath in through my nose and out through my mouth. There was no reason to get off track. "This is early for you. Why did you call?"

"Just checking on you." There was something off in her voice.

I stepped out of the kitchen. "Millie, there was another reason you called at the crack of dawn."

She took a deep breath. "I'm missing you. I'll be out there as soon as I can."

"Millie, I'm here. Anytime you need me."

"I know. You're the best."

"You too."

Hanging up the phone, I closed my eyes for a second. I knew there was another reason Millie had called, but something stopped her. What was it? When her mind was made up there was no changing it in the immediate future. Laughter came from the kitchen as I returned.

"London, do you want an omelet?" That voice had only gotten sexier with a few more hours of sleep.

Ty cocked his head to one side, watching me. "Daddy makes the best omelets. You can sit by me, London. Daddy is really big, but he's nice. He's old."

Jaxson and I looked at each other as I raised my eyebrow. There was no way I could keep it in any longer as I laughed. Jaxson pointed the spatula at Ty. "You told London on me and I'm not old."

Ty giggled into his hands. "I knew she wouldn't want you on her phone and she'd come straight to the house. You said I couldn't wake her up unless it was a good reason."

"Give me a high-five, Ty." Satisfied, Ty slapped my hand as hard as he could. I pretended it stung, which made him puff his chest out.

"London, will you be my best friend?"

"I think that sounds good."

All attention returned to Jaxson. "She's my best friend until I get old. Then we'll get married. Don't you think she's pretty, Dad?"

I coughed as Jaxson laughed while I felt the heat creep across my face. It was a fact—I would never be able to go five minutes in front of this man without being mortified. The heat in Jaxson's stare warmed me more. "She's beautiful."

Only the sizzling of the skillet could be heard for a few seconds before he asked, "What can I get the beautiful lady this morning?"

"Just a cheese omelet. I can get the glasses."

"Perfect. Glasses are to the left of the sink. Ty will want apple juice. There's a fresh pot of coffee. Mugs are on the top shelf."

I gave a nervous laugh. "I'll stick with juice. Caffeine makes me jittery. And that's the last thing I need right now." Why was this man affecting me this way?

As I made my way to the sink, Ty scrambled off the chair without saying what he was doing. There was no telling. Leaning up, I grabbed two glasses. "It was hard falling asleep with your scent all around me last night while I slept in the bed you were in."

Tingles erupted over my skin followed by goose bumps as I felt Jaxson's breath against my ear. Barely above a hoarse whisper, I said, "Is that so?"

"Yes." That one word had me nearly dropping the glass as I sat it on the counter.

"Jaxson . . ."

"London . . ."

Footsteps brought me back to the here and now. When Jaxson moved, the lack of heat was noticed. I wanted him near me.

"London, I'm ready to go see Sparkles do her tricks." I took a second before turning around and facing Ty. When I did . . . I wanted to squeeze him with how cute he looked in his roper jeans, boots, and T-shirt.

"Breakfast first. Who is Sparkles?" Jaxson asked.

Ty walked between us. I was still recovering from our earlier encounter. "Sparkles is London's horse. She said she could do tricks. I told London I don't ride horses after you got thrown and hurt yourself because you were old."

Jaxson's eyes shot to mine for a second before he took Ty's omelet out of the pan. I raised my eyes again to say, *see this was why I thought you were old.* He mouthed to me as he stirred the eggs, *I'm not old.*

I raised an eyebrow and gave a noncommittal shrug. "Sometimes it's best to simply embrace the truth."

The new egg batter popped in the butter as it cooked. To keep from smiling, I bit down on my lower lip. As I passed by, Jaxson grabbed my hand while turning my way, his back to Ty. He mouthed again, *I'm not old.*

"I guess you'll have to prove it . . ."

Oh-my-gosh. Did I just challenge him . . . again? I was in trouble. Serious trouble.

SPARKLES WAS SADDLED and grazed a few feet away in the field next to the barn. The red saddle pad against her black coat looked amazing. A few other horses grazed in this pasture, but they were at the other end, leaving plenty of room for us. I knew Sparkles wouldn't take off.

Jaxson had excused himself to check on a few of the horses in the rehab clinic. Afterward, the plan was to show me what my job entailed while Ty did some rounds with Levi. Impatiently, Ty stood on the fence rail.

"Sparkles, are you ready to show Ty some tricks?" The horse stood tall and nodded her head. "Before we start, can I have a hug and kiss?"

My horse loved performing. Dad and I worked with her for tireless hours. While I was in prison, Dad kept up all the training. Trotting the few steps to me, Sparkles puckered her lips to my cheek. "Aw, I love your kisses." Next, she reached around with her neck to hug me. "That's a sweet girl. Do you want to blow a kiss over to Ty?"

This trick was always done in the direction I motioned with my hand. I had four fingers extended with my thumb against my palm.

Sparkles shook her head, puckered her lips and let out a big gust of air. Ty couldn't stop laughing.

"Sparkles! It's not nice to be rude." I put my hand on my hip. A neigh escaped right on cue showing how much Dad worked with her. I was prepared to improvise if some of her tricks weren't practiced. "Sparkles, time out for you."

With her head down, she walked a few feet and looked back. I kept pointing. "Timeout, Sparkles."

I turned back to Ty. "I'm sorry she was so rude. I don't know what happened to her manners."

Ty barely kept his laughter contained as he watched Sparkles walk sideways back to me ever so quietly. I turned quickly and she stopped and looked up. Focusing back on Ty, he laughed again. "What's so funny?"

He shook his head. And I repeated what I'd done before. After two more times, Sparkles rested her head on my shoulder. "She snuck up on you, London. She didn't go to timeout."

I patted the side of her face while giving her a sugar cube. "Sparkles, Sparkles, Sparkles, what am I going to do with you?"

She shook her head. "Why don't you take a bow since you snuck up on me?"

Backing away, Sparkles leaned forward as Ty clapped. "She really does do tricks, London! She's the bestest horse ever."

I gave her another treat. "I think so too. I need to ride her for a bit as a reward. Do you want to watch?"

Brows furrowed as he thought hard. "Do you think I could ride with you?"

"Sure, let's go." This seemed like good progress if Ty was willing to ride her. Per the McCole's, he hadn't ridden in a while.

Sitting Ty high up in the saddle, I mounted behind him. "You promise she won't buck, London? I'm scared."

I wrapped my arm around his middle. "If you want off, tell me and I'll stop immediately. I promise she won't buck. I promise, Ty."

"Okay, London. I trust you." Those three little words did more for me than I could have imagined. To have someone trust you was a gift beyond anything money could buy. I knew what it was like to lose someone's trust. To have this child believe I would take care of him was a gift I would treasure—a sign that there was the chance to heal.

We set off at an easy pace. At first Ty had a death grip on the saddle horn, but it loosened as we walked along the rail of the white fence. I picked up the pace to a slow trot and didn't see any signs of distress in Ty's body posture. The pace increased to a cantor as Ty said, "Can we ride some more, London? This is the most fun. I love horses."

"Sure thing, kiddo." We rode until Sparkles had nearly exhausted all her energy. Jaxson, Pam, and Levi all stood at the fence and watched. Levi and Pam had huge grins. Something was off with Jaxson's expression. I didn't know him well, but he wasn't the carefree person I'd met last night and this morning. As we arrived at the fence, Ty excitedly said, "Dad! Dad! Dad! I rode on Sparkles and wasn't scared. She can do tricks. Dad, did you see how brave I was?"

Handing Ty off, Jaxson brought him into a bear hug. "I sure did, son. I'm so proud of you. That was very brave."

"London is my bestest friend. She helps me be brave. I love her lots."

Jaxson's eyes locked onto mine. There was so much emotion there, I wasn't sure what he was trying to convey with his eyes. I shifted uncomfortably on the saddle. Opening his mouth, he closed it and focused solely on Ty. "Come on, Ty. I think this calls for ice cream."

"Yay! Can I get chocolate fudge too?"

Scrubbing a hand down his face, he nodded while Ty jumped for joy and took off toward the house, making it to the front porch in no time. The odd silence had me unnerved, so I said, "Let me brush Sparkles and get her tack put up. I'll be right in to get to work if that's okay, Jaxson."

Turning my way for a mere second, Jaxson nodded, barely giving me a second glance. I wasn't sure why that bothered me. The intense flirting drew me to him. This new side left me feeling bereft. I dismounted. "I hope I didn't overstep or do something wrong with Ty. I wasn't thinking."

Pam pulled me into a big hug. "Don't be silly, you precious girl. You were exactly what that little boy needed when he needed it the most."

Levi gave me a nod. "Thank you, London. We've been worried about him."

The way Jaxson acted still left me confused, but that was something I would need to talk to him about, not his parents. The last thing I wanted was to be one of those girls. The mental loop-da-loop with that sexy-as-sin cowboy was wearing on me. I focused back on his parents. "I'm not sure what to say. I didn't do anything. But thank you for all you've done for me too."

They left and my phone vibrated with a text message.

Dad: Pulling out with the new horse. Should be home by mid-afternoon. I figured you would be working and didn't want to call.

Me: Just took Sparkles for a run. About to brush her down and start work.

Dad: Call me when you're done.

Me: Will do. Love you.

Dad: Love you too, punkin'.

The message from Dad helped ground me.

After getting Sparkles settled back in her stall, I headed to one of the rehabilitation rooms. It was where they kept the Aqua Equine Treadmill. The horse walked into a clear rectangular box that surrounded him. A belt on the bottom moved as the water climbed up to about eighty or ninety percent of the horse's leg height. Jaxson stood tall next to a long, blond-haired man up on the platform. They looked at me at the same time. The blond man's blue eyes were a crystal clear as he gave me a friendly smile. Jaxson motioned for me to wait. "That's looking good, Dwayne. Go for another fifteen and let him rest."

"Will do."

Dwayne waved to me and then focused intently back on the horse as Jaxson's footsteps could be heard on the metal steps while descending the platform that gave a good view of the horse in motion. The earlier warmth I felt was still gone, and I felt my palms become clammy. I was more nervous than I had been after screaming in his face and waking up almost the entire house.

It was best to clear the air. "I'm sorry if I overstepped by taking Ty for a ride. I'll check first with anything until I know the parameters."

"No, thank you. I've been wracking my brain on how to get him on a horse again after he saw me get thrown." Jaxson scrubbed a hand down his face. "We'd taken on a flighty as shit racehorse for rehabilitation. He'd broken his leg in the holding area at the starting gate before coming here. It was his first ride since the accident. I didn't want anyone else to ride him. Ty happened to walk into the arena at the worst possible time."

I followed Jaxson. He didn't say another word as we walked down a corridor. "What was wrong with the horse on the treadmill?"

"Another racehorse. Fracture to his left cannon bone on his leg. He's worth about ten million dollars, so the owners are trying to salvage his racing days. It'll take time, but that horse will see a racetrack again."

We walked past two guys taking another horse into the room with the pool. I asked, "Why did you choose the Aqua treadmill for that horse versus the pool?"

"I like a slow progression. I think it helps take the strain and allow for a more natural healing in serious cases." Healing horses was his passion. It was evident as he spoke with fervor.

"Dad has that philosophy too."

Jaxson slipped back into mechanical mode as he explained the operations of the business. For now, I was helping with the grooming side since I was used to it. I'd float between areas to learn the different aspects and help where I was needed. Something fun, interesting, and different from what I was used to.

ELEVEN

ONE WEEK PASSED. LIFE WAS settling into a routine which was good. The McCole's welcomed me with open arms—more than I ever imagined. I talked to Dad and Millie every day. Since arriving, no additional notes were left that I knew about. My apprehension lessened more each day and made everything easier.

I sighed as I gazed out to the pasture in front of the McCole main house while early evening approached. It was a therapeutic gesture. Picturesque was the only word I could think of as horses meandered about grazing. Ty begged for me to stay and eat dinner with them daily. Tonight was the first night I accepted. Through the week, Pam took me to get groceries, but she wanted to assure me I had an open invite to dinner anytime.

Jaxson was a doting father, committed to the business, helped anyone who needed it. There had been a man broken down on the side of the road. Jaxson was late picking up Ty one evening because he helped the man get a new battery. He was genuine and the love of his family was evident. He watched out for all of them. I'd never met a man, besides my father, who exuded such qualities.

It would be easy to fall for someone like him, but it was apparent there was no interest.

Things with Jaxson were off. Or maybe they were right. I wasn't sure if maybe that first couple of times was him having lack of sleep. *Who knows.* It shouldn't have bothered me, but things had heated up quickly. Millie was baffled like me as she assured me there was interest from his end when they spoke the one time. I agreed there had been an unmistakable chemistry between us. I saw it in the way our bodies gravitated toward each other without thinking the first night and morning.

Then, something had doused his fire. Maybe he found out about my past. At times this week, it was as if he was restraining himself as I thought back to one of the many instances, but I wasn't sure.

Ty and I were swimming in the pool. A splash war against each other was underway his giggles filled the air as he used all his might to send as much water as he could my way. At the end of each lesson, we played until he was worn out. Today we focused on his backstroke. As one of my summer jobs in high school, I was a swim instructor to help pay for all the dance fees. It seemed like I remembered most of it.

"Ty, we need to head to town."

We stopped and saw Pam leaning against the rail. Ty swam as fast as he could to the steps. Pam was taking him to get some new boots and out for ice cream. The kid would do anything for ice cream.

"Bye, London. I'll see you later."

"Bye, Ty."

He waved and ran up the steps while dripping wet with water. Wrapping a towel around him, Pam picked him up and smothered him with kisses. The smile that spread across his face as he pretended to not want the affection was picture perfect.

Picking up all the toys, I saw the Dr. Seuss book Ty always read at night on the lawn chair. He'd brought it this morning for us to read together. Quickly drying off and then leaving the wet towel, I headed into the main house to leave the book on the kitchen counter. As I came around the corner, Jaxson stood in the kitchen sipping a cup of coffee.

His eyes shot to mine and they roamed over my black-bikini-clad body. "London."

Every time we were in the same proximity, electricity intensified around us. But then, Jaxson would abruptly leave or barely look at me while he gave his next set of instructions.

As usual, I tried to stay relaxed. "Hey, Jaxson. Ty left his book outside and I knew he'd want it tonight."

Setting the coffee on the counter, Jaxson held his hand out. I took a few steps closer to where I was within reaching distance and slipped on the floor. Quicker than I would have thought possible, Jaxson's hands shot out to catch me, bringing us chest to chest. The book clattered to the floor.

"Are you okay?"

"Yes, thank you. Seems like we have a lot of situations occur in the kitchen."

A gorgeous smile lit up his face. "We do."

The feeling of his body next to mine felt oh so right. More right than I cared to admit. I missed him being near me even though we'd only touched a couple of times.

Our breaths were labored as we got lost in each other's gaze. "London."

"Jaxson."

His eyes darted to the side and he let me go, taking in an audible breath. "Thanks for bringing the book. It saved me a lot of time hunting it down."

Feeling rejected, I took a few steps back. "Anytime. I'll see you at the barn tomorrow."

As I left the kitchen, I heard a muttered curse. I wanted to say something but knew it wouldn't do any good. It was for the best. At least that's what I kept telling myself.

Now, we were amicably friendly. Maybe sterile was a better word. Jaxson was pleasant, helpful, and a gentlemen. *Ugh, I wanted him out of my thoughts.*

Through the days, I learned more about the rehabilitation side of the business. The staff was fantastic, especially Dwayne. He had an easy charm about him that made it comfortable.

Ty sat beside me. "What are you thinking about, London?"

He still had traces of spaghetti sauce around his mouth and I smiled. "Nothing much. Just tired. Are you about to head home?"

Ty nodded. "Do you have a mommy? You only talk about your dad, like me."

I gave him a sweet smile. "I do have a mommy, but she's sick. She doesn't know who I am anymore."

His hand grabbed mine. "My mommy left me too. Does it make you sad, London?"

This was a hard question to answer, especially since I knew some about his past. "I miss my mom. But, I know how much my family loves me and I think about that instead."

Taking a deep breath, he looked up at me with sad eyes. "Do you love me?"

"Yes, sweetie. You've stolen my heart. I love you across the whole wide world." It was true. Unexpectedly, this bundle of energy had crept inside my heart.

We lapsed back into silence as his brain thought. "Do you think my mom loves me?"

"I think every mom loves their child. Sometimes a mommy is sick and can't be there for her kids."

"Do you think my mom is sick?"

Ty had a loving family, but there was no substitute for a mother's love. I wasn't sure how to answer, but a deep voice my body was highly attuned to saved me from fumbling through an answer. "Your mom was sick, Ty."

As I attempted to stand, Ty's grip tightened on mine. "Don't leave, London. I like you here."

Glancing up, Jaxson nodded as he took a seat next to Ty. He put his arm around his son and my heart burst for the millionth time around this man. "I love you more than anything, Ty."

Ty leapt into his dad's arms. "I love you too, Dad. I don't think I want to marry London. I want her to be my mom."

My eyes became as big as saucers as I blushed. This only added to the awkwardness of the last week. Jaxson glanced my way, and for a minute I saw the hunger I had the first day, but it quickly disappeared. "That's not how it works, buddy."

I touched Ty's back. "How about we be the bestest friends ever, like my friend Millie? You've heard me talk about her. That's even better sometimes."

"Yes! I'm telling Grama and Grampa." He scampered off.

Standing, I said, "Night, Jaxson."

Tomorrow was Saturday. It was going to be nice having a day off from all this confusion. I planned on avoiding Jaxson if possible to decompress and get my act together.

"Yeah. Thanks, London. Night." I wanted to scream at how cold he was being. He barely made eye contact with me. It was as if I was a stranger.

The night air was heavy. This whole situation irked me. I should have never let my guard down. I was barely two weeks out of prison. I shook my head admonishing myself. I knew I was being ridiculous having feelings this quickly. Part of me was embarrassed and the other part didn't understand why he changed toward me. I shook my head.

"London, wait." My heart jerked in my chest. Footsteps fell behind me. I turned and Jaxson was closer than expected. "I know I came on strong and pulled away. I'm an ass."

With a fake smile plastered on my face, I responded. "It's okay. We were super tired. I get you're my boss and I also watch Ty." I knew better than to flirt like I did. The attraction to Jaxson had knocked me over unexpectedly. "It's not an issue. I'm going to get some sleep. Have a good night."

I attempted to walk away, but Jaxson grabbed my shoulders and backed me against the stone wall of the house. The dying embers between us roared to life. It was hard not to reach up and run my fingers along his scruff. "Fuck, London. I can't get you out of my head. I'm a damn wreck thinking about you."

My head swam. "What? We've been so distant to each other. I thought . . . I don't know . . . what?" His body pressed against mine. All I wanted was to be close to him again and see where the attraction went. The connection was strong. Overpowering. Almost unbearable.

Was this happening?

His breath danced across my lips. "There's no denying how attracted I am to you. I couldn't stop wanting you, but knew I could fuck everything up if we kept moving at the pace we were. Then, I saw you on Sparkles with Ty."

His nose touched mine and goose bumps danced across my arms. I kept my hands to my side, resisting the urge to feel him. "Go on."

I wasn't sure what our situation had to do with Ty riding Sparkles.

"He got on a horse, London. I couldn't mess that up for him with how scared he's been. He truly has attached himself to you. If we dated, then it didn't work, he would be heartbroken. Tonight he wanted you as his mom." Jaxson stepped back and ran his hands through his hair. "I haven't wanted anyone like this in a long time . . . well, really—" He stopped himself from whatever he was going to say next. His tormented eyes searched mine.

My back was still plastered against the wall. "Jaxson, I don't know how to respond. What are you saying?"

"That I want to kiss you so bad it consumes me. That I want to take you on a date and see where this goes. That I'm scared shitless my boy will get his heart broken because I couldn't stay away from the one woman I've wanted something else with if things don't work out."

I stepped forward and placed my hand on his chest. "At least I wasn't crazy about how things initially went and what I felt between us."

Crowding me again, Jaxson leaned in, barely leaving any space between us. "No, you weren't. Not at all."

The sound of the screen door opening nearly had me jumping out of my skin and Jaxson stepped back. "I'm heading to the house, Jaxson. We can talk later." He nodded and I jogged to the guesthouse. There were things Jaxson needed to know.

What in the hell just happened? Where did that leave us? Unlocking the door with the code, I hurried inside, letting out the breath I'd been holding. The last few minutes felt like a roller coaster. *Jaxson liked me. He couldn't stop thinking about me. I consumed him.* A dopey smile spread across my face.

With Charles we had always . . . been.

There was never the anticipation, the build, the desire to be consumed.

This was more . . . so much more, and it hadn't even started.

A knock startled me from my thoughts. I cracked open the door to see Jaxson standing there. "Jaxson, what are you doing here?"

"I couldn't leave with everything still unsaid between us." Those words caused me to open the door wider. Jaxson stepped closer, piercing me with his eyes.

"Where's Ty?"

He looked over to a truck disappearing in the distance. "My parents are watching him. They're taking him to feed the sheep in the north pasture."

"He loves feeding the sheep. I went with him and Levi once this week." Jaxson stared at me for a few beats and I started to get nervous. To fill the silence, I asked, "What did you tell them you were doing?"

"Coming after you."

Those tingles erupted again as my lower stomach tightened. I opened the door wider to let Jaxson in. Briefly, I smiled. "We haven't talked—"

He cut me off as his hands came to each side of my face, obliterating my train of thought. The emerald-green of his eyes captivated me. Lost in his stare, he slowly lowered his lips to mine. The wait was excruciating. As his warm yet firm lips pressed against mine, not a single fantasy over the past week compared to the reality. *I want this. He wants me.*

A quick swipe of his tongue had me opening up to him and his tongue danced along mine. Without thinking, I intertwined my hands into his dark hair. He moaned in my mouth as he deepened the kiss. On the cusp of it turning into more, he pulled away.

This was going fast. Too fast.

As our breathing subsided, Jaxson trailed his nose along mine. "A thousand kisses from you a day wouldn't be enough."

I blushed at his words. "They're yours. Anytime."

But . . . we still needed to talk.

As if he read my mind, Jaxson grabbed my hand and led me to the couch. Jaxson asked, "What did you want to talk about earlier outside?"

Nervously, I tucked my escaped hair behind my ear. "My past. The threats. I can't start something with anyone if they don't know everything."

Jaxson took a deep breath. "I know about the accident. I know all about the threats. I know about it all, London. I just never expected . . . you."

"Jaxson, you have a child to think of."

The brush of Jaxson's hand along my arms soothed my nervous energy. "London, I know what the courts and evidence said, but I agree with your dad. I think there's more to the story."

"What makes you think that?" The words Mom said at the nursing home came back. *Someone did something to her.*

Jaxson watched me. "I don't know, but people don't change who they are at the core. I can't imagine you going on a bender because something upset you after the time we've gotten to know each other. Were you ever like that?"

"No. Never. It never made sense, but the evidence is there. I've accepted my actions."

"Think about this . . . should I be punished for the rest of my life for abandoning my son?"

I closed my eyes, abhorred by the image my brain conjured up of a neglected Ty. "It's not the same. I took a little boy's life while driving. I was behind the wheel."

"Ty could have died if his mom hadn't been lucid enough to drop him off. We dated for a few months. The last few times we didn't use a condom. Then, I realized she was crazy and unbalanced. I found out she was conning me. Crystal wanted to find a wealthy man to set her up for life. I tried to get her help. She refused and I ended things. I never checked to see if she got pregnant. I should have checked, knowing we were having unprotected sex. The only reason she dropped Ty off was because her latest rich boyfriend didn't want a kid." I went to protest. "London, I'm not saying what you did was okay. I know a boy lost his life and you served time in prison. You'll carry that burden for the rest of your life, more so than a true drunk and you have no recollection of it. I'll always carry around how Ty came to us."

I nodded, not sure what to say.

"In regards to the threats, I think someone wanted you gone, which leads to me still believing you don't have the full story."

Sometimes opening old wounds only left more scars.

"If I ever thought I would put Ty in danger, I would leave. I promise. I only think they wanted me gone from Guin."

Jaxson's jaw tightened. "Just talk to me first. Okay? We do this together. I would never put my son at risk, but if we try this, we do it together."

"Together." It was hard after being on my own for four years in prison to be connected with someone. "What about Ty? Jaxson we've known each other for all of two seconds. What if you don't like the way I chew my food? Or I don't like the way you put on your shoes?"

I knew my examples were stupid, but I wasn't sure what else to say to get my point across.

Trying to be serious, Jaxson pressed his lips together before he burst into laughter. "If I get past your chewing, I think we can get past my shoe habits."

I slapped his chest. "I'm serious. Maybe those were bad examples. Let's talk about everything. Figure it out. Not say anything to Ty."

He scrubbed his hand across his chin creating a delicious friction sound. "I'm not dating you in secret, London, like we're ashamed. This affects Ty too. He's a lot to handle, London. A lot. You've seen it. He's part of the deal. It's our relationship, but he's part of it too. Fuck, I don't know how to do this."

"Have you ever dated with Ty around?"

"No. Not ever."

Tightening his arms around me, I leaned on his shoulder. "We'll get to know each other. Find out more. Not tonight. Not when I have to leave in a bit and your thoughts could talk you out of us. London, let's see where it goes. For both of us. All of us. I don't make commitments lightly, but I take them seriously."

"Me too. I like the sound of that." I sighed.

"Good." A finger grazed my cheek and I shivered.

I lifted my face and involuntarily licked my lips. Without missing a beat, Jaxson brought my face to his. The kiss intensified. I needed to be closer. In one swift movement, Jaxson flipped me on my back and hovered over me on the couch leaving me breathless. A vibration sounded from his pocket. "That's Dad. They're on their way back."

It was too soon for my time to be over with Jaxson, but I understood. He kissed me hard once more before his piercing green eyes watched me. "I want to take you on a date as soon as I can get a sitter for Ty."

"We could go to a park or ice cream parlor altogether?"

Feeling his lips against mine told me he liked the idea. The cell phone rang and I heard a regrettable groan. My core ached for more, but it was too soon. *Slow. Slow. Slow.* We needed that. There was still so much we needed to learn. And our attraction was catapulting us fast down the relationship road.

Fishing the phone out his pocket, Jaxson answered. "Hey. Yeah, that's fine." He chuckled. "Okay."

"What are you going to tell your parents?"

"That I got a second chance."

We smiled at each other. This was happening. This wasn't a dream. Beeping from the keypad was the cue for Jaxson to stand. I righted myself as Ty entered. "London, you missed feeding the baby sheep. It was awesome." He crashed into me.

Instinctively, my arms wrapped around him as Jaxson watched. "It sounds like it, little man. We'll have to go again sometime."

Ruffling his hair, Jaxson said, "We'll take her, buddy. We need to get you home and in bed."

"Aw, Dad. I want to stay here."

"Not tonight. We'll see London bright and early tomorrow."

Arms came around my neck. "Night, London."

"Night, Ty."

As they left, Jaxson looked over his shoulder and blew me a kiss. I caught it and returned the gesture before he walked out the door. My heart melted into a pile of goo. I hoped I kept this one piece of happiness I found.

TWELVE

A T THE TABLE IN THE kitchen, I ate granola and cereal. The silence comforted me as I processed what happened with Jaxson last night. Ty would be arriving in about two hours for me to watch until Jaxson was done with his rounds at the barn. Jaxson had controlling interest in the therapeutic part of the business while Levi controlled the McCole Classic. Both seemed to be lucrative business operations.

Even though it was Saturday, and my day off, I'd offered last night via text to help Pam since she needed to run a few errands in town. Originally, she was to watch Ty today. Glancing at the clock, I figured there was enough time for a run in the fresh country air. With my constantly changing schedule, it was hard to always fit a run in. Especially since today was my first day off since arriving.

Staying busy kept me focused and not dwelling on what couldn't be changed.

Since being released, I could see a difference in my body from eating better and being able to exercise more. I loved it. Hopefully soon I would have time to dance again.

Mid-bite of granola, a knock sounded. Around the food I tried to yell, "Just a second."

It was too early to have anyone here unless there was a problem. Quickly, I wiped my mouth and headed to the door. The early-morning angle of the sun blinded me for a second before I was able to focus. Two figures before me held a bouquet of wildflowers. I gasped as my hand gravitated toward my mouth.

"Dad says you bring a girl flowers when you like her. We like you, London." Ty thrust the wildflowers at me and I smiled. "Do you like us?" Before I had the chance to answer, he looked up to his father. "Dad what do girls bring guys they like?"

His green eyes pierced mine and those familiar butterflies returned. I had it bad for this man. "They give us their love."

My heart exploded. I'd never been romanced before. Of course, I went on dates, but Charles and I dated for so long we were complacent. Kneeling, I took the bouquet from Ty with his eyebrows puckered. I gave him a hug. "Thank you for the flowers."

The sweet delicious smell permeated the air. I loved wildflowers. They were perfectly imperfect with their beauty.

Tiny fingers motioned for me to come closer for a secret. In a loud whisper, he responded. "It's okay if you want to give me more than love. Like a super hero or something."

I busted out laughing as Jaxson ruffled his hair. "One day you'll understand, buddy. One day love is all you'll want."

Knocking his father's hands away, Ty gave him a you-are-crazy look.

The wooden screen door of the main house creaked open. Pam called from the back porch. "Ty, we need to get going."

Going? I thought I was watching him. Once Ty was out of earshot, I'd clarify. Ever-changing plans were definitely part of my daily schedule.

"Gotta go, Grama is calling me."

Before he could escape, Jaxson picked him up and gave him a hug. Jean-clad legs and cowboy boots kicked as he tried to wrestle free from Jaxson's hold. "Listen to Grama. Love you."

"Love you too, Dad."

Ty raced to the house. In his yellow shirt he looked like a lightning bolt. "I wish I had that much energy." Even standing, Ty bounced. I cleared my throat. "Do you need me to watch Ty at all today?"

A devilish smile appeared on his face. Those dimples. That scruff. It was all enough to make a girl go crazy. "Change of plans. I thought I could go with you this morning on your jog. I heard you mentioning it to Mom last night. Maybe spend some time together this morning before I have to work."

It wasn't until now I noticed Jaxson wore low slung black running shorts with a light-blue wicking shirt. "You're running with me?"

Jaxson was taking an interest in me. Things I liked to do. It wasn't a one-way street, but the beginning of building something else I wasn't used to. Charles never took an interest in my hobbies.

Hesitantly, he responded, "If you want company." Jaxson's confidence trailed off.

The thought of running with Jaxson nearly had me bouncing in place like a little girl. "Yes. Yes. Of course. It's just unexpected. I didn't mean to sound like I didn't want you to come. Let me grab my watch."

Traipsing inside, Jaxson followed. As soon as the door shut, my body was gently pushed against the door. Jaxson's mouth was on mine. Slightly pulling away, we smiled against each other's lips. Our breath mingled as I asked, "Did you sleep well?"

"I thought about us all night."

The kiss deepened for a few seconds before he stepped back, taking a deep breath.

"You really know how to swoon a girl. How is it you didn't date before?"

Part of me dreaded the answer. Was I the same as the girls before me?

Jaxson watched me closely while making sure he had my full attention. "I messed around from time to time. I wasn't interested in anything more. I'm not messing around with us, London. This isn't a casual fuck. I've never misled anyone. I want you to understand this. I wouldn't have my boy involved if it was."

In one swoop, Jaxson helped ease my apprehension. I gave him a small kiss before saying, "Well, I'm glad you changed your mind."

With my hand on his stomach, I felt his rigid abs. His subtle spice smell nearly had me wanting to sniff him, but I remembered myself. There was no need for the already long list of embarrassing acts I'd committed in front of him. Time for a subject change. We needed to get out of here before our obvious attraction took us to the next level sooner than intended. "Are you ready to be put through your paces?"

"You bet." He wagged his eyebrows and I blushed at the verbal innuendo I'd walked right into.

Sex. Wow, it had been a long time. My libido was ready to cash in the rain checks. And trust me, it was becoming more outspoken by the moment. Just the thought had me panicking. What if I wasn't any good when it was time? I'd only ever been with Charles. *Behave. Maybe the Thunder Down Under Vibrator Millie gave me should be used to calm me.*

Hands touched my shoulder. "London, baby, breathe. We're not rushing this. Why do you look scared shitless?"

It was best to be honest. "I'm nervous. I've only ever been with one person. What if I'm terrible? What if—"

Lips silenced me and I melted into the man who captivated my attention. "It's me and you. Anyone else in our past doesn't matter. I'm one lucky bastard to have another chance with you. London, I want to know everything about you. No secrets."

I beamed. Honesty was something I thrived on. "No secrets."

THIRTEEN

THE HEAT FROM THE SUN felt good on our morning jog. The air smelled fresh after the slight rain passed through last night. I tried to keep my eyes on the ground as we jogged in order to not look at the way the shirt clung to Jaxson's sweat-sheened body. He was in insane shape. Nearly done with the jog, it felt good to run for an hour.

At the quarter-mile mark from home, we slowed to a walk for the cool down. The whole time I'd spilled my guts about everything from Charles, to dancing, to prison. Around Jaxson it all came out—almost lifting a weight, knowing he knew everything. Patiently, Jaxson listened.

Finishing with my journey to Colorado, I asked, "So, have I scared you away yet?"

He raised his eyebrow and scoffed. Our bodies moved closer. "Hardly." Fingers wrapped around mine. I licked my lips to hide the insane smile that wanted to spread across my face. The pace slowed.

As the silence lingered, I wasn't sure what else to say. Saving me from rambling, Jaxson said, "Crystal, Ty's mom, was not who I thought she was. She knew all the right things to say and was interested in the same things. Then, I found out it was all an elaborate lie when she accidentally texted me versus her friend. I started digging and found out our relationship had been a setup from the beginning." He took a deep breath. "After that . . . from time to time, I heard about her drinking and doing drugs with her new richer boyfriend from mutual friends. No one ever said anything about a baby. She told them the baby was someone else's, so they didn't mention it. Ty had been born tiny and she said he was premature. People bought it."

The muscles in Jaxson's throat bobbed as he swallowed. "Almost a year later, Ty was dropped off on our doorstep in the middle of the night. I made it to the front door in time to see taillights disappearing. Ty was screaming. Turned out he was nearly starved to death. He was the size of a six-month-old when I first got him."

Jaxson stopped for a second and gazed out onto the field with the horses. Sparkle stood at attention at seeing me before going back to eating. The pressure on my grip tightened. "There was a note, sloppily written saying he was mine and she didn't want him. She purposely stopped using birth control to get pregnant and trap me, but I found out her plans too soon. She was mad and kept him a secret to punish me. We nearly lost him, London. He was hospitalized for almost a week. Those images will forever haunt me. If I had known—"

Shaking his head, he cleared the dark memory. I understood the need to escape being pulled into the past. It only leads to places that never wanted to let go. "I have full custody and Crystal has a restraining order against her. She may not even know about it. I've tried to locate her to simply know where she is but haven't had any luck. The last thing Ty needs is a crazy drugged-up mother showing up and shaking up his life."

"Jaxson . . ." Understanding filled my tone.

Pinning me with his eyes, he asked, "Have I scared *you* away yet?"

"No."

He gave me a quick kiss. "Good. Come have breakfast with me at my house."

"I'd like that. Let me grab my phone first so I can tell my dad good morning."

Nearly to the guesthouse, butterflies danced in my stomach. Hormones were out of control anytime I was in the vicinity of Jaxson. *Concentrate on the chlorine smell from the pool.* Yes, chlorine. It's very clean. His body. His sweaty body. *I need an orgasm.*

Shit.

This was bad. So very bad. I pressed my legs together as I entered the code. *Hold off for the thunder stick.* Millie was a godsend having the foresight that I would need something. Tonight I was putting that stick to good use.

Jaxson's hand rest underneath my breast as I messed the code up hitting a six instead of a nine. *Thunder stick. Thunder stick. No need for a dick.* Was I rhyming? Please, no.

Another swipe of his hand and I nearly melted. Involuntarily, I leaned my head back as his lips sucked a path down to my collarbone. "I think breakfast may have to wait, sweetheart."

"Yes. It can wait."

What's better than a thunder stick? Dick. Oh my gosh, I needed help or an orgasm.

I messed up the code again. His hand trailed down my stomach. I messed it up for a third time. Strong hands laid on top of mine and depressed the numbers for me. The lock blessedly opened. Before the door closed we were on each other tumbling to the floor. Lust exploded between us. Jaxson's hands were under my shirt as mine touched his chest. Pushing my sports bra up, he touched my nipple—a straight line to my inner need. *It's certain, I need a dick, not a thunder stick.*

"Of fuck, London. You are responsive."

Who cared about slow? Not me. Not my body.

He rolled my nipple while he kissed me. My phone rang. I called out. "Don't stop, don't you dare stop. I don't care if we're on the floor."

Fingers stopped their movement. My eyes sprung open. "What are you doing?"

A swift breath left Jaxson. "Sweetheart, the first time is not happening on the carpet in your living room. I can't control myself around you." His words were calm and collected. The exact opposite of his strung-tight body. He kissed my lips and I enjoyed having this effect on him. "Let me make it special for you. For us. Something to remember for the rest of our lives. Let me undress you. Devour you. Let's have breakfast first."

He traced his finger down my arm, eliciting that dipping feeling in my stomach.

I let out a breath, the ache in my lower abdomen nearly unbearable. "Well, when you put it that way, how is a girl supposed to argue? Breakfast it is."

Need filled my voice and Jaxson's lips pressed against mine. The bulge pressed against my leg hardened. "I promise to make it good, London."

My phone rang again and I let it go to voicemail as I slowed my breathing. I looked over to Jaxson. "You better."

Fingers glided over my still exposed stomach. "I'll more than make it up to you. I don't want us to look back and think we moved too fast. I want you more than anything, but I won't chance fucking this up."

A knock interrupted us. There was no such thing as privacy here. I huffed in frustration. Jaxson swore under his breath as he righted my sports bra and yanked down my top. "Next time we have a second together, I'm making sure we aren't interrupted."

Hopping up, Jaxson opened the door. "My word, you must be Jaxson."

Millie. I scrambled to the door. "Millie! Oh my gosh! You're here!" I threw my arms around her neck. "I can't believe you're here. I missed you."

It was unbelievable . . . Millie was here . . . standing in front of me.

"I missed you too." She pushed me back. "So, he decided to stop being stupid? Saw what was in front of him?"

I kept Millie updated on what was happening with Jaxson through our talks. And of course she was hardly ever subtle.

"Millie!" There were times I wanted to kill my best friend as I said her name with irritation.

Jaxson came up beside me. "I did and damn glad it didn't take me longer. It's nice to meet you, Millie."

Millie threw her arms around him and I heard her whispering something. I thought I heard something about frank and beans. Good grief. I was going to have a word with her.

Jaxson looked straight at me the entire time; those green eyes ensnared me as he answered Millie. "I promise."

A heat crept on my face guessing what Millie had said. Turning to me, Millie got serious. "I need to talk to you. I have something to show you. I couldn't tell you over the phone. I found it last night. I know this is shitty timing, but it's important."

Dread dripped into my stomach. Millie's eyes darted to Jaxson, silently asking if he could stay. Whatever it was, I would tell him. If we had any chance of making it, there wasn't room for secrets. "He can stay."

Of course, Jaxson looked confused. Even more so when Millie led me to the couch. This was bad. So bad. Bile tasted bitter in my mouth.

Jaxson sat beside me. The warm embrace helped soothe me minutely. "Millie, what the hell is going on? You're scaring the shit out of her."

"Shit, London. I'm sorry. I'm not trying to scare you. I'm still trying to process it myself. This isn't bad like you think. I promise."

She pulled out a manila envelope and handed it to me. Numbly, I opened it while she nervously rubbed her dark-clad jeans. They were medical records.

My medical records.

From June third.

"I don't understand. Why did you bring this?" The past took hold as the images I'd seen from the accident replayed in my mind. I looked away for a second as a tear slipped free. Jaxson's grip tightened on me.

"Flip to the finding's page." Millie's voice was shell-shocked. How was this not bad?

Quickly, I thumbed to the back. The blood drained from my face as my eyes shot to Millie's. "London, you were framed."

I was going to be sick. My stomach revolted as I shot off the couch, barely making it to the toilet. I was framed. It wasn't my fault. The dry heaves continued. Tears left salty tracks down my cheeks. Millie wet a washcloth as I calmed down. Strong soothing hands rubbed my back. "What's going on, Millie? What did you show her?" There was an edge to Jaxson's voice—defensive and ready to strike.

Deep slow breaths abated the nausea. The cool tile was relief against my hot clammy skin. Millie handed me the wrung out washcloth and wasn't answering Jaxson. She wanted me to have the choice of how much he knew.

Hoarsely, I spoke before Jaxson lost it. "All the evidence submitted at the trial supported I only had alcohol in my system." Tears made fresh tracks against the old down my face. Holding up the paper I continued. "This was the real report. There was more than alcohol in me."

Millie replied as I wiped my face. "There is no way you would ever drug yourself."

I started sobbing. "This wasn't my fault. This wasn't my fault.

I never felt I could do something like that."

Jaxson picked me up and cradled me against his chest. "Shh, sweetheart. I have you."

As Jaxson set me down on the couch, I reached for Millie. "Thank you. Thank you. Thank you."

Millie sat in the chair next to the couch and held my hand. "Anything for my bestie. Anything. I'll always believe in you. I wish we could have found this prior to the trial. It would have changed everything."

More sobs came. There were a million questions swimming around in my head, but all I could focus on was I had been drugged. Nurse-mode kicked in from my best friend. "London, with the amount of Rohypnol in your system, there is no way you were coherent for long. No way. You couldn't have driven from your house to Alec's neighborhood. You would have been barely conscious to do anything. Someone put you in that car and did who knows what."

I shivered. Someone had done this to me. To Alec. To my family. To Alec's family. "I'm not a murderer. I'm not a killer."

Jaxson clutched me closer to him. "No, sweetheart. You never were."

"How did you find this?" Jaxson asked the next question I would have if I hadn't been trying to process everything. I was innocent. Innocent. The word rattled in my head as the shadow that suffocated me faded. Alec. Sweet Alec. A life stolen for a reason that wasn't revealed. An ache formed thinking how we were bystanders. Both robbed of our innocence.

Millie picked up the report. "I've been dating the sheriff." I scrunched my eyes. Wasn't he old? She responded to my facial gesture. "Not Norman. He passed away nearly three and a half years ago. His son, Chris, is now Sheriff."

"I remember him. He was a few grades older."

Anytime I asked about the cop, she had been vague over the last week or so. Now, it made sense.

She winked. "Yes, he was. We had some fun back in the day." Waving her hands she cleared her thoughts. "I'm digressing. Anyway, I've been dating him since I sent that text last week. I've been staying over some at Chris'. After he would leave for work, I would snoop."

My eyes widened and Millie shrugged. "We made it clear it was casual. Yesterday, I found the file in his father's things. It was an old manila envelope in a box of stuff buried in the back of the closet. I can't believe it was still there. I made a copy and put everything back before heading to work. Then, I booked my ticket and came here since I have the next three days off work. I didn't want to say over the phone. I got a bad vibe when I thought about it. There's no telling what the person responsible is capable of. I couldn't take a chance."

This still seemed like a dream. *Why would the sheriff not have shared the files? Who wanted to do something like this to me . . . to Alec . . . to my family? With every truth, more questions unearthed themselves.*

"There's more."

"What?" There wasn't much more I could take. This was all too much. The forced reality I made myself believe crumbled around me.

Millie took out a notepad. "Norman died five months after you went to prison. The same doctor who tested your blood, Dr. Michaels, oversaw Norman's autopsy. Three months after that, Dr. Michaels died in a car crash. London that is not a coincidence. Everyone died who helped cover up whatever this is except . . ."

I finished her sentence. "Whoever framed me."

"Yes."

My hands shook at the realization that the person behind all this was more dangerous than I ever imagined. "They wanted me out of Guin."

"I think so. Has anything else happened since you came here?"

"No." A lead weight dropped in the pit of my stomach. At least three people lost their lives because of this person.

Jaxson was quiet through this whole thing. I glanced up at him. He watched Millie as he asked, "Who do you think it is?"

Sitting back in the chair, Millie responded, "I think it's Rachel. The fiancée of London's ex. Her family has the pull to do something like this. They wanted the political affiliation and made that clear all through school. Hell, Rachel practically threw herself at Charles every chance she got when London wasn't there. She secured Charles pretty easily after you were sentenced. After four years of schmoozing and laying the foundation, Charles is running for Mayor. Supposedly, he'll go for the presidency when he's eligible per the rumors his dad is spreading to fuel his own campaign. And guess who is the perfect person to be by his side as the perfect politician's wife?"

My head spun. Abruptly I stood. "I need to brush my teeth."

Quickly, I left the room to find my toothbrush and toothpaste. *How could someone do this to another human being?* The loss. It was too much. All to get Charles. His political connections. The life of a politician never intrigued me. I actually preferred not to be part of it.

Vigorously, I brushed my teeth. Hands eased on top of mine. "I think they're clean."

I spit the toothpaste out and rinsed my mouth. "Everything is a lie. Was a lie. I've spent four years convincing myself I killed him. For four years, I believed I drank and drove. Four years."

Wrapping his arms around my waist, he took a deep breath. "If Charles wants you back when all this comes out, do you want him?"

Without hesitating, I knew the answer. It had been the truth right in front of me for so long, but I hadn't been ready to face it . . . to give up another piece of what had been. I turned and placed my hands on the side of his face. "I would have never started something with you if I still loved Charles. Or if I wanted to rekindle something with him. If Charles showed up three days ago before we admitted our feelings for each other, nothing would have happened."

Lips pressed against mine. "I like that answer."

"Me too."

"Let's go back out there and finish talking this out. Are you okay?" Jaxson's eyes were filled with concern and it warmed me.

I shrugged and exhaled wanting to give him the truth but not sure how I felt myself. "I don't know. It's a lot to take in."

Guiding me back to the living room, Millie sat on the couch worrying her lip. "London, I'm so sorry."

I hugged her. "Don't be. You gave me back something I never thought I would get." Relief washed over Millie's face as she visibly sagged in the dark leather chair. Sitting next to Jaxson, I laid my head against the back of the couch. "What do we do with all this new information?"

Jaxson leaned forward. "We have no idea who actually set this in motion. All we have is a medical report that proves London was drugged, but not by who. The police were in on it before. So was the doctor at the hospital. Fuck."

He popped his neck as he took a deep breath. I knew where he was going. Continuing Jaxson's thought, I said, "If we share what we have so far, all our cards will be on display. And whoever this is may do something else. Potentially worse. Especially if they feel threatened."

Millie's phone rang. "I need to take this. It's work."

My stomach turned again thinking about them hurting people I loved. Hurting Ty. The muscles tightened within me ready to spring. Jaxson's jaw clenched in my peripheral vision. He squeezed me tighter. "I know what you're thinking. Don't."

There was nothing to say. I couldn't lie to him. If I needed to leave, I would. The pressure from Jaxson's hold didn't let up. "London, don't do anything rash."

I turned. "What if they come after Ty? Or you? To hurt me. We barely know each other." A few more tears escaped. "Alec died because of someone wanting to hurt me."

"Let's talk this out. Okay? No rash decisions."

Nodding in agreement, I took a deep breath. "Okay." That was something I could promise.

Millie came back in the room. "Sorry, they were checking if I could be at the hospital tomorrow afternoon for a department head meeting. Apparently, there's a big announcement coming on Monday they want us to be prepared for. I think the administrator is resigning unexpectedly. There's been a lawsuit the hospital has been dealing with and it seems like they're taking action upon some findings. They're paying for the change fees. I'm going to have to change my flight to the early ass one again. Ugh. After dinner I'll staying at a hotel near the airport. The hospital is making the reservations."

"You can stay here." I hated I would only have today with her, but some time was better than nothing.

Resuming her seat, Millie responded, "I know, but it'll be easier. Getting up at four is better than three in the morning."

"Well, you're always welcome here." Millie grabbed my hand and gave it a loving squeeze as I asked, "What's the next step?" Obviously, I wanted the person responsible behind killing Alec to pay, but we needed to be smart about this.

Thumbing through the medical records again, Millie pointed to a small faint line. "You were treated in Guin, but Doctor Albertson worked at Northwest Medical. My hospital. They sent your blood work to Winfield to have it done in the orders on the first page. The Guin hospital lab was backed up, which happens from time to time."

As I looked for more answers within the documents I stated. "The Guin records were forged to make it look like the blood tests happened there."

Papers shuffled. "Yeah, I'll see if I can find anything which shows the lab was backed up. I think whoever the mastermind behind this is didn't get the doctor to cooperate until after. Why have blood tests done at all if they planned to forge them? Let me see what I can find."

"Millie, I don't want you to get hurt." The thought of Millie hurt because of all this was too much to bear.

She leaned forward. "If we keep it only between the three of us then no one should be the wiser until we find something else. Enough to take the asshole down. We'll have to keep everyone else in the dark."

A headache loomed in the back of my head. I wanted my name clear, the real killer to be convicted, but not at the cost of other people getting hurt. "For now I think that's a good plan."

FOURTEEN

I T WAS EARLY EVENING AS Millie and I sat on the couch, curled up next to each other watching *90210*. Jaxson left mid-morning to work. I could tell he hated leaving me but knew I needed time with Millie. The reality still felt like an illusion.

Innocent.

That was now my verdict.

Whoever caused Alec's death, I wanted them to pay. But, we had to be careful. Surprise was our biggest ally at this point.

I checked the time. Dinner would be here soon and Millie would be gone. Seeing my best friend helped in more ways than one. She approved of Jaxson and thought he was a good guy.

The *90210* show ended as we finished the last of our hot chocolate. Millie took a chance because she believed in me. "Thanks for all you did, Millie. Even if only the three of us ever know, I know."

"That's what besties are for. We'll keep looking to see if there's anything else." Pensively, she tucked the strand of blonde hair behind her ear.

"What made you decide to start looking?"

In all the commotion, I hadn't thought of getting the backstory.

"I never stopped, but I wasn't close enough to dig deep and not bring attention. The evidence said it was your fault, but it never made sense. Two nights after you left for Colorado, I watched an episode of *Criminal Minds*. Then, I started thinking about the facts."

After I was convicted, I asked Millie and my parents to stop saying I was framed. It only made the guilt worse and felt like I wasn't dealing with the repercussions of my actions. I raised my eyebrow. "*Criminal Minds?*"

Shrugging, she said, "You can't help when a stroke of genius happens." She took a sip of water as I laughed. It felt good to be able to be happy without any guilt. "Anyway, I thought about how the accident didn't make sense. And then the note that was sent to the businesses. While you were in prison, there were no threats. Nothing. Not hardly twenty-four hours after being released, you're threatened."

Her finger raised in the air to emphasize the point. "And that didn't happen until after you saw Charles with . . . Rachel and her parents while you were at Caroline's. The next day, threats happened. The only other person you saw was Alec's mom, who I don't see having the pull to blackball you. Rachel's family have hidden scandals before."

A vague memory took shape as I filled in the gap. "Oh, I remember. In high school, there was that article about Rachel's mom getting arrested for drunk driving. Then, the newspaper printed a retraction in a special edition which ran that afternoon." It had been forever since I'd thought about that. One day the town was abuzz with the gossip, then there was nothing. No one spoke a word about it.

Millie snapped her fingers. "Exactly. And now that you've left Guin . . . had no contact with Charles . . . the threats magically stopped. That's more than a fucking coincidence. I knew we needed to get creative and relook at the facts. There was something we missed. There's always a loose thread that unravels the rest of a plan. No one is perfect. At the Piggly Wiggly, I ran into Chris and remembered Norman was the officer in charge. My plan hatched when Chris asked me on a date."

"You're crazy, but I love you dearly."

"Forever and always. So . . ." Millie waggled her eyebrows. "Jaxson McCole."

I knew this was coming. The one-liner approval I received earlier today was not enough for Millie. Keeping it simple, I responded, "Yes."

"You know I want more details than *yes*. You seem different with him. I mean different from how you were with Charles."

Unconsciously, I bit my lower lip as I thought about the man working his way past my defenses. "I feel different. There's something deeper there that brings me to life. We have to be smart about this because of Ty. Letting our hormones take control like today is not the answer."

"Or let things happen how their supposed to."

The words were easier said than done with my over-chaotic brain that circled around and sometimes wasn't sensible. The threads of the afghan danced between my fingers as I confessed what happened. "We came close to sleeping with each other today. It stopped right before you got here. He wants to make it special."

A warm hand landed on mine, stopping the thread's movement. "London, it should be special. You deserve special. But . . ." She waited for me to look up. "Don't overthink it. You've over-thought things your whole life—every decision with the pros and cons and the effects. You lost four years. Don't risk losing something else because you are scared."

"When did you get so wise?"

She bumped my shoulder. "I've always been older and wiser."

"By two months. You're only older by two months."

We laughed. Taking a more serious note, I asked. "How's your mom?"

"As good as can be expected. Her spirits are high. The last CT Scan showed the tumors were shrinking."

I held Millie's hand. "Good. Keep me posted and let me know if you need anything."

On the other side of the door I could hear the code being entered. I had a feeling it was a certain five-year-old boy. Jaxson and Pam offered to change it to keep Ty out, but I thought it was adorable. Millie watched as the door swung open and slammed shut. Ty took a deep breath in his cute jeans and blue super hero T-shirt while closing his eyes. "I think I tricked them."

"Who are you tricking, Ty?"

Ty saw me, and his eyes lit up. "Grama and Dad. They said you had a friend and I couldn't bother you. I figured you were missing me. I told them I was going to the bathroom, but ran out the back door to you. Was I right?"

He hopped on my lap.

"I was missing you something fierce." I squeezed him and kissed the top of his head. "This is my friend, Millie."

Holding out his hand, Ty said, "I'm Ty McCole."

Millie shook his hand and gave me a he-is-so-adorable look. "Nice to meet you, Ty. London has told me a lot about you. Said you guys are best friends."

He stood straighter. "We are. Did you know my dad likes London a lot?"

Conspiringly, Millie whispered like it was top-secret knowledge. "Really? How do you know?" This piqued my curiosity. Five-year-old intel was truthful.

He leaned in closely and whispered. I leaned in to make sure I heard everything. "I can tell by his goofy grin when he talks about her. He talks about her a lot. He says—"

A knock at the door had us all looking like we were caught doing something bad. Ty and I looked at each other as Jaxson's voice came through. "Ty Edward McCole! I know you're in there."

"Save me, London. Make him give that goofy grin."

Giggling, I said, "Stay here, buddy. I'll try and get the goofy grin."

I tiptoed to the door and glanced back. Ty could barely keep his laugh in as I innocently said, "Who is it?"

"Jaxson." *That voice was sex on a stick and then some.*

"What can I help you with?"

"I'm looking for an escapee. About three feet tall, dark hair, green eyes."

Engaging the safety chain, I opened the door. A huge grin met me. "Hmm . . . it may sound familiar, depending on if he's in trouble."

Lowering his voice, he replied, "He is. But, I'm willing to take volunteers for his punishment."

Many *punishments* flitted through my mind. Punishments I would gladly endure.

"What do you have in mind?" The breathiness in my voice couldn't be missed.

"Come out here and see, sweetheart."

Complying, I opened the door after taking off the safety chain. "Will I get the goofy grin Ty told me about? He thinks that's the way I'll save him from his daddy's wrath. He says you've been talking about me a lot."

Jaxson leaned in, his outdoor woodsy smell engulfing me. *Yes, I want to be punished. Wickedly punished.* Dazed by the thoughts, smell, and Jaxson's presence in general, it took me two seconds too late to register his intentions as he scooped me up. We were headed to the pool.

"Jaxson McCole! Don't you dare! Put me down!" Everyone came out from the main house and guesthouse. I refused to get distracted by the sinewy abdominal muscles I could feel through his shirt. I could barely stop laughing to sound serious which only fueled Jaxson's grin. "Jaxson! I mean it! Put me down."

"Dad! What are you doing?" Fractionally, we turned to face Millie and Ty who were grinning like fools.

"Showing London what happens when a man has a goofy grin over a girl." The grin appeared as our stares locked onto each other. The world slipped away.

Ty giggled and it broke our trance. "There's that goofy grin, Dad. Am I saved?"

Remembering my eminent swim in the pool, I struggled in his arms, which was no match for the iron grip on me. I needed a new plan. I worked on getting a straight face as we made it to the edge of the pool. "Jaxson, let's be reasonable. Talk this out."

At the edge of the pool, Jaxson watched me with a twinkle in his eye. He loved this foreplay. "Go on."

"All I did was harbor a refugee for a bit. A cute refugee. He was being kept prisoner from seeing me. Don't you think that's the bigger crime?"

"Millie, dunk her or save her?" Jaxson called over his shoulder.

I locked my gaze with her, imploring the best friend guilt. "Millie! We've been best friends for years. I've never contested your claim over Dylan! Do not betray me!"

"I'm talking this out with the refugee. Hold please." Millie leaned down to Ty and they whispered back and forth.

"Ty! I'm your bestest friend. I rescued you! I give you ice cream!"

It was as if I wasn't talking as the whispering continued. My pitiful pleas were falling on deaf ears. The deep rumble of Jaxson's laugh vibrated through me straight to my core. His lips touched my ear. "I think you're about to get dunked."

I moved my head to brush my lips against his, deploying my ultimate weapon. "It may keep you from getting lucky later."

"Are you challenging me?"

Oh shit. Jaxson angled us to where they couldn't see his mouth barely nibble my earlobe. "It's taking everything I have not to kiss you in front of everyone." The desire to have his lips was overwhelming. He didn't stop weaving the spell. "I want you, London."

"DUNK HER! DUNK HER!" The chanting broke the spell.

At their words, I latched on to Jaxson. "You don't have to listen to them."

"Sweetheart, they've spoken."

"We can get a second opinion."

The time for words was over. Jaxson easily unhooked me and swung my body as if I weighed nothing more than a sack of sugar. The laughter bubbled free. Right as he released me, I grabbed on to him, bringing him with me.

"Shit!"

The water splashed around us, cool and refreshing. I swam underwater a few feet away, out of reach. Just as Jaxson breached the surface, I splashed him. Through all the water, he shook his head and said, "I'm coming for you, London."

I squealed and took off to the side of the pool. Being barefoot had its advantages as I quickly made it to the edge. Jaxson was slower. Lifting myself up, I barely made it out of the pool when Jaxson's hand grazed my toes. More giggles as I heard them chant, "Run! Run! Run!"

"London, I will get you."

Jaxson hoisted himself out of the water. *Do not look at the wet clothes clinging to his muscular body.* Sassily, I taunted him. "I can run a long ways, remember?"

"I know, but—"

I took off across the pavement to the yard. Literally, we had lost our minds as we shamelessly flirted in front of anyone who joined the show. As I hit my stride, I was tackled to the ground. Jaxson took the weight of our fall while cradling me before flipping me on to my back.

"You were holding out on me this morning during our run," I accused.

"No, I wanted to stay near the girl I like. A lot."

I loved those small professions. "What are you going to do now that you've caught me?"

"Make you fall in love with me."

Fall in love with him. The words thrilled and scared me at the same time. Breathlessly, I responded, "I can't wait."

And I meant it.

A satisfied smirk appeared on his handsome face. Helping me up, Jaxson and I walked back to our audience with his possessive hand on my back. Jaxson announced, "All is good. She declared me as hers."

I smacked his stomach as everyone else laughed.

"Would you and Millie like to join us for dinner in town?" Pam called from the deck.

"Sure. We'd love to." I knew Millie wouldn't mind going. I was nervous going out with his family since this was moving at what felt like an exponential speed. But it felt right. "Do I have time to take a quick shower and change?"

"Yes, dear. Come to the main house when you're done."

A sweet smile graced my lips as an idea formed. Without any warning, I pushed Jaxson and he tumbled into the pool. I took off past Ty and Millie. "You guys are either with me or against me. Make your choice quick."

Pam called after her son. "Jaxson, you deserved that! Leave her alone."

I quickly entered the code on the keypad. Millie and Ty were with me, jumping in excitement for me to hurry. Good choice. The door flung open and we got inside as Jaxson came toward me with an ecstatic smile, not listening to his mother. He loved this. I loved this. Slamming the door, I engaged the deadbolts.

Outside the door, I heard him make it to the porch. "I definitely have the goofy grin, sweetheart."

"Me too."

"Hurry up so I can see you again."

"I will."

High fives were exchanged as I made my way to the shower. Life was perfect. Well, as perfect as it had been for as long as I could remember.

FIFTEEN

DINNER PASSED BY IN A blur in the rustic dance hall diner. In the middle was a dance floor for families to dance. Tables surrounded the area. Two kids with their father were currently dancing to a country song on the old wood floor. It was adorable.

I focused back on our table. Everyone was smiles and laughing as they talked. The McCole's were truly a family—a family like mine had been. Sydney and I were still getting to know each other as she had been traveling extensively with Mallory for dance competitions. The whole family supported each other regardless as I witnessed over the last week. Jaxson went by Sydney's house daily to make sure everything was okay.

Leaning back, I pushed my burger away. "That was incredible."

The moment we walked into this place I knew the meal would be delicious with the savory smells. A slow song came on I didn't recognize. Couples danced in the center of the room while the music played from the jukebox. I loved the family fun environment the restaurant provided.

Jaxson's arm draped along the back of the chair. "The three of us need to come back on Sunday for Sunday Sundae. It's one of Ty's favorites."

Across from us, Ty sat with a huge grin on his face the entire time while he watched us. "Can we bring London here tomorrow?"

"I think we can if she's free."

"I'm free."

All eyes were on us. Suddenly, I felt subconscious and refolded my napkin. Thankfully, Millie broke the silence. "Why don't we pick out some songs to listen to, Ty?"

It was overwhelming feeling like I was on display. More importantly, the last thing I wanted was for Ty to be upset if this didn't work out. Maybe this was too fast?

"Yes!" Ty's loud response brought me back from my thoughts.

Jaxson quirked an eyebrow at me and I focused on the blue checkered pattern of my napkin.

Ty followed Millie up to the red vibrant music box. "That boy has more energy than a firecracker." Levi chuckled. "He takes after Jaxson. Nearly the spitting image of him."

"You'll have to share some stories some time." I was excited to see baby photos and hear embarrassing stories.

"Oh, I will."

Jaxson groaned. "None of it's true."

"We'll let London be the judge of that."

Again, Jaxson and I got lost in our gaze. A tap on my shoulder caused me to turn and see a smiling Millie. "I think it's time we got our dance on."

My eyes widened. "What? Here?"

"Yep."

An anxiousness came over me. Part of me had been avoiding dancing for a reason I hadn't wanted to admit. But now, there was no reason I shouldn't be able to enjoy things without guilt. Determined, I stood. "Let's dance."

The beginning to "Burn" by Ellie Goulding played as the dance floor filled with other strangers. The beat infiltrated my bones as I let it seep in. My muscles remembered as they moved to the beat.

Millie and I loved to dance. We fed off each other. A light thin sheet of sweat coated my skin. I missed this. I missed dancing. I missed feeling alive.

The song came to an end. "Welcome back, London. You've still got it."

"It's good to be back."

The song shifted to "Superman" by Bon Jovi. Familiar arms wrapped around me. "Can I have a dance with my girl?" Jaxson asked Millie.

"She's all yours."

Millie walked back to the table as Jaxson moved in closer to slow dance. "I'm glad you started dancing again."

"Me too."

Our bodies moved as one. Only Jaxson stayed in focus as the rest of the world drifted away. "Isn't the first song a couple dances to their song?"

The tempo sped up and Jaxson twirled me in and out as excited squeal bubbled out. Jaxson had moves. "I think we now officially have a song."

As the song came to an end, he leaned to my ear. "I'll be yours for a lot longer than tonight."

"I hope so."

A tug on my shirt brought my attention to Ty on the dance floor with a hopeful looking face. "London! London! Will you dance with me?"

"Yes, little man. Let's dance."

Leaning over, we started moving haphazardly as I mimicked Ty's erratic moves. Levi and Millie with Pam and Jaxson soon joined as we danced to "Sweet Home Alabama" by Lynard Skynard. There was no doubt Millie's selections were still playing.

A few songs later, we wrapped it up and headed outside. The cool breeze felt good against my heated skin. Time drew near for Millie to leave. I hugged her tightly to me. "Thank you for all you did. Be careful."

"I promise. Be happy, London. We'll figure this out. We'll use our code."

If Millie found something new out about me being framed, she would tell me about a new ice cream flavor she tried. It was simplistically stupid, but would keep anyone unaware of what we were doing. With not knowing who was behind this and seeing the depths they went, we weren't going to take a chance our phones were tapped.

I waved as she drove off and took a deep breath as hands wrapped around my leg. "Night, London. I'm leaving."

Kneeling, I gave him a hug. "Night, Ty. Don't let the bedbugs bite."

"Night," I said to Jaxson, who was right next to me as I stood.

Jaxson picked up Ty putting a few feet between us. "Love you, Ty. Listen to Grama and Grampa."

"Love you, Dad. Make sure London gets home."

"I will."

Skipping away, Ty got in Levi's mammoth sized truck before leaving. Crickets chirping filled the silence between us as Jaxson moseyed closer to me. We were alone at the edge of the parking lot. "Did you arrange this?"

"Mom and Dad offered to give us some time together."

Time alone . . . with Jaxson. I smiled at the thought. "It's been pretty crazy the last couple of days."

"It's why we need to have a date . . . some time for us."

Jaxson helped me in his big truck. Like father, like son. Nervous butterflies drifted in my stomach. *Let things happen naturally. See where this goes. No pressure.* With my hand held in his, he rubbed soothing circles as the truck bounced along the dirt road.

"How are you doing after this morning?"

The realizations of the morning felt like a lifetime ago. "It's surreal. I'm scared. It's a new reality for me."

"We'll figure it out."

I stared out the window. "I know. It means a lot." And it did. More than Jaxson would ever know. The truck came to a stop. "Where are we?"

"A field. Come on."

My eyes rolled heavenward at Captain Obvious' statement. In the moonlight the grass swayed to its own beat as the wind rustled about. It was peaceful. At the back of the truck, Jaxson spread a blanket. "I thought we could spend some time watching the stars."

"I'd love to." Snuggled into the side of Jaxson, I gazed up into the sky and asked, "Do you worry this is too fast?"

"No. Not at all, London. It feels wrong to hold back."

"Yeah, it does." That was true. When I let my heart lead me, things felt right.

We lay under the stars and talked while stealing kisses. A shooting star raced across the sky. "Make a wish, sweetheart."

"You."

"I wish—"

I silenced him with my finger. "You can't say it out loud. It's bad luck." A brow raised and I explained. "Before Mom got sick, we wished on every shooting star. We always said them out loud and our wishes didn't come true. Don't say it out loud. Please."

Lips found my forehead. "I'll keep it to myself but let you know when it comes true."

"Perfect." Jaxson got me and wasn't pressing to push me to wish.

The intensity grew. Fingers crept up my stomach. "London, I want you to come home with me. Only if you want."

Desire flooded me.

I wanted this.

I wanted him.

Without hesitating, I responded, "Yes."

In a swift movement, Jaxson had me in his arms as he walked to the truck. Something grew stronger between us like I had never imagined. A connection solidified.

The drive to his house felt like it took forever. Holding hands wasn't enough. I needed more.

Finally, his house came into view. The truck stopped. Jaxson hauled me over to the driver's seat from the passenger side and nibbled on my neck. *Yes! Yes! Yes!* I closed my eyes to absorb the sensation.

"From the moment you screamed that night, I've wanted you, London."

A moan escaped. "Me, too. Hurry, Jaxson."

I was lost in the touch of his lips. "Are you sure you want this, London?"

"Yes. I'm sure. I don't want to fight what I feel is right."

We were all hands and touching as we made our way up the driveway and to the porch. The rest of the world drifted away as Jaxson's touch consumed me. Devoured me.

Fumbling with the key, the front door finally opened. Hungrily, he kissed me as we zigzagged our way back to his bedroom. While I'd watched Ty, I'd looked in Jaxson's bedroom wondering what it would be like to be in his arms. I was about to find out.

The house was masculine, lacking a woman's touch but filled with Jaxson's cologne. The open floor plan only added to the vastness.

In the bedroom, Jaxson flipped on the dimmer switch before setting me down. I missed the warmth of his body. A soft glow bathed us. This was it. This was the moment our relationship would change.

A finger trailed down my cheek eliciting a gasp. "If this is going too fast between us, London. Tell me."

"I promise it's not."

Hands grabbed the hem of my dress and slowly pulled it over my body, the cool breeze elicited goose bumps across my skin. Thank goodness, I had the foresight of wearing some of the sexy lingerie Millie gave me. Tonight was a matching see through pale-pink panty set.

"You're gorgeous. Absolutely stunning, sweetheart."

"I wish I could say the same, but you're fully clothed."

Jaxson removed his shirt and I could barely focus as his taut chest and finely-tuned abdomen came into view. Tentatively, I touched the ridges and felt his skin quiver beneath my touch. "That's better. So much better."

Lips touched my neck as I felt pressure on my sex and he backed us toward the bed. His bed. The mattress met me and I leaned back, earning a groan from Jaxson as I put myself on display. "Jaxson . . ."

With his other hand, he unsnapped the front of my bra, freeing me. "Beautiful . . ." The words sounded as if he'd never seen anyone like this before. Warmth engulfed my nipple followed by sucking. I arched off the bed. "So responsive. I love how your body reacts to every touch."

More pressure.

The amazing sensation built.

More pressure.

The orgasm neared as I lost myself to the pleasure. A moan escaped me. He switched nipples. It had been so long that my body detonated quickly and my eyes fluttered shut. I felt the fabric of my panties slide down my legs and the sound of Jaxson's zipper. Then nothing. I opened my eyes as Jaxson removed his jeans in fluid movement, releasing himself.

My word. He was . . . blessed.

From the drawer he pulled out a condom and laid it on the bed table. "First, I want to taste you, London. Then, I'm going to make love to you."

He captured my mouth. Before I was ready, his lips moved down the base of my throat and to my erect nipples, leaving a trail of fire in their wake. The sensations were so strong I thought I was going to combust. His tongue toyed with my nipple bringing moans of pure pleasure from me. He spent ample time between my breasts before trailing kisses down my stomach which tightened in response as he neared his goal.

Arousal, lust, and desire were rampant through me. At the top of my apex he kissed me and I writhed against the bed. "So responsive, sweetheart."

His tongue traced around my nub. "So beautiful."

"Jaxson, please."

Warmth flooded me as Jaxson licked me before dipping his tongue inside my core. There was an intense pressure building as his thumb made contact with my clit. The orgasm washed over me without warning. Tendrils of pleasure spiraled through my body as I became boneless in the moment of ecstasy.

Jaxson's lips moved back up my body before he kissed me. I tasted myself on him. It was erotic and the need for more made itself known.

"Sweeter than honey, baby. I already have a condom on." I felt him at my entrance.

"Please, Jaxson." The tip nudged my entrance. Our eyes locked and I took a deep breath. "Jaxson, I want this. I want it with you."

It felt like my first time as he achingly pushed in ever so slowly, stretching me, filling me—making us one. Sparks flew between us, tying me to him deeper than I was able to admit to myself. Fully in, he put his forehead to mine. "I could spend the rest of my life right here like this. Are you okay?"

"Yes. Feels so good. Don't stop."

Ever so slowly he moved in and out, drawing out the pleasure, kindling a need. I clawed at his back demanding more, not able to wait. His teeth nipped my shoulder.

The pace picked up.

The friction warmed me.

It wasn't near enough. "Faster, Jaxson."

He pumped into me. I met him thrust for thrust.

Faster.

Deeper.

Harder.

I was nearing my orgasm. The strained muscles in Jaxson's neck told me he was close as we both climbed to the pleasure awaiting us. A light sheen of sweat coated our bodies. He shifted and I exploded around him while arching my back, the beaded tips of my breast brushing against his chest as he pumped into me before finding his release.

This was more intense than I'd ever experienced.

More emotion.

More feelings.

More everything.

He collapsed on me, keeping the weight off with his arms. "I'll never be the same again after having you."

"Me either. Jaxson, I'm falling fast."

"I've already fallen, sweetheart."

Rolling to the side, he disposed of the condom and brought me to him. I felt safe. I felt loved. Soon we dozed off, basking in our lovemaking. This was perfect. Beyond perfect.

SIXTEEN

I FELT ACROSS THE BED to snuggle closer to Jaxson, feeling a chill in the air. I was greeted with cold sheets. I was alone. "Jaxson."

My heart hammered wondering what the next step was. I wanted more but how much more did Jaxson want?

"I'm out here."

I took a deep steadying breath. Taking the sheet with me, I walked to the balcony in his bedroom that faced the mountains. The cool night air helped awaken me. "What are you doing out here?"

He pulled me onto his lap. "Thinking about us." Apprehension filled me again. "You're tensing. It's nothing bad." Kissing my neck, I gave him access and relaxed as his lips soothed me. "I don't know how I'll make it a night without you in my bed."

"Jaxson." He wanted me. The smile was impossible to suppress.

"I'm serious, London."

Fingers traced down my stomach and I arched needing the contact. "We'll figure it out. Tomorrow. Let's focus on this moment right now. Hell, I know you're thinking this is fast, but I want to be honest with you."

"Me too. I need the honesty, Jaxson. Even if it scares me."

"I promise."

More nibbles along my neck as Jaxson murmured, "I'm going to taste every inch of you."

RAYS FROM THE open balcony door beamed into the room. We'd left the doors open when we came in from outside last night. There wasn't a part we didn't know intimately about each other now. I touched my lips remembering Jaxson's against mine as we made love through the entire night. The memories flooded me. Perfect memories. Jaxson treated me as if I was the most precious thing to him. I smiled to myself remembering his lips whisper sweet nothings against my skin. I turned my head to see his face peacefully asleep.

Warmth surrounded me as Jaxson held me to him while he slept. This was peace.

Last night was how my first time should have felt. The connection and intimacy was beyond anything and it was only our first time. With Charles it was more . . . platonic, lacking the soul-shattering depth I felt with Jaxson. Charles had always been attentive but our connection had been a spark versus the flame Jaxson and I shared. For so many years in prison, I'd thought I'd lost the love of my life.

I was wrong.

Charles wasn't the love of my life. Things with Jaxson would take their course, but what we had was more . . . so much more.

Pressure increased on my stomach as Jaxson brought me closer to him. His frank was ready for more. I nearly giggled out loud adopting Millie's terminology mentally. "Morning. What are you thinking about? I can feel your wheels turning." That sleep-ridden voice had my thoughts turning to lust quickly.

"Last night. How different it was."

Kissing my shoulder blade, he asked, "Different good?"

"Yes." I turned to face him, my breasts rubbed up against him, turning into pointy peaks. "Different fantastic."

His worried face relaxed. "I meant what I said last night. I don't know how I'm going to survive without you with me at night."

I stroked his face and took a deep breath. "It will make the times we have together more special. You know I can't stay over. That will confuse Ty."

"I know." Lips brushed mine. "We need to make sure we make time for us. I know I'm in love with you."

The breath caught in my throat. Love. *Did he just say he loved me?* I searched his eyes as Jaxson waited for my response. "London, it's okay if you're not ready to say it. I know it's quick."

His thumb brushed my cheek and I closed my eyes, organizing my thoughts. When I opened them I was greeted with a smile and patience. Jaxson was willing to wait until I was ready. I took a leap and told him how I felt. "I'm scared to admit I'm falling in love with you. For as long as I can remember I always lose everything I care about."

"Don't be scared. I'm not letting anything happen to us."

Take the leap, London. I kissed him as I murmured. "I love you, too."

Moving positions, Jaxson hovered above me while showering me with kisses. "I'll never tire of you saying that. I'll make sure you feel my love every day."

I BRACED MYSELF as we entered Pam and Levi's house. The smell of freshly baked biscuits wafted through the air. There was no doubt they would know we had sex last night. In the light of day, maybe being so obvious was a bad idea. A warm hand was placed on my lower back. "Don't worry, London. We're adults."

"I know, but . . ." I stopped.

Laughter erupted in the other room. Jaxson's hands came to

my face bringing my attention back to him. "London, I'm a grown man. You're a grown woman. My parent's adore you even with the misconception of your past. They trust you with my son. I trust you with my son."

"Jaxson, London. You're here." I stepped back from Jaxson as Pam walked in. I felt like a teenager being caught kissing. What was wrong with me? I was an adult. An adult who slept with this woman's son all night long. Stop. Get a grip.

She brought me into a hug. "I'm so glad you guys are giving this a chance."

I nearly choked at her comment. "Me too."

Maybe things weren't awkward after all. I was a mess and out of practice with the whole dating thing. "Be aware Ty's been asking numerous questions about boyfriends and girlfriends."

On cue, the little man ran in here. "Dad! London—" He stopped. "You found her. I went to see if she wanted breakfast and she wasn't there. Where were you?"

I tensed at the question and heat flooded my face. How was Jaxson going to answer him?

Jaxson picked Ty up and brought him to the office off of the front door motioning for me to follow him. "Ty, I took London to breakfast. She's my girlfriend. But we're going to eat with you guys again."

Well, we hadn't had food for breakfast. A light heat graced my cheeks at the thought.

"Are you getting married?"

Both men's eyes darted to mine, Ty's full of curiosity. The question made me fiddle with my hair while Jaxson answered him, "No, son, we're not getting married. We like each other a lot. We'll be boyfriend and girlfriend at first. Like Mallory has her boyfriend."

A huff escaped. "Don't take too long, Dad. Mallory and her boyfriend broke up. She told us this morning. Aunt Sydney and Mallory are here for breakfast."

"I promise I won't take too long." There was a definite vow spoken that had nervous, excited flutters racing through me.

"Good. We don't want to lose her, Dad."

"We won't."

Ty grabbed my hand while Jaxson's went to the small of my back before going into the living room. The family sat around while Mallory stood in the middle with her dark hair in a ponytail. I remembered my days of being a teenager and dancing. Pam clapped. "Oh good, Jaxson and London can see your routine you learned at dance camp."

"I'd love to see it." The excitement in my voice was evident.

Mallory, wearing a pink and black dance shirt, centered herself as Pam hit play for the music to start. The routine was fairly standard with a few free spins, kicks, and heel turns. During the heel turn, Mallory's balance faltered slightly and she stopped. "Sorry that part keeps throwing me."

"Turn your right heel out slightly to help counteract the weight balance on your supported foot." Mallory's brow crinkled. The attention turned to me, but I ignored it as I walked free of Jaxson's embrace. "If you keep the weight more balanced it won't throw you off. Try this."

Slowly, I demonstrated the step and she mimicked it, executing the maneuver perfectly. I loved that feeling—when a move became fluid to the point it was merely an extension of your body. "Now try that and see if it transitions into your next move easier."

I took a step back. The music played again and Mallory executed it with perfection. Quitting the dance, she ran to me. "Thank you, London. Where did you learn that?"

"I used to dance a lot back in the day."

"Will you help me with some other moves?"

With Jaxson's hand on my lower back, I felt complete. Another piece of what I'd given up slipped into place. "I would love to."

SEVENTEEN

T WO MONTHS PASSED SINCE JAXSON and I had our first night together. Nothing new had been discovered about the accident or who was behind it. It was frustrating, but at least whoever it was hadn't bothered me anymore.

The heat of late August was upon us. Before I came, Jaxson decided to wait a year for Ty to start kindergarten since he was in the gray area for age. Made complete sense to me. Pam supported Jaxson's decision, but thought Ty should try it and if he was too young, repeat it. Jaxson wanted Ty to have an extra year at the farm.

My eyes drifted to the flowers on the counter from the two men I loved. Every week, Jaxson and Ty brought me flowers. The word *perfect* was subpar to how the last couple of months had been. Everything was falling into place. Jaxson. Ty. Dancing. On the side, I helped Mallory and a couple of her friends with dance moves. I was in heaven.

Dad arrived last night and was sleeping in the guest room. My phone vibrated on the counter as I made biscuits for breakfast. Jaxson and Ty were joining us in about forty-five minutes.

Jaxson: Good morning, beautiful. How was your night?

Me: It was lonely.

Stolen moments was all time afforded us as of late. Last week, Jaxson traveled to Birmingham for three days to see some therapy equipment demonstrations. Ty stayed with me in the guesthouse which had been fun. The ever-inquisitive mind of a five-year-old constantly asked about what was next for Jaxson and me. He was getting tired of the answer, *we're getting to know each other.*

Jaxson: If you were in my bed it wouldn't be.

I shook my head. That was something I didn't budge on with Ty being in the house. With Ty already wondering how relationships worked, it would blur the line between me being the girlfriend and a wife.

Me: I know, but it'll make it that much better someday.

Jaxson: Someday better come quick.

Me: Patience, my love. Patience. Breakfast will be ready in about forty minutes.

Jaxson: We'll be there. And you know I don't have any patience.

Me: I know. Love you.

Jaxson: Love you, too.

Smiling from ear to ear, I sat the phone down as I patted out the biscuits. "I take it that was Jaxson?"

I looked up at Dad with a slight heat gracing my cheeks. "Yes. I know it's fast, Dad."

He shook his head. "Your mom and I met and were married within five weeks. As long as you're happy, that's all I care about."

"I am happy. Happier than I ever was with Charles."

"I think so too." With summer here, dad switched out his normal flannel long sleeves for short plaid button ups. "If you and Jaxson got married, you'd have a son. Are you ready for that? It's a big responsibility."

After placing the biscuits in the oven, I sat next to Dad. "I love that little boy. It would devastate me not to be a part of his life if something happened to Jaxson and me."

"That's how it should be if you love him. One can't exist without the other."

I leaned my head on Dad's shoulder. "I do love them, Daddy. I really do. Did something happen to make you concerned?"

"No, punkin'. Just checking up on you. I know we talk all the time on the phone, but I wanted to talk about it in person—make sure you're following your heart."

The doorbell stopped our conversation. "I promise I am. Let me get that. There's no way it's Ty, because he doesn't know the meaning of knocking."

We chuckled. Yesterday, Dad experienced Ty running into the guesthouse as soon as he got here. Ty was enthusiastic to question Dad. He wanted to know if Dad could make me marry Jaxson since he was my father and I had to listen to him. Opening the door, Ty stood there, which was odd. "London, can you come to Grama's house. She needs help."

"Is she okay? Why didn't you come in with the keypad?"

He started bouncing and moving his hands. "I can't say anything else. I've promised to keep my lips shut. She needs help. Are you coming?"

This was getting stranger. But sometimes a five-year-old never made sense. "Okay." I called over my shoulder. "Dad, I'm going to help Pam real quick."

"I'll come too." Dad slid off the stool and fell into step beside me.

Moseying to the main house, Ty was practically bursting at the seams. More so than normal. There was no telling what was going on. There was a chance Pam hadn't asked for help, but nevertheless this child had stolen my heart.

Things became more awkward as we entered the kitchen with the entire family staring at me, including Sydney and Mallory in a line beside the counter. Sydney's husband was currently deployed overseas and due home by Christmas. It was his last deployment before he retired from the marines.

All eyes were on me and I felt like I'd interrupted something. Tentatively, I said, "Good morning. Ty asked if I could help Pam."

It was like a rehearsed speech as the group called out, cheerily. Too Cheerily. "Good morning!"

The room fell silent . . . again. I peered back at Dad who looked at everything but me. "Umm . . . Ty said you needed help. Am I interrupting? I can come back later."

Giggles came from beside me. "London, it's a surprise for you."

Glancing at my dad, he grinned from ear to ear. "Surprise?" I asked confused. It wasn't my birthday or any special event I could think of.

Had this family lost their mind? Where was Jaxson? He was the only one missing. Levi and Pam stepped aside to reveal Jaxson on one knee. He looked gorgeous as he grinned at me, the dimples showing.

Was this happening? Was Jaxson asking me to . . . marry him? Here? Now? In front of all our family?

Without thinking, I walked toward the man who captured my heart. Tears threatened to spill over.

"Jaxson . . ." His name died on my lips when he popped open a black box. A beautiful, square sparkling diamond sat nestled among the black velvet.

Strong fingers touched my hand, beckoning me closer. "London, I'm here before you and all our family, in the spot where we first met, asking you to be my wife and—"

"My mommy. Don't forget that, Dad. We talked about this."
That precious voice filled with immeasurable hope broke the dam
as a few tears trekked down my face. Everyone laughed. Ty stood
beside me, looking up at me with a grin on his face. "Don't be sad,
London. Dad and I love you."

My voice came out slightly broken. "I love you too, little man.
I love you and your dad so much."

Ty beamed. "She's going to say yes, Dad."

Happiness filled the room as Jaxson squeezed my fingers, bringing my attention back to him. "Will you marry me? Will you be
our family?"

I threw my arms around him. "Yes. Yes, I'll marry you."

The tight embrace from Jaxson felt like home. Nothing in the
world would ever compare to what it felt like in his loving arms.

"And be my mom?" The voice was precious.

My head swiveled while Jaxson kept me in an iron grip. "Ty, I
would love to be your mom."

His legs brought him crashing into us. Jaxson adjusted his hug
to include Ty. "We're a family. London loves us, Dad."

The ring slipped onto my ringer. "We are, son. We are." Jaxson
and I gazed into each other's eyes. "I love you, sweetheart."

"I love you, too."

Whoops and hollers filled the space between us, but I was lost
in the green eyes of my future husband. All roads were supposed
to lead home, and I was finally where I was meant to be. A familiar
voice caught my attention. "Millie?"

A tablet screen appeared before me. *Millie had been here.* "Hey
there, bestie. I'm so happy for you. Jaxson stopped by the hospital
last week after seeing your dad and asked me for his permission."
She leaned in closer. "Psst . . . I think he's a keeper."

Now the quick flight out to Alabama made more sense. I giggled.

"I think so too."

"I'll call later. I'm on shift and couldn't leave. Can't wait to see you again. Miss you."

"Miss you too."

The screen went blank and it all clicked. "Wait, you saw my dad this week when you were traveling?"

A feather-light kiss touched my lips. "I wanted this to be perfect for you. I wanted his and Millie's blessing. I talked to your Mom also."

"Mom?"

I sobbed. He included everyone special to me in my life. Everyone I loved.

"Thank you, Jaxson." Another kiss and I buried my face in his neck, composing myself. Though Mom wasn't aware, she'd been involved.

Ty's arms tightened around me. "Don't be sad, London."

I pulled back. "I'm not. I'm the happiest girl in the world."

"Share her, Jaxson. We want to see the ring!" Pam and Sydney both crowded around.

Standing, Jaxson kept his arms possessively around me as I held out my hand. "My word, my baby brother knows how to pick them. It's beautiful. Welcome to the family, London."

"Thank you."

Dad approached next. "I'm proud of you, punkin'. I think you've found one of the most upstanding men there are."

"I think so too. Love you, Dad." Jaxson briefly let me go while I hugged him.

Speaking into my hair, Dad was choked up. "You'll always be my little girl."

"Always."

Congratulations flowed as we basked in the perfect moment. Pam and Levi seemed genuinely happy about the proposal. The first night here, Pam had told the truth about basing judgments on what was in front of them versus the actions of my past.

Before we left to go back to the guesthouse, Pam approached me after I helped Ty tie his shoes. Breakfast was moved to the main house so we were able to celebrate the engagement as a family. "Thank you for making Jaxson and Ty so happy. They love you dearly."

"I love them."

She hugged me to her tightly. "I can see it. Ever since that first night you and Jaxson met, I felt the connection. That first week when he backed off, he talked to me about it a lot. How he'd never experienced something so strong before. He was scared for him and for Ty, especially with how fast Ty attached himself to you. He asked what he should do."

I waited for the response on bated breath as she pulled back. "I told him those feelings can be once in a lifetime and to take a chance on love was worth everything. Then when you find your perfect match, don't wait."

"He's my match too. I'm glad he listened."

"Me too."

Dramatically, she sighed and placed a hand on her heart. "Now, we have a wedding to plan. I love weddings."

We were planning a wedding. I had no idea where to start. What was needed? This was something my Mom would have helped me with which brought on a somber thought. How was I going to do this? Breaking my chaotic thoughts, Pam said, "I'm here however you need me. But know there's no pressure. This is your and Jaxson's day."

"I'd love your help." She had no idea how much.

Wrapping my arms around me, Pam said, "We're so blessed to be getting a daughter like you."

Mom and I always talked about what she wanted to do when I got married—a mother-daughter weekend to look for a dress, bridesmaid luncheon, and go to showers with me. It was bitter-sweet while preparing for a wedding to a man I was desperately in love with.

Having a mother-figure in my life soothed what could not be.

My heart overflowed for the millionth time today. I had everything I ever truly wanted, just not exactly how I imagined it.

Love.

Family.

Hope.

EIGHTEEN

AFTER BREAKFAST, JAXSON AND TY came back to the guesthouse. Dad was leaving this afternoon with Levi to head to a convention. They'd be back tomorrow. Then, Dad would head home the next day.

Ty was currently watching Dad shave in the bathroom. From the kitchen, I heard, "Do I get to call you Granddad, now?"

"I'd love that." It was weird hearing my dad called granddad.

At the counter, Jaxson came up behind me. "Are you happy?"

"Deliriously so." And I was.

His chin rested on my shoulder. "I'm one step closer to having you in my bed every night. Of course, I'd rather you move in now."

Facing Jaxson, I kissed him. "Won't that confuse Ty?"

Before he could answer, Dad's phone vibrated on the counter. "Can you get that, punkin'? Ty's helping me shave."

"Sure thing." As I picked up the phone without looking, I looked at Jaxson with mock horror on my face. "I hope Dad knows what he's doing."

A smirk with that sexy grin showed me how happy Jaxson was as I answered the phone. "Hello. This is London McNally answering for Ken."

"London. Thank God. I've been trying to reach you. No one will give me your number." The blood drained from my face at Charles' voice. *Why was he trying to reach me?* A once soothing voice now only brought dread. All the anguish connected with my past came rushing back.

Jaxson sensed something was wrong as he held me tighter and mouthed, *Who is it?*

"London, are you there?"

The sandpaper lacing my throat made it hard to talk. "Why are you calling my dad, Charles?"

Another female voice sounding like Rachel was in the background and spoke. "Darling, Mom and Dad arrived. Your parents have to stay in DC for two more days."

Charles muffled the phone. "I'll be right out. This is the endorsement for the candidacy."

More lies.

I wasn't able to hear the response.

Bastard.

Dirty rotten bastard.

He was lying to his fiancée like he had me.

Anger burned through Jaxson as his muscles went rigid. He didn't move as he watched me. I angled the phone for him to hear. "London, I've been wanting to talk to you. Explain some things. See where we stand. I fucked things up. I want to set it right." He sighed. "I haven't been able to get you out of my head since the day at my parents."

I felt sick to my stomach. There was no part of me that wanted anything to do with Charles.

"London, don't say yes to whoever you've met."

My voice barely came out audible. "How did you know?"

"I saw him last week when he was here. London, don't make the biggest mistake of your life. I've been trying to find you."

I looked into Jaxson's eyes. He watched me closely, and me him. The pulse thrummed in his neck. "Charles, I've already said yes. I love him. He's my future."

There was no need to talk about Rachel. Charles being engaged or not had no impact on my decision.

A smile spread across Jaxson's face. In prison all I could imagine was Charles begging to get me back. Admitting he made a mistake. But, he wasn't whom I wanted. Not anymore. In comparison, Charles was a dim light compared to the bright shining star in front of me.

"London, for fuck's sake. You just got out of prison. Does he have any idea you killed someone?"

The phone was yanked from me. Jaxson's face was steel as his equally matching cold tone spoke, "Charles, this is Jaxson McCole. You will not talk to my future wife that way. She's made her decision." He paused. "That may be true, but I have her future." Through the line I could hear Charles' voice raising, but I couldn't make out what he was saying. "You're a real piece of work. Of course, I know she was in prison and I love her. Nothing you say will change that, asshole."

My fists balled. Charles had tried to ruin my relationship. As Charles was still speaking, Jaxson ended the phone call and crouched to look me in the eyes as I glanced away. "London, I love you. That bastard won't change it."

"I know." I took a deep breath. "I hate that I can't shout the truth from the mountain tops. That the past can still be thrown in my face. It hurts. Charles was never that mean. Not when we dated."

"Because he had you."

Dad walked out with Ty. "What's going on?"

Giving a pleasant smile, I avoided Dad's questions. "Hey Ty, would you see if your grama has any spaghetti sauce I can borrow?"

"Yes!" Ty took off.

When we were alone I explained what happened. Dad nodded. "He's been trying to get ahold of you. Millie and I refused to give your information. We should have asked or let you know."

"No, it's fine. I would've asked you to not give him my information. Don't let him know. I'd rather disappear from his mind."

We agreed it was all for the best to continue as is. Dad still had no clue about the blood tests which showed I was drugged. When he got back from the convention, I wanted to tell him the truth.

Taking one last sip of coffee, Dad gave me a hug. "It's time for me to go. I'll be back tomorrow evening. Maybe in a few months, the three of you could come to the house."

Dad released me and shook Jaxson's hand. "We'd like that, sir."

"Ken, call me Ken or Dad or whatever you want. You're family now."

Family. I was beginning my own family. The thought was daunting, but I loved it. Immensely. As Dad left, Jaxson's phone rang. "Hey, Mom. Yeah. Is she sure? Okay, we'll come up to the house to say goodbye."

My curiosity was piqued when Jaxson prowled toward me. "Sydney offered to watch Ty tonight. Looks like I get you in my bed after all."

The perfect day was about to become the perfect night.

NINETEEN

I STRETCHED APPRECIATIVELY, MY LIMBS SORE from Jaxson's sexual appetite. "Morning, my beautiful fiancée."

"Morning."

"I loved having you here."

Rubbing my hand up his chest, I saw the sparkle from my diamond. "Pretty soon, you'll be stuck with me forever."

"Good. I'm ready."

Glancing at the time, it was past seven. "We promised Ty we'd take him to breakfast this morning to celebrate around eight."

"You'll be a good mom."

Mom. That word still felt foreign to me but I welcomed it. I always wanted children and was blessed to have Ty. Beyond blessed.

I closed my eyes. "I hope so. I'm afraid of messing up."

"You're perfect for Ty and me. We'll figure out how we fit together. I'm not worried."

Jaxson's phone rang on the bedside. It was Sydney's ringtone. He stretched, leaving me cold where his body once was. "Hey, buddy. Yeah, we'll be there. Yes, she's still going to be your mom. And my wife. Me too. We'll be there shortly."

Mom. I was about to be a mom.

Jaxson hung up. "He's anxious."

"Let's go to breakfast early. Maybe we can do the park today too."

"Perfect. I'll text Syd to meet us at Mom and Dad's in like twenty minutes."

Quickly, we got ready and headed down to the guesthouse. Last night, when I packed my overnight bag I forgot the right color flip flops to go with my jean shorts and T-shirt.

Ten minutes later we pulled up to the back of the guesthouse. "I'll be right back," I whispered.

Jaxson was on the phone talking about the new equipment coming from Alabama he ordered on his last trip to be installed late next week. I traipsed over to the door while sending Millie a good morning text.

Something caught my attention and I stopped dead in my tracks. A knife was stabbed into the front door with a note. The same type of knife which was used in Dad's barn. The note was sloppily scrawled.

I dropped the phone. Everything slowed as I looked at the angrily scrawled words. Jaxson called my name, but I wasn't able to answer.

They found me.

They were here.

It wasn't over.

Pressure on my shoulders cleared the fog. "London, sweetheart, look at me." Our eyes connected as Jaxson turned me to face him. "You're safe here. We're safe."

"Jaxson—" I couldn't breathe.

A voice sounded from behind and my eyes grew wide. "Hey, Syd. Take Ty in the house. We'll be there in a sec." There was no mistaking the urgency in Jaxson's voice.

"Sure thing."

I heard Ty calling for Jaxson. For me. I wasn't able to answer. The words stuck in my throat. Jaxson called over his shoulder. "Buddy, give us a few. We'll be right there. Everything is okay."

Ty. I was bringing this on Ty.

"London, look at me." I stared him in the eyes. What if Ty got hurt? Jaxson? My dad? "London, I see the look in your eyes. You're not leaving."

I swallowed hard. Jaxson pressed on. "We'll figure this out. I'll protect you. Protect our family." Panic kept setting in. "London, you have to promise me. I can't lose you. Ty can't lose you. We love you." Jaxson sounded panicked. "I love you. Dammit, sweetheart, I love you. I can't lose you."

The breath I held expelled from my body. Thoughts snapped into place. "I won't leave. I promise. I love you both too much to leave."

Jaxson's lips smashed against mine as he claimed my mouth. "I need to call the cops. Get this documented. And we need to tell our parent's what's going on."

Numbly, I responded, "I agree. Pam's at her hair appointment, but I can make us breakfast. I'll call Dad and tell him we need him to come back."

Arms became like a vise grip around me. "I won't let anything happen to my family. I swear it."

I believed him, but *at what cost?*

DAD AND LEVI came home as soon as I called. The only thing I said was that there was a threat similar to the one at home. When Dad went back to Guin, he would be able to fill Millie in as to what happened.

After the cops came, we ate breakfast in Pam's kitchen. Sydney was a lifesaver keeping Ty away from seeing what was going on. The last thing I wanted was for my life to taint his.

Currently, Ty was feeding the sheep with Levi and were due back in about a half an hour. My nerves were raw, exposed.

I sat nestled into Jaxson's frame on the couch in the guesthouse as we alternated filling in Dad on what Millie found when she visited. After we finished, Dad sat back. "Your mom and I always knew something else had happened. We kept searching for answers after you went to prison, but couldn't find anything. She thought there was something wrong with the reports. But, shortly after she got sick, I wondered if we were causing you more harm by chasing what could have been figments of your mom's imaginations. I'm so sorry we stopped looking."

I stood and Dad followed suit. "We didn't know. This isn't your fault, Dad. Yours or Mom's. We're all victims of this. Alec. His family. Me. My family. The list goes on."

Dad scrunched his brows as Jaxson stood. "How did they find you? This was the first you'd heard from them, right?"

My spine stiffened. "Yesterday, on the phone, Jaxson said his full name to Charles."

"Fuck." Jaxson's head lolled back. "I did. Fuck. Fuck. Fuck."

Millie was right as I said, "Whoever this is has connections somewhere here. Yesterday, I heard Rachel in the background while Charles was talking to me. Her parents were there. They have the connections."

Squeezing me to him, Dad directed his attention to Jaxson. "We need to come up with a plan to keep London and Ty safe while we figure this out."

Dad released me and Jaxson intertwined his fingers with mine. "I think London should move in with me. I can up security at the house. Keep her and Ty safe at the same time." I raised my eyebrow. "Ty will be fine. Staying in the guesthouse is not an option anymore. Hell, I'll marry you right now if it keeps you safe, but I know you want a wedding."

Dad interjected. "London, I want you safe. I'd feel better with you at Jaxson's."

Never in my wildest dreams did I think Dad would give his blessing to live with a man before marriage. Of course, in my last relationship, I'd been barely twenty and in college. I looked at Jaxson. "What about Ty and the example we're setting? I can sleep in another room."

"He's five. You're already his mom in his eyes. I promise he'll be fine."

Mom. The word was still sinking in and I'd had no time to process all of this. My life was on fast forward and not stopping. Maybe moving in with Jaxson, catching our breath, being a family would bring normalcy to our lives while we prepared for the wedding. "I'll move in with you and Ty."

A huge grin spread across Jaxson's and my face.

Dad scowled. "Son, try not to look so damn happy. She's still my little girl."

The smile instantly dropped from Jaxson's face and I giggled. "Sorry, sir."

Dad said, "I think we need to tell your parents, Jaxson. Bring them up to speed. I understand why you guys didn't say anything before, but they don't need to be exposed either. I'm taking Ty out to feed the horses while you guys talk."

Dad left us and the clawing feeling returned. "Jaxson, what if they don't want you involved in all this? What if they regret us being together? What if—"

Silenced with a kiss, Jaxson brought me to him. "Family doesn't bail when things get tough. I chose you as my wife. You're part of this family. Understand?"

"Yes."

Before we left to see his parents, Jaxson pressed me against the door. "Tonight, I'm going to savor you. You're officially mine. Forever is about to start, sweetheart."

"Now that you're getting the milk and cookies for free, will you be one of those guys who won't agree on a wedding date?" There was a teasing tone to my voice.

A breath away, he responded, "I meant what I said. As soon as you have the wedding you want planned, I'll be at the end of the aisle. The sooner you're my wife the better."

"Really?"

"Yes. Let's talk to Mom and Dad. Then, we'll tell Ty about you becoming our new roommate."

MY PALMS SWEATED as Jaxson finished telling Pam and Levi everything. We sat in silence as the attention centered on Levi. I grew more anxious waiting to hear that I wasn't good enough for Jaxson and Ty. He rubbed his chin. "I think there's some changes we need to make to monitor who's in and out of here."

Wringing my hands out, I said, "I'm so sorry about this. I didn't mean to bring this on you."

Levi pinned me with a stare. "Do you love my son and grandson?"

"With all my heart." There was no doubt. I loved them. I would die for them.

He nodded, satisfied. "Then, it's what needs to be done. I'm not taking away their happiness because of some spineless bastard who feels threatened and robbed my soon-to-be-daughter four years of her life. London, you're family now. That means you're my daughter too."

Not being able to help it, I stood to hug Levi and Pam. "Thank you. I love you both."

Family was worth more than anything else in this world.

TWENTY

ALL MY BAGS WERE IN Jaxson's house after dinner. Dad and Levi were getting some of the security implemented. Jaxson would have to meet with the security company tomorrow, but it was important for him to be here as we spent the first night as a family in our house. Our house. It was crazy to think this was now my home. I looked around the place like I was seeing it for the first time. Two boys definitely lived here with the lack of warmth. The walls were bare and only the minimal furniture was present. No additional knickknacks.

Surprisingly, I was calm about this part of my life. This felt right. However, knowing someone was still watching me, waiting for me to do something, had my nerves frayed.

Jaxson was upstairs putting the last suitcase in the closet. Later I would unpack my stuff. Tonight I wanted to spend it as the three of us.

Currently, Ty was at Pam's getting something. A secret. For me.

In the living room, I took in my new home. Dump trucks filled a toy bin next to the television. Of course, I'd been here countless times, but it felt different now. I was going to be permanently part of this.

Warm arms came around my waist. "Welcome home, sweetheart."

"I like the sound of that."

His breath tickled my ear. "I thought later this week, when things calm down, we could look at redoing the house. Something our style."

"Jaxson, I don't want to waste your money. I'm not here to cause havoc on your and Ty's lives."

My body spun around before I could process it. Jaxson's firm body moved me against the wall, soliciting desire through me. "What's mine is yours, London. All of it. Our house. Our money. Our son. Our decisions. You're not causing havoc on our lives. You're the missing piece that sets it all right."

I closed my eyes and his lips brushed against mine. "I don't know what I did to deserve you, but I fall more in love with you every second of every day."

"Good. I'll make sure that never changes." His tongue mingled with mine and I moaned.

Tires came up the front drive and Jaxson pulled away. "Later, sweetheart."

I kept my face serious. "Do you think I should stay in the guest room?"

Fingers trailed down my stomach and dipped in my pants. "Do you want to stay in another room?"

"It might . . ." I wasn't able to finish my thought when his fingers touched my clit. "Jaxson . . . I want you."

"Good. You'll get me in our room."

The door opened and his fingers retreated, leaving me wanting.

"London! I have a surprise for you." Ty yelled through the front door. Giving me a wink, Jaxson headed to the foyer to give me a second to collect myself.

My word, was it bedtime yet? Taking a deep breath, I walked to where Ty called my name. I knelt down as Ty ran to me full steam ahead. "What do you have?"

A big grin greeted me. "Grama and I made cookies to welcome you to your new house. I made a card." I took the card proffered and saw a picture of Jaxson, me, and Ty in the middle drawn in crayons. The word *My Family* were written at the top.

Emotions swelled within me. This was really happening.

Holding it to my chest, I said, "I love it. I'm finding the most special place for this so I can see it all the time."

"Your's and Dad's bedroom. That's where it should go. Then, when you wake up you'll see it."

Well, that solved my worry about the bedroom situation. In Ty's mind we were together and I belonged with his dad.

"I think that's the perfect place." He gave me a kiss on the cheek when I agreed with him.

Pam walked up and I stood. "Night, sweetheart. I'm going to let you guys get settled. Call if you need anything. How does breakfast sound in the morning before Ken takes off?"

I responded, "Perfect."

The subtle lavender scent of Pam already became a comfort. My mom always smelled like roses. It was amazing how you connected yourself to smells. I missed Mom terribly. She would have loved Jaxson and Ty. I could only imagine how she would help me get settled in my new home and give me tidbits of advice. Mom always wanted a big family but was only able to have me. Now her family was growing. I took a deep breath and focused on everything I had.

Jaxson gave his mom a hug. "Thanks, Mom. Breakfast sounds good. Security will be here at eight to rework the houses."

"Perfect. I'll let Levi and Ken know."

We watched as Pam left the house. We were left alone. It was surreal. Okay, it was a lot more than surreal. Earlier, Pam offered for Ty to stay the night with her, but I thought our first night here as a family should include all of us. Jaxson agreed.

"Hey, London?"

Ty looked at me with his big green eyes. He was barely able to contain himself. "Yes, little man?"

"Can we watch a movie as a family?"

Jaxson picked Ty up over his shoulder as giggles emanated from him. "I think that sounds like a great idea. Which movie do you want?"

"Shaun the Sheep! London, it's so funny. He's a naughty sheep."

"I can't wait." And I really couldn't. We'd watched movies together over the last few months, but this was different. Blinking a few times, I willed the tears back.

Sitting on the couch, I watched Jaxson move around as he inserted the DVD. My word he was hot. Those muscular thighs. The ass. I wanted him all to myself. A devilish smirk appeared when I was caught ogling.

Jaxson sat on the couch and wrapped his arm around me as Ty climbed on my lap. A contented sigh left Jaxson's lips and then a feather light kiss brushed the side of my head. "My life is complete with both of you in it." Jaxson always knew what to say.

I turned to stare into Jaxson's eyes filled with love and warmth. The screen flickered to life, interrupting me echoing Jaxson's. "Dad, can I sleep with you and London?"

I held my breath. "We'll do a campout this weekend. How does that sound, buddy?"

"Yes!"

Jaxson winked at me.

The movie began and Ty snuggled between us, causing the subject to drop thank goodness. The feeling of us all together as one brought a joy I'd never experienced before. I loved it.

As the opening credits ran across the screen, a yawn escaped from the nearly tuckered out Ty. Jaxson scooped Ty up. "Let's go to bed, buddy."

Tiredly, Ty asked, "London isn't leaving is she?"

Piercing me with his eyes, Jaxson responded. "She's not going anywhere. Ever."

Guilt assuaged me as I thought about my earlier selfish thoughts. "I promise, Ty. I'm not leaving you or your dad. You're stuck with me."

Ty was insecure from knowing his mother left him even though he had no recollection of it. I gave him a kiss on the head. "We're going to your Grama's house for breakfast tomorrow before my dad has to go home."

"Okay." Eyes shut as I followed Jaxson to the bedroom to lay him down. He rolled over with his hand tucked under his cheek. Children were a precious gift and I was blessed to have one as part of my life. Something I never thought would come to pass. Thoughts of Alec flickered through my mind. I would always remember him.

The door quietly clicked shut and I threw my arms around Jaxson's neck. "I promise I'll never leave. I'll never let Ty doubt my love for him or that he won't have me in his life. I don't know what I was thinking."

Jaxson picked me up, carrying me to his room. "I know. It's been a long day, sweetheart. I want to focus on us tonight. Just us."

"We're engaged."

"We are."

"We're living together."

"We are."

"We're in love."

"We are."

His breath touched my face and my lower abdomen cinched with remembered desire. I wiggled my fingers, catching the sparkles from the ring. "I want a short engagement."

Slowly, Jaxson let me slide down his body. His rigid length pushed against me. "Whatever you wish. I want to make love to you as you wear my ring, future Mrs. McCole."

Tilting my head back, he tenderly kissed the base of my neck. "I like the sound of that."

TWO WEEKS PASSED. No more threats were received. Dad spread the word around town I was happily engaged and planning a wedding. Security was definitely increased. There was a guard posted at the front gate who checked deliveries during the day. A few more did perimeter checks on a regular basis. Key cards were issued to all the employees for entrance to and from the barn. All visitors were logged. All houses had upgraded security systems.

I felt safe. Or at least had the illusion of feeling safe.

"Sweetheart, this is delicious."

My two men sat at the table devouring the cheese quiche I made. I loved cooking for them. Mom and I spent hours cooking together through my childhood. "I'm glad the recipe turned out and you guys like it."

"London, you're the bestest cooker ever." Ty pushed his plate back and held his stomach dramatically.

I ruffled his hair that was getting longer and needed a trim as I sat to join them. "Thank you." Since the engagement and explaining how the wedding happened, I noticed Ty still called me London which was fine. I would never pressure him to call me anything more.

The doorbell rang and Jaxson stood. "That'll be Grama. Grab your shoes, buddy. She's going to take you to get a haircut."

A groan emitted.

This morning Pam was watching Ty while I helped muck the stalls after my morning ride on Sparkles. Two of the employees called in sick, leaving the facility in a jam. But, I loved going to work with Jaxson. He was teaching me more about the therapy business. I felt like his true partner.

Jaxson returned and finished the couple of last bites. "Are you ready to head to the barn?" Heading to the sink, Jaxson was preoccupied with his thoughts.

Casually, I said, "So, I was thinking about a wedding date."

That stopped Jaxson in his tracks and he whipped around. Frequently, I was asked if I had any dates in mind. Until this morning, I was still trying to decide.

"And when were you thinking, sweetheart?"

"Let me preface this by saying, if you don't think we can pull it off, we can wait."

He pulled me to my feet. "You're killing me with anticipation." I felt the heat of his hands wander to my ass.

"Millie and Dad are planning on coming out together next weekend. I don't want the stress of planning a wedding. I've heard of too many drama stories. I want it simple and meaningful. I want to spend our first holidays in the house together as Mrs. McCole, not your fiancée."

"Are you absolutely sure this is what you want?" Jaxson searched my eyes.

"As long as you do."

Lips mashed against mine. "I don't care what we have to do to make this happen. All I want is you to be my wife."

"But what if—"

He silenced me. "London, I mean it. All I want is for you to be my wife. What do you want?"

"A beautiful dress and cake. For Millie and Dad to be there. Then whatever you want and whoever you want to invite."

Spinning me around, I squealed in Jaxson's arms. "You've made me the happiest person in the world. Where do you want to get married?"

Last week at lunch, Pam brought out the family albums of their weddings. There was a place special to the family. "At the chapel where your parents, grandparents, and great-grandparents got married."

The spinning stopped. "Are you sure, sweetheart? If there's some place—"

I put my fingers to his lips. "I want it there. I want to be part of the tradition with you."

"It's you and me, London. Together."

"Together."

Instead of going to the front door, Jaxson pulled out his phone. "Dwayne, I'm going to be about an hour late."

As he shut the phone off, I knew what was coming next and warmth spread through me as Jaxson took me to the bedroom.

TWENTY-ONE

"**L**ONDON, DEAR, WHAT DO YOU think?"

I stood in front of the mirror in an all-white princess gown. Tulle flowed in layers upon layers and sparkled with the intermittent crystals reflecting in the light. The sweetheart bodice hugged my figure.

"I think you look beautiful, punkin'."

"It's gorgeous, bestie."

I turned around to see Pam, Dad, and Millie sitting on opposite ends of the couch. Dad was out of his element, but I loved him for being part of this process since Mom wasn't able. Through all this, not having Mom by my side was the hardest part. Harder than I ever imagined. It helped having a short engagement.

The wedding was in two days. Earlier in the week, I came with Pam to pick out the dress and get it altered. From the moment I tried it on, I knew it was the one.

Everything sunk in. I was getting married. Really getting married.

"London?" Dad's voice had emotions spilling over.

I walked to him and threw my arms around him. "Dad. Is this really my life? Did I really finally find happiness?"

"Yes, punkin'. This is real. It's yours and no one is taking it."

I took a deep breath. "It's perfect."

Everyone broke out into excited chatter. Pam and Millie took over the entire wedding planning. Jaxson and I wanted to be surprised. The only thing we'd been involved with was the cake. It was an Italian crème flavor to die for. We were only doing one cake since our wedding consisted of about twenty people.

Pam touched my shoulder. "It's beautiful. I can't wait for you to officially be my daughter."

"I can't wait either. Thank you for all you did this last week."

We checked out and left the dress at the bridal shop to be steamed. Millie would pick it up tomorrow and keep it at Pam's house. Jaxson was dying to see what I picked out and there was no reason to tempt him.

Jaxson, Ty and Levi were at the ice cream parlor. The store was a block over. Pam refused to let them be on the same street in case Jaxson walked by the window and saw the dress.

As we entered the ice cream parlor, the sweet dairy smell filled the air. Jaxson rose to greet me with a kiss on the cheek. "Is everything good with the dress?"

Eagerly, I nodded. "Yes. It's beautiful."

"Oh, Jaxson. It's gorgeous. Simply stunning on London." Pam had been wonderful through all of the planning. She documented every step to show Mom at some point. I knew it was more than likely pointless, but the memories were captured nonetheless.

Ty's chocolate face lit up. "So, you really are going to be with Dad and me forever?"

"Forever and ever. In two days."

Grabbing a napkin, I wiped off his face. Ty craved motherly attention and let me always dote over him.

An hour later, we were headed back to the ranch. Dad and Levi left to go on an afternoon fishing trip. Pam and Millie left to run a few errands, which left Jaxson, Ty, and me in the truck.

There was nothing new to report from Millie's investigations, which I was glad. By all means, I wanted the person behind this caught, but I wanted a drama-free wedding also. Millie's mom received good news. The cancer was gone and now she'd be having a double mastectomy.

The quiet hum of the radio filled the background while I filled Jaxson in about Dad's invite. "Two weeks after the wedding, Dad has an awards dinner he's presenting at. He asked if we'd be available to go, but understood if not. I think he wants to show off his new son-in-law."

Typically, kids weren't able to attend events like this.

Jaxson gave me a brilliant smile. "We'll make it. I'll take any opportunity to show off my wife." There was pride in his voice. "I'll talk to Mom or Sydney to see if they can watch Ty."

The event was in Mobile, Alabama. After all the shame I brought on my family, or that I thought I had brought on my family, this was going to feel good to have something to be proud of to show everyone. "I'll tell him. Our first event as husband and wife."

"We'll have the McCole Classic a few weeks after that." Over the past month, I'd been helping Pam prepare for it but there was a lot to do between caterers, cleanup crews, security, and more.

I sighed contentedly. "I can't wait."

The vehicle fell back into a comfortable silence.

"So, Mom. Can we bake cookies this afternoon?"

Mom, he called me Mom. A lump formed in my throat. *Don't overreact, London. Be natural.* I wondered why out of all the times, Ty now decided to start using that name. The words came out filled with emotion. "I would love to."

As if reading my mind, Ty continued. "Since I know you're not leaving us, I can call you mom now."

I glanced over to Jaxson who looked straight ahead. He took a deep breath. Needing the contact, I reached for his hands, which he gladly took. "I love that, Ty. Thank you."

"I like it too. I finally have a mom like the rest of my friends. They're going to like you. Dad, can I tell them all?"

"Yes, buddy. You can."

Jaxson squeezed my hand. This was one of the most cherished gifts a child could bestow upon me . . . their unconditional love, trust, and belief. The drive home was filled with emotion and elation combining into one. We were a family. A true family. Ty accepted me as his mother.

As the truck parked in front of the barn, Jaxson looked over at me. "I need to check on a few things. Are you okay?"

"More than okay. Check on Sparkles for me. I haven't gotten by there yet today. We'll get some lemonade from your mom's and sit on the front porch."

Jaxson kissed me. "I will. I love you."

"Love you more."

"Not possible."

Ty and I left the vehicle and headed to the porch. After fixing our glasses we went to the swing. The lemonade was cool and refreshing as we swung, letting the birds chirping fill the silence until I spoke. "I used to sit on my porch at home with my mom and sip lemonade when it was warm. Hot chocolate when it was cold."

"Really?"

I nodded. "Yep. Every day after school we would talk about what happened. Mom said it was our time to talk about whatever I wanted."

"When I start school, can I do that with you?"

"Of course. We can start now."

Ty leaned his head against me as the creak from the swing echoed through the air. "I love you, Mom. Thanks for being my mommy."

From the hillside the sun reflected on something moving toward us. A car? It was fast. Too fast. Going through the pasture. There was something wrong as my instincts told me to get out of the situation.

I pulled out my cell phone to speed dial Jaxson. Something was off. "Ty get in the house."

"Mom . . ."

"Ty, please listen to me."

By the tone of my voice, Ty scurried through the front door and I followed. Jaxson picked up. "Hey, sweetheart. I'll be just a few."

"There's a car speeding toward the house through the field. Are you expecting someone?" I clicked the deadbolts into place.

"You and Ty get in the house. I'm on my way."

The urgency wasn't missed as I moved us to the couch.

"We're already in here and I've locked the door. Be careful, Jaxson."

I could hear him running. "I will. Stay on the phone with me until I get there. I need to make sure you guys are okay."

"Mommy, what's going on?" Ty clutched my hand, worry evident in his tone.

I kept an outer calm. "I'm not sure, buddy. Your dad is checking it out. Let's wait in here together."

My number one priority was to make sure Ty was okay. I contemplated going upstairs, but that left us trapped if we needed to leave out the back. A tightness seized my chest, but I forced myself to remain rational.

Jaxson broke through my thoughts. "I'm out on the front porch. Stay on the couch. The car is almost here."

"Please be careful."

Tires screeched to a halt on the concrete section of the drive. Ty climbed on my lap. Muffled voices, one was Jaxson and one I wasn't able to make out. "It's okay, Ty. Your dad is fine."

A door slammed and then a woman screamed. "Tyler! Tyler! It's your mommy! Come see me!"

My defenses instantly kicked in. I was Ty's mother. Was Crystal out there? No. No. No.

"Get in your car, Crystal! There's a restraining order!" The hatred in Jaxson's voice was unlike anything I'd ever heard from him.

Crystal, Ty's biological mother, was here. She hadn't seen him since the night she dropped him off. I remembered the stories from Jaxson of how Ty was left on the front porch. I'd seen the pictures one night as Jaxson showed me the restraining order in case I needed to know. She'd been gone for a long time, but Jaxson was cautious.

Ty broke free and ran to the window.

"Ty!" I ran after him as he pulled back the curtain. A bone-thin woman with dirty-blonde hair waved her arms frantically at Jaxson while she spoke. I was unable to make out what she was saying as her words were rushed. Jaxson corralled her back to the driver's side. My heart thudded in my chest as I saw the out of control female struggling against Jaxson.

She looked dangerous.

The movement caught her attention before I could remove Ty from her view. "Tyler! Tyler! Come with me! It's your mommy!"

Jaxson looked back our way, worry and anger etched on his face as he talked on the phone and restrained Crystal with one arm against the car. She thrashed against him.

Gasping, Ty sunk to the floor. Crystal's eyes caught mine. "Jaxson who is she? Who is that bitch? She can't have my baby! They said she was taking my baby."

I picked up Ty. "Let's go upstairs, okay?"

He didn't answer. We needed away from all the screaming. From Crystal.

Sniffles came from him as I carried him, and my heart broke. At the second floor, I went to his room. He clung to me with a death grip. More sniffles. "Was that my mom?"

"I don't know. Let's see what your dad says. You're safe. I promise.

I won't let anything happen to you."

Jaxson had sole custody. From the looks of Crystal, she wasn't clean and sober. Ty only clutched me tighter as we waited for Jaxson. I picked up a few books and read to him, but he was lost in thought a million miles away.

I lost track of time until my phone rang. It was Jaxson.

"Jaxson?"

"I'm coming inside and didn't want to scare you guys. Where are you?"

The door opened as the alarm chimed. "Upstairs. Ty's room."

"How is he?

"Upset."

Jaxson took an audible deep breath. "Okay. I'm on my way."

I kissed Ty on the head. "Your dad is on his way up." No response.

Footsteps came up the stairs. Jaxson had a weary look on his face. "Ty, everything is okay. I promise."

He clutched me tighter. "I don't want to give London up. She's my mommy. I don't want that mean woman as my mom. I want London. Don't make me give her up because that mean lady wants me now."

My eyes grew wide as Jaxson looked at me. "Buddy, you're not giving up London. She's not leaving. London is still your mom."

"Then who was that person? She said she was my mom. Dad and moms are supposed to get married. I don't want you and London not to get married."

Jaxson sat next to me after pulling Ty to him. "That woman is sick, Ty. Sometimes . . . moms and dads don't live together. I'll never let her hurt you or take you away."

Ty raised his tear-streaked face. "I don't want her to be my mom. I don't want her to take me."

"She won't. I promise she won't. Ty, you are safe with London and me."

Ty looked at me. "Will you still marry my dad?"

The quivering lip of Ty had me hugging him in Jaxson's arms. Crystal would never get her hands on him. Never. "I love you and your dad. I'm not going anywhere. We're still getting married."

Ty then looked at Jaxson. "Are you still going to marry London?"

"Yes. Nothing is changing. I love London. She loves us."

A tired sigh escaped Ty. "Can we go home?"

"Sure thing, buddy."

TWENTY-TWO

I CLOSED THE DOOR TO Ty's bedroom. It had been a long day after Crystal's visit. Jaxson called the cops and they arrested her. Apparently *they* were the voices in her head that talked to her last night saying I was going to steal her baby. When pressed how she knew about me, Crystal said she saw me in the window. Her ramblings were incoherent. Underneath the broken woman, I was sure at one time was a vibrant one. It saddened me she lost herself along the way. Lost it all. Like I had at one time.

Rubbing my hand down my face, I let out a breath as I leaned against the wall, processing everything. Jaxson had kissed Ty goodnight, but Ty asked if I could lay in there awhile. Endless questions to ensure I married Jaxson and I would be his mom happened until he closed his eyes. He was concerned something would happen to us like it had with Jaxson and Crystal.

I wanted to throttle Crystal and shake some sense into her. How could a mother cause a child so much harm?

Hopefully, his young mind was able to process the difference between being sick versus love. It would take time.

Voices came from down the hall in the study . . . probably Jaxson with the lawyer. Apparently Crystal drove through the fence in the south pasture and straight up to the house between the security rounds. More security patrols were being added to the expansive property. Levi and Pam were out checking the patch on the wooden fence the stable workers made.

I heard Jaxson's voice rise for a second, so I pushed off the wall. The last thing we needed was Ty waking up again. He needed the rest. In the dim lit study, Jaxson scrubbed a hand down his face. "Larry, I understand." I held a finger to my lips when Jaxson saw me. He nodded and continued in a lower voice. "But, I need to make sure there's no fucking way Crystal will get any type of visitation with Ty. She was still strung out on something today. She threatened coming after him."

Motioning for me to come closer, I walked up and sat on the desk. Jaxson nestled himself between my legs as he cracked his neck. "I'm not sure except what she mentioned about the money. Okay. We'll touch base tomorrow."

Crystal also said she would take ten-thousand dollars and leave. Of course, if Jaxson went down that avenue she would always be coming around when the money ran out.

Tossing the phone on the desk, it clattered. "Jaxson, we'll get through this."

Face stricken, he stared at me. "There is no way in hell I will ever let that woman near my son. No way."

"She won't. It's obvious she's barely coherent." I paused. "Do we need to move back the wedding? I don't want to cause you extra stress."

"London, no fucking way. That bitch is not getting in the way of my future." His hand crept along my thigh, eliciting the electrical charge within me. "We'll talk to the lawyer tomorrow. Right now I want to get lost in you."

My hands went down to Jaxson's pants and I released the button.

"I want you too."

He tore the panties from me and I moaned at the sound of fabric tearing. There was no foreplay. Jaxson needed a release. Now. His erection sprung free and pressed the tip to my core. Nibbling my ear, he said, "We need a condom."

"No, we don't. You know I'm on the pill. We're getting married in less than two days."

Pushing in slightly, our gazes locked. "Fuck, you feel good."

"Please."

He thrust in and picked me up. "I'm taking you to bed." I ground down on him, needing the friction. "SIow down, sweetheart. I'm going to enjoy you bare."

"Yes."

Nothing felt better than when Jaxson was inside me.

LYING IN BED, legs entwined, Jaxson trailed his finger along my hip. He'd woke me up as dawn approached to make love to me. We'd stayed up relishing the touch of each other. "I'll never tire of having you."

"I'm glad, since you're about to have me for the rest of our lives tomorrow. I'll be Mrs. Jaxson McCole." I giggled.

He kissed me hard and whispered against my lips. "Music to my ears."

The stress in Jaxson's voice was still apparent. I touched his taut stomach. "We'll get through this. She won't get Ty."

"I know. I never wanted him to be affected by my poor decisions. Now he's afraid of losing you." He sighed. "I want him to feel safe and secure."

Lips teased my nipple followed by his breath blowing as he moved between my legs. "Jaxson . . ."

The doorknob turned and I froze, Jaxson's tip touching my clit.

"Dad? Mom?"

I became stiff, but Jaxson didn't move.

"Coming, buddy. Give me just a second." Jaxson gave me a devilish grin showcasing his dimples while he nipped my ear and pushed in farther. "We'll have to pick this up later." Pulling out, I felt the loss. I was worked up, beyond worked up. Quickly, Jaxson put on lounge pants and a T-shirt. He tossed me my pajamas. I needed a release.

After I was dressed, Ty opened the door and came running in as he threw his arms around my neck. "You stayed. You didn't leave."

I stroked his back as Jaxson's face contorted in pain. "I'm not leaving. I promise, Ty. I don't break my promises."

His body relaxed. Jaxson sat beside us. "Ty, I'm sorry about what happened yesterday."

Ty went to Jaxson. "You promise I don't have to ever go with that lady?"

"I promise." The words were a solemn vow spoken from Jaxson's lips.

The brows on his forehead scrunched for a minute. Then relaxed. "Okay. Can I have some breakfast before Grama comes and picks me up?" The conversation was a large swing, but children were resilient. I knew we weren't through all the insecurities, but the worst of the storm seemed to be behind us.

"Sure thing. How does cereal sound?"

Ty cheered for getting the sugary goodness he was only allowed on occasion. As the two of them disappeared to the kitchen, I brushed my teeth and freshened up a bit more. As I walked, the fabric of my pajamas brushed against me, reminding me of my earlier need.

I took a deep steadying breath as Jaxson appeared at the door. "You're looking flushed."

"Umm . . ."

Casually, Jaxson leaned against the door. "Do you want me to help?"

Facing Jaxson, I smirked at him as I leaned against the counter, my hand slipping down my pants. "I think I've got it. No assistance required." My head fell back as I moaned. My own fingers worked me up.

A strong hand stopped my movement. "This will have to be fast, sweetheart."

"Yes. Where's Ty?"

"Watching cartoons."

I smirked at Jaxson through my reflection. Ty never got to watch cartoons while he ate, which assured us some privacy.

Jaxson spun me around to face the mirror and ripped the T-shirt over my head. My nipples beaded and my core tightened. "I want you to watch yourself fall apart while I fuck you. Lean forward. Hands on the mirror."

I followed his instructions precisely as he pulled my pants off and spread my legs. His hardened length pressed against me. A moan escaped.

"You have to stay quiet." He pushed in while his hands moved up my sides, finding their way to the underside of my breasts.

I closed my eyes to absorb the sensation as Jaxson withdrew and then pushed in. "Keep your eyes open."

At his command, they sprung open. Jaxson's muscles on his chest were strained. The hard pinching sensation of my nipples made me gasp. The pressure increased as Jaxson quickened his pace. Within me, Jaxson hit that spot that built me up faster than anything. I was close. So close. He rolled my nipples, creating a zing to my core.

Jaxson shoved into me hard, sending the pleasure-filled orgasm spiraling through my body. He stilled as he released himself in me. As my arms gave out, Jaxson grabbed me. Between words, he kissed my shoulder. "Perfect. Every. Single. Time."

"I love you. I can't wait for tomorrow."

"Me either. Then I'll have you for three days to myself."

Jaxson rented a cabin up in the Rocky Mountains for the honeymoon. Now with Crystal in the picture, I was glad that we decided to go for a shorter amount of time. After pulling up his pants, Jaxson gave me one last kiss before heading back to the living room to check on Ty.

Dressed, I headed out to the bedroom. My phone vibrated. Checking the message, an icy feeling surged through my veins followed by cold dread.

Unknown: Glad you're now listening and staying away, I'm still watching.

I dropped the phone as it clanked on the wood floor. "Jaxson." My voice came out hoarse. I sank to the bed, numb.

"Mom is here. Ty is—" Jaxson was in front of me, kneeling. "London, what's wrong?"

Deftly, I pointed to the phone on the ground. Jaxson picked it up. "Fuck that fucking asshole." He took my face in his hands. "London, we'll report this like the note. Give me a second."

Jaxson left the room, leaving a pounding headache in its wake. All I wanted to do was leave the past behind and live my life. Why was the past refusing to let me go?

TWENTY-THREE

IN FRONT OF THE MIRROR, I looked at the woman who stood before me. *It was me.* A complete difference from when I first was released from prison. The hollowness of my features were filled in. The lifelessness in my expression gone. I was happy. Healthy. And in love.

My best friend rested her chin on my shoulder with blonde curls piled on top of her head. "You look beautiful, London. Are you ready to become Mrs. Jaxson McCole?"

"I am." Last night, I'd stayed in the guesthouse with Millie and Dad. We'd watched Donna's wedding on *90210*. We even talked Dad into watching an episode. He'd fallen asleep within five minutes of it starting. It was like old times as Millie and I lay in bed later that evening while we talked.

Backing away, Millie affixed the comb of the veil in my hair. "How are you feeling?"

Since yesterday when I got the text message from the unknown person, I wasn't able to shake the looming headache trying to ebb its way forward. My body felt achy. This morning I'd taken some cold medicine to help me get through the day without feeling terrible.

There was nothing that would ruin this day.

Nothing.

"I'm okay. I think the stress from the text message toppled me over the edge along with Crystal."

I shuddered at the thought of Crystal being out there or causing any more trouble. She'd been released from jail. Plus nothing new had been found regarding who was behind my drugging or the notes. Currently, Millie was volunteering in the records department in order to investigate other patients the doctor had seen. Between Crystal and the phantom stalker, I was stressed to the max and knew that was the case behind me feeling ill.

Millie snapped her fingers in front of my face. "There will be no negative thoughts on your wedding day. The crazies are not allowed to be part of this day."

Saluting, I said, "Yes, ma'am." For some unknown reason the gesture elicited a laugh from us.

"Here, take this. It's full of vitamins and will help keep the cold at bay."

With gratitude, I took the medicine. At first, Millie thought I was pregnant. Considering my period ended just under a week ago, I knew I was in the clear. The thought of a baby was the last thing we needed right now.

The door opened. "Punkin', Pam says it's time."

"Okay, Daddy. I'm ready."

This was it.

I stood and pushed the queasiness aside. Jaxson and Ty awaited me. My family. My future.

With my arm in his, Dad led me out of the room. "You have a fine young man waiting to marry you. Your mom and I are so very proud of you."

A bittersweet smile passed over my features. It was doubtful Mom realized I was getting married or that I was released from prison for that matter. At least there would be video. With her condition, the doctor advised against moving her to attend the wedding. I understood, but wanted her here. Dad promised at some point he would bring her, thinking the mountain air might be good for her despite what the doctor said. With the threats looming over us, we thought it best for me to stay away from Guin for the time being.

Dad placed his hand over mine and I relaxed.

Walking the short distance down the stone floor, Millie stayed a few steps in front of us. Faint strains of classical music played through the air. This would be the first time I would see the church. Everything but the cake and dress were kept a secret from me. Millie looked back from her emerald-green dress, eyes sparking with excitement. "Are you ready?"

"I am."

A flowery smell wafted through the air as the doors were opened to the church. I remained out of sight beside the door. Before Millie took off down the aisle, she whispered, "I love you, London."

"Love you, too."

Emotion swelled within me. Dad led me in front of the doors as I kept my eyes closed. Upon the slight pressure from Dad, I opened my eyes and gasped. White twinkle lights hung from the beams of the ceiling in the old, gray stone church. White flowers of every kind covered the surface. It was like a dream come true.

Jaxson moved to the center of the aisle, awaiting me with Ty. The sight took my breath away as I gazed at the strong man who captured my heart. Millie stood slightly off to the left after walking the short distance. The melody changed to "Jesu, Joy of Man's Desiring," the song Mom walked to Dad on their wedding day.

The entire world faded away except the man I was about to pledge my undying love to.

I took a deep centering breath as Jaxson impatiently waited for Dad to deliver me to him. We arrived and I stood only a few inches away from Jaxson. The preacher said something but all I was able to focus on was Jaxson as he searched my eyes with his green ones. This was right. I was meant to be his.

My heart thudded in my chest as I anxiously awaited to be in his arms.

As Dad handed me over to Jaxson, I turned back to him realizing he'd given me away. "Dad, I love you forever and ever. I'll always be your little girl."

"That'll never change, punkin'. Never."

A tear slipped free. Kissing his cheek, I whispered, "Never."

Jaxson took my hand and the energy flowed between us. Our gazes locked. This was right. He was the man I was meant for all along. The ceremony progressed in a haze. Quicker than I imagined, but slow at the same time. Ty stood there enamored with the entire process with a huge grin on his face.

All my thoughts were consumed by the man in front of me and the child I was becoming the mother of. As we said our vows, Jaxson broadened his shoulders as he declared his love for me. My voice was steady and strong, unwavering as I pledged my thoughts.

"You may now kiss the bride." Cheers erupted and a fire danced within Jaxson's eyes.

Our lips met.

We were one.

I was his.

He was mine.

We were forever.

A hand touched my waist. I broke the kiss. "You're really my mom forever."

I knelt down and hugged my son. *Son.* It all felt real now. "Always and forever, Ty. I won't leave you."

He squeezed me tighter, then looked at his dad. "Does this mean I get a little sister or brother now?"

Frozen, I glanced at Jaxson while the few people laughed. "One step at a time, buddy."

A huff escaped my son. "That's what you said about London being my mom and that took *forever.*"

More laughter.

We stood as Jaxson picked up Ty and held me close. The moment was perfect. Incredible. Facing our families, they rushed to give us hugs. The voices melded together as congratulations were given. Jaxson never faltered with his hold of me.

The reception was in the small room off of the chapel. The same twinkle lights gave the fairytale feel. The cake was stunning as the crystal beads embedded in it sparkled mimicking the pattern of my dress. The sweet confection filled the room with a sweet, savory smell.

The Italian crème flavor exploded on my tongue while Jaxson fed me. As we shared our first drink of champagne, the bubbly concoction did not sit well with me as the adrenaline from the day receded, leaving a dull ache within my body.

I will not be sick on my wedding night. I will not.

"Are you ready to leave, sweetheart?"

"Never been more ready," I said.

A devilish grin appeared. "Words every man loves to hear from his wife."

Heat crept on my face as the anticipation built of our night together. Ty hugged me tightly as we said our goodbyes. Over the last week it was explained repeatedly what would happen after the wedding. Of course, Ty wanted to come and we planned to take a family vacation sometime this fall. He was going to go fishing with Levi and Pam for a few days to help keep his mind off of everything. "Promise to call me every morning and every night, Mom."

"I promise." He kissed me hard on the check. "Love you, Ty."

"Love you too, Mom."

Jaxson took Ty and they whispered the same sentiments. Levi hugged Pam as they watched the scene unfold, approval on their faces. Millie approached. "Was your day perfect?"

"Yes, because of you. I'm still in awe over what you guys did. It was beautiful." A huge grin appeared on Millie's face at the praise. They had worked tirelessly to make this wedding stress-free and stunning.

Pam and Levi gave hugs. "Welcome to the family, London. You're perfect for our son."

"Thank you." Pam's words resonated through me as Levi spoke to Jaxson. I was like a daughter to them now. A true family member.

As we made our way to the car, Sydney and Mallory gave us one last hug. The atmosphere only heightened as news was received that her husband would be home for Christmas from his tour. We were blessed. Dad waited at the car in his tux, an abstract difference from his flannels and jeans. The worry wrinkles that were pronounced the day I was released had lessened and been replaced by joy.

The familiar woodsy scent wrapped around me as I prepared to get in the car. "I'll see you soon in Mobile. I'm so proud of you, London."

"Thank you, Daddy."

Dad turned to Jaxson as he handed me off. The significance of the moment formed a lump in my throat. "Take care of my little girl."

"I swear I will."

Dad dipped his head in acknowledgment. "I know."

Getting in the car, I sank against the seat as my body felt warm. "Are you ready for your honeymoon, Mrs. McCole?"

"Yes. I like the sound of my new name." I closed my eyes for a second. Exhaustion was making itself known.

Light touches of my husband's fingertips slid along my cheek. "Are you okay, sweetheart?"

"I took some cold medicine earlier today. I think I'm getting a cold. But, I'll be fine."

A hand rested upon my thigh. "Rest. We'll be there in a couple of hours."

"I can't wait." Sleep was welcomed and would give me more energy. *I will not be sick on my wedding night.*

As my eyes closed, I relished in this moment of happiness.

"LONDON, SWEETHEART. WAKE up. You have a fever."

I felt terrible. Achy. Hot. "Jaxson. Where are we?"

Cold hands touched my face. My eyes adjusted to the dim light. We were pulled over on the side of the road. Jaxson had his phone up to his ear. "No, I'm bringing her home. She'll be more comfortable."

Home? I wanted my honeymoon. Hoarsely, I tried to speak, then felt the queasiness take over. I needed out of the car. I needed out of it right then. I hurled myself onto the side of the road while Jaxson swore. My stomach wretched as I lost everything from the day. Jaxson was beside me in a second. I was thankful I'd changed out of my gown.

"London, we're going home."

Soft strokes ran along my back. "Jaxson. Our honeymoon." More retching occurred and I nearly collapsed. Strong arms kept me from colliding with the gravely pavement.

A handkerchief appeared in front of me. "London, we'll have a honeymoon. But, you're sick. We need to get home. Millie is going to look you over."

I wanted to argue. But I was weak and lacked the energy. "Promise?"

Hoisting me up, Jaxson cradled me to him. "I promise you."

Relaxing, I let my eyes drift closed as the cold leather seats cooled my blistering body. The last thing I heard was the muffled sound of the car door closing before I drifted off.

THE MORNING LIGHT shone through the windows as I glinted into the bright sun coming through the balcony doors. The soft breeze created a fresh smell which waned the grossness I felt from being sick. Maybe it was the afternoon light. Bits and pieces came back over who knows how long. Millie was here at some point and said it was the flu. Hopefully I was over it.

I stirred to sit up. Jaxson was there with a light hand on my back to help me. Pillows were propped behind me. "You're awake. How are you feeling?"

"Tired. Weak. Better."

Someone beside me stirred. I heard a whimper. Peeking my eyes open, I saw Ty. I remembered him coming home too. Sick. "How's he doing?"

Lightly I brushed my hand over the back of his Superman pajamas.

"Better. You both were sick. It was easier to take care of you guys in here together. Millie said it would have to pass. There wasn't much we could give you guys because it was viral. All I could do was keep you hydrated and give you fever reducer. He's about a day behind you."

My body ached as I threw my arm across my face. "I spent my honeymoon . . . with the flu. That's terrible."

I felt the mattress dip and my arm removed. "It'll be a memory we'll never forget. Something to tell our grandkids one day."

A chuckle escaped. "Jaxson, we haven't even . . ." I glanced over to Ty who was fast asleep catching myself before I said consummated our marriage.

Soft lips touched mine. "We will. I promise, sweetheart. We will. Rest. I'll get you some food."

FIVE DAYS PASSED since I recovered from the flu. By some miracle, Jaxson avoided it. Mallory had it two days after Ty. So far, that was the end of the contamination. I sat on the back porch gazing at the mountains as the sun set, sipping a cup of hot tea. The fall mountain air felt good as I took a deep breath and watched the gray puffy clouds roll in. A storm was brewing. I loved the distant rumble.

"It's getting cold. Why don't you come inside? I don't want you getting sick again." Jaxson nuzzled me while his deep voice vibrated from within. The outdoorsy manly smell infiltrated my senses and my libido came to life.

Slightly turning my head, I kissed him. "Let's head inside."

Marriage was wonderful; well, the few days I'd been married were. Jaxson was attentive to my every need while simultaneously working on the McCole Classic and running the clinic. Today was the first day I felt like a human. Same with Ty.

Jaxson nibbled my ear. "Are you feeling better?"

"Yes." My breathy reply conveyed everything. Since being sick, Jaxson hadn't touched me intimately. I needed him.

With an extended hand, Jaxson helped me up and we walked inside with his hand on my lower back. He filled me in on what happened today at work. As soon as he'd gotten home, he took Ty to feed the sheep.

Thinking of the little man. "Where's Ty?"

"He's occupied. I want to show you something."

I quirked a brow. "This sounds intriguing."

No further reply came as Jaxson led me back to our bedroom. A gasp of air left me as I saw rose petals sprinkled on the floor and onto the bed. Candles burned on every surface. The curtains from the deck billowed with the impending storm. "Jaxson . . ."

Arms came around me as Jaxson's hand caressed my stomach. "Ty is with my parents tonight. He's decided to make a list of why we need a dog. Dad's helping him come up with convincing reasons."

I chuckled. Since explaining a brother or sister would be a ways down the road, Ty decided we needed to practice on a puppy to show how responsible he was so he could get a sibling.

"You know you're going to get him a puppy." Then it registered. We were alone. "We're alone." Tilting my head back, I gave access to my neck as I felt the warmth of his lips press against the pulsing vein in my neck.

My shirt lifted and Jaxson turned me toward him. Slowly he undressed me as I him. I touched his hardened muscles that quickened under my touch.

"I will never take your touch for granted." Jaxson's words elicited goose bumps along my skin. We took a few steps back until the back of my knees hit the mattress. "I will never stop loving you." Tenderly he laid me on the bed and positioned himself above me, waiting to join us together. "I will cherish this moment for the rest of my life."

TWENTY-FOUR

W E WERE IN MOBILE, ALABAMA at the Healing with Horses event. My parents always donated to the cause as it helped children with disabilities learn to cope. It was an amazing organization. Last year, Dad won the award he was presenting this year; *Healing with Horses Humanitarian Award*. I saw pictures but wasn't able to attend since I was in prison. Dad donated several horses as well as his time to the organization.

Jaxson called from the other room of the hotel suite as I put the last touches of makeup on. "London, are you almost ready?"

We were running ten minutes behind schedule. I texted Dad to let him know, since we were meeting him for the event. "Coming. It's your fault I'm late."

"That's what you were doing a bit ago."

"Jaxson!" I mock scolded from the other room and heard a laugh. It was true; Jaxson's lips coerced me to stay in bed longer than I should have. But the rewards of his tongue were worth it.

Putting in my dangling earrings, I took a look at my elegant black dress that sparkled in the light with an underlying gray tone. A few wisps of dark hair framed my face. The theme color was black and gold this year. Pam and I found the dress in Denver. It was stunning.

The tall, black stilettos clicked against the marble tile on the floor as I made my way to the living room.

Jaxson paused as he put down the remote. "You take my breath away, London. Truly."

I stood motionless as I gazed at the sight of my husband dressed in a tux. His messy hair rumpled in a way that screamed sex.

A broad smile spread across my face. I walked up to him. "I sometimes can't believe I have you as mine. All those years in prison, I never imagined—"

"Sweetheart, you deserve everything you have and more."

Softly, I kissed his lips. "I love you so much."

"And I'll never stop loving you."

Guiding me out of the room, we headed to the ballroom. Guests dressed to the nines were arriving as we stood in line to enter the room. As we stepped over the threshold, the smell of begonias filled the room; their petals sprayed with the theme colors. Dad waved to us and we made our way toward him. The beautiful gold-glittered black table dressing gave a royal feel. I felt like a princess in my dress. I remembered as a kid how much Mom always loved these charity events. I missed her not being here. I missed her not being part of my life and seeing the woman I was becoming. But, we sent videos for Dad to play for her when he visited.

Dad hugged me to him. "You look beautiful, punkin'."

"Thanks, Daddy. I missed you."

Whispering in my ear, he said, "I think marriage suits you."

"I have to agree."

The night proceeded with several speeches as well as videos from the year. Tender moments brought tears to my eyes as children overcame obstacles in their lives through the tender touch of a horse. Seeing the children light up while brushing the horses, riding them, and caring for them.

For a couple of summers before dancing took over my schedule, I spent time helping these children. It was near and dear to my heart. I smiled to myself as I thought about Sparkles putting on many a show for the kids on the opening day to help ease the apprehension of being around such a large animal. From time to time, with the more difficult cases, Sparkles was brought out to work with the children. It was something we did as a family. Mom baked treats for the kids after the lessons.

The memories were good ones I hadn't thought of in a long time.

The announcer cued my dad to walk up on the stage. He greeted the audience, accompanied with a gentle smile. This year he was starting a scholarship fund in my mother's name to help children who weren't able to afford this type of therapy. The McCole's already made a generous donation. Several children would get the help they desperately needed because of this.

The crowd applauded. He looked dashing as he waited for the cheers to calm down. I was unable to wipe the grin from my face.

This time last year, I wasn't able to attend. Dad was alone. The thoughts were sobering with how far life had taken me.

Dad finished the speech and a classical song played by the three-piece band filled the air. I leaned in to Jaxson. "I'll be right back. I need the ladies room."

"Hurry. I want to dance with my wife. Then later, I want to take you to bed."

Heat graced my face as Dad sat next to me. Quickly, I excused myself after giving him a congratulatory hug. With the crowd, it took me a bit to make it through as people remembered me from my days of involvement. Finally, I made it to the hallway where the restrooms were before my bladder exploded.

"London!"

I stopped as unease slid down my spine.

My feet were rooted in place for a mere second before I

remembered myself and whirled around at the familiar voice. The man I knew for many years stood in front of me. I wasn't sure how I felt, but there were no feelings of regret or wishing he chose me like there had been—only confirming my feelings.

Stiffly, I greeted him. "Charles."

Glancing around, I saw no one else. We were alone. The last thing I wanted was to irritate whoever was behind the notes since Charles seemed to be the trigger. So far, after heeding their warning, nothing more happened. I wanted it to stay that way until there was concrete evidence pointing out who the culprit was.

He took a step forward while unbuttoning his suit jacket. I took a step back. There was an illuminated exit sign behind me if I needed to leave. I wasn't trapped, but my phone was at the table within my clutch.

Dammit. Why hadn't I brought it?

I forced myself to remain outwardly calm while my insides shook with apprehension.

"London, I've been trying to reach you. I figured you would be here tonight."

"Who's with you?"

A wrinkle crossed his brow and his shoulders slumped. Resigned, he answered, "Rachel and her family." He took another step forward and I backed up twice as many. "I know how this looks, London."

He was a piece of work keeping Rachel on the line while trying to find me on the side. However, it was what happened to me while I was in prison. Maybe Charles needed two women in his life. One for presentation purposes and one for fun. The thought sickened me. I remained silent.

"You look beautiful. You always were the most gorgeous woman in the room when we went to events together. I loved having you on my arm." He paused before I had a chance to set him straight on my availability. "London, can we talk? Are you still seeing that fucker?"

The sarcastic demeaning voice fueled my irritation. Raising my hand, I showed my wedding ring. "I'm married to Jaxson. We were married two weeks ago."

Charles rushed me in a flurry. A sharp pain radiated through my back as he pushed me against the wall. "Let go, Charles. You're hurting me."

A pained expression tore across his face. "How could you not give us a chance? How could you not give me a chance to escape the hell I've found myself in? How could you give up on us? Our love? We were the real thing, London."

"Get your fucking hands off my wife, you son of a bitch." The menacing no-nonsense voice was steel through the air. This was the second time I had ever heard Jaxson this mad. The time before had been on the phone with Charles.

Charles' blue eyes continued to penetrate mine. "She was mine. Is mine. I had her first."

Before I was able to push Charles away, he was yanked from me. Anger flowed through me. Jaxson stood furiously protective in front of me. "Come near her again and I'll have a restraining order and whatever the fuck is needed to keep you away. I have no issues taking it public and ruining your chance at office. Stay. Away."

Stepping slightly to the side, but staying behind him, Charles clenched his jaw. Losing my temper would only increase the tension. I changed tactics. "Charles, I fell in love with Jaxson. I am his. We have a past like everyone does. It will always be the past."

Incredulously, Charles looked at me. "London, you can't mean that. I meant every word I said the last day at the prison. Every. Word."

I ignored the last part of the sentence. "I love Jaxson, Charles. With my whole heart or I wouldn't have married him. You know that about me. I don't do anything unless I'm being true to myself. That hasn't changed, even with prison."

Backing away, Jaxson put his hand on my lower waist and guided me out of the hallway. Charles said nothing to our retreating backs. This was too surreal. Nervously, I glanced around to see if anyone else was there watching us.

The corridor remained eerily empty. I hoped this incident wasn't another trigger.

Concerned, Jaxson asked, "Are you okay? I got worried when you didn't come back after a few minutes."

"A lot of people stopped me to talk. It took me longer than expected." I leaned against Jaxson. "I want to go to our room after I say bye to Dad. I'm exhausted."

Searching out my father, we gave our goodnights. "Great speech, Daddy. I'm tired from all the travel. I'm going to go rest. Don't forget Millie and her Aunt Diane are coming for breakfast in the morning."

For a second I thought about mentioning Charles, but that would only add worry when it had been handled.

Dad gave me a kiss on the forehead. "I won't. That flu really took it out of you. Rest up."

"It did. I'm almost back to new."

"Night, punkin'."

"Night, Dad."

After giving me a quick kiss, he and Jaxson exchanged goodbyes.

A few people stopped Jaxson or me as we left because of his connections in the horse world. There were a few who expressed interest in attending the McCole Classic. Underneath the calm friendly exterior, I knew Jaxson was boiling from what happened earlier with Charles with his barely contained restraint.

A chill ran up my spine as I felt an unwanted stare. My eyes caught Charles' pleading ones while he stood next to Rachel while she was otherwise engaged with her parents. *How could you not give me a chance to escape the hell I found myself in?* The words from the hallway echoed back in my mind.

Hell? What kind of hell had he found himself in?

The elevator dinged with its arrival and we stepped into the mirrored walls, all watching me which left me feeling on edge as if the stalker was monitoring my every move.

What was Charles saying? Was it in reference to Rachel? Running for office? Leaving Me?

Would it have mattered?

I looked up at Jaxson as he stared ahead. No, nothing would have changed. Jaxson was who I was meant to be with. Nothing stirred within me while I was in Charles' arms. Even now with only Jaxson's arm wrapped around me, the energy was felt at every connecting point. More than I ever felt with Charles.

"What are you thinking about?"

The elevator opened and we stepped into the ecru with gold trim corridor. "Just something Charles said. How could I not give him a chance to escape the hell he found himself in?"

The card reader to our door made a beeping sound as it granted us access. As soon as the door closed, Jaxson turned to face me. "So, is this your subtle way of saying you made a mistake?"

Fury erupted to the surface that I pent up downstairs. Some of it was misplaced, but this hurt. I pointed at Jaxson and took a step forward. "Don't take this out on me! Have I ever once given you the impression I thought I made a mistake? I'm not like that! It hurts you don't know me better since I'm your *wife* and think of Ty as *mine!*"

Tears threatened to spill over. Jaxson was shocked at my outburst. Momentarily stunned. Turning on my heel, I headed to our bathroom and locked the door behind me. The hurt was deep as my heart felt like it was breaking in two.

Marriage was trust.

Marriage was love.

Marriage was forever.

I slid down the wall as the tears tracked down my face. The

handle on the door moved. With the lock engaged, Jaxson was kept out. I needed a minute to collect my thoughts before more hurtful words were spoken.

One thing I learned from Mom, *"Words can never be unheard, London. Make sure you mean everything you say."*

"London, open up." The muffled voice came through the door.

My eyes closed shut. "Not right now." The tremble in my voice was evident.

The door rattled again while Jaxson pleaded once more. My silence I'm sure spoke volumes as I lost myself in my thoughts.

How long had Jaxson doubted my feelings for him? I took my wedding vows seriously. Maybe we rushed into this? Even as I tried to believe we had, I knew I hadn't.

But was Jaxson rushed?

A hand touched my face and I jumped. Jaxson dropped the door key which was probably hidden above the doorframe. "Sweetheart, I'm so fucking sorry. I was so wrapped up in that asshole, I wasn't seeing reason. He had his hands on you and it took everything I had not to hurt him." Hands cradled my cheeks. "I know you, London. I know you would never make a lifelong commitment without being sure. Charles may have known you longer, but I know your heart. I have it forever."

I nodded as more tears fell. "The hell Charles referenced may give us more information as to what happened. That was why I was thinking about it. I may not love Charles, Jaxson, but if he's in trouble I want to help."

Jaxson swallowed hard and brought me into his lap. "If he was coerced to leave you because of someone's agenda—"

I put my hands to his lips. "Jaxson, it wouldn't change my feelings for you. My life is with you and Ty. Not Charles. But as a human being, I feel compassion for someone I once shared a relationship with. That's all."

Lips pressed against mine. "I don't know what I would do if I lost you. I'm so sorry I jumped to conclusions."

Nestling into him, his thrumming heartbeat centered me. "Jaxson, talk to me first next time. I'll never lie to you. I promise."

"Never again." In one fluid movement, Jaxson stood with me in his arms. "I'm going to make love to my wife all night long. You'll never doubt how much I love you, London. Never again."

TWENTY-FIVE

N EARLY HOME, I GAZED OUT at the mountains still thinking about this morning after breakfast. With Jaxson on the phone since we landed regarding the upcoming McCole Classic, I recounted this morning's events. Would we ever have answers?

Sitting at the breakfast table of the hotel, Dad along with Millie and her Aunt Diane, ate with us. I loved Millie's aunt. Claimed her as my own. She was a kind-spirited woman. Since I was released, Aunt Diane had been up north visiting her children since Millie was able to help with her mom, who was continuing to recover. We hoped for a cancer-free report at the next appointment.

I took the last bite of French toast and pushed the porcelain plate away. "I'm stuffed. That was delicious."

Time to leave approached as our plane left in three hours. Diane pressed the mauve-colored cloth to her mouth. "Me too. I'm glad I got to see you, London. I missed seeing my girls together. And your husband is quite the catch."

Jaxson captured Aunt Diane's attention from the moment he walked into the room. She was a feisty lady. A chuckle escape Jaxson as he winked at me.

"She has impeccable taste." Jaxson winked at me while Aunt Diane laughed.

We all joined in as Aunt Diane fanned herself. Not answering and only giving me a devilish smile, Jaxson had me giggling. Millie stood. "Let me help you guys with your stuff before you have to leave."

Millie mentioned a new ice cream flavor she tried last night on the phone. I hardly slept wondering what had been found. Dad offered to keep Aunt Diane company while we brought down our stuff. I'd let him know after I heard from Millie what was going on.

Leaving the restaurant, I acted as natural as possible. From the corner of my eye, I saw Charles with his parents, Rachel and her parents. Caroline waved and excused herself. I focused my attention on Caroline and not the malice stares from Rachel. Charles Senior gave me a wave and I smiled. I still hadn't seen him since I got out. He remained in his chair, talking more animatedly with Rachel's parents. If he left the table, the awkwardness would only amplify. I was grateful for Charles Senior's help in distracting the Graves.

Before I brought my attention back to Caroline, I saw the pure hatred in Rachel's eyes and I knew somehow she was involved. Jaxson's arm protectively went around me.

"London, how are you doing? I couldn't believe that was you. What are you doing in Mobile?"

Last night, I hadn't seen Caroline or Charles Senior. When had they arrived? Had Charles told her nothing? Her features only exuded delight and surprise in seeing me. She was pristinely dressed in a light burnt-orange suit, not a blonde hair out of place. "Dad presented an award. We flew in to see it and are about to head to the airport." Caroline's eyes moved to Jaxson briefly. I introduced them. "This is my husband, Jaxson McCole."

The warm answering grin eased my nerves. "Husband? Oh London, I'm so happy for you. Jaxson, it's nice to meet you. I had no idea London was married or I would have sent something. We've been on the campaign trail. I'm afraid I always get behind on what's happening at home with all the events. I'm Caroline Paddington."

It was true. I had spent a few weekends on the campaign trail. Every minute of every day was allotted to something that hopefully would either ensure or bring in votes. Everyone wanted their time, their moment. It was exhausting. Not the life for me.

"It's nice to meet you, Caroline. London has spoken warmly of you." Jaxson extended his hand.

"My husband and I have a special place for London. She's like a daughter to us."

Rachel appeared beside Caroline dressed in black slacks and a long sleeve blue silk top—campaign trail ready. I remembered Charles critiquing my wardrobe before events. I hated it. Why had I stayed in his life for so long?

The voice was like nails on a chalkboard. Rachel was a mean-spirited person. "Caroline, I hate to interrupt, but the wedding coordinator has arrived to discuss the last of the details."

With her hand extended, Caroline made introductions to Jaxson. Rachel appraised him for a second, and I felt Jaxson's hand around my hip.

Rachel extended her hand. "Nice to meet you also. I wish we could have married quickly like the two of you, but planning the wedding of the century takes time."

No one said anything until Caroline broke the silence.

"I need to go. We have some last-minute details to wrap up before everything is finalized for the October wedding. Charles Senior and I flew in early this morning before we leave for our next stop." Caroline gave me a quick hug. "I'm glad you found happiness. You deserve it, London. Let's make a date to do lunch if you're back in town anytime soon. I'll get the details from your dad in case we're in your area also."

"Perfect. Thank you."

Caroline walked away. Rachel looked back with a hatred glare on her face followed by a sinister grin. "Well, I wonder how Rachel really feels about you," Millie said sarcastically as she watched Rachel swing her hips with sass.

Rolling my eyes, I caught a glimpse of Charles before I turned away. A haunted look crossed his features.

Maybe we were victims of the same circumstance? We neither knew nor willingly participated in the game we were unknowingly drafted to play.

As the elevators door closed, Millie muttered, "I hate that woman. She was envious Caroline talked to you. You're married. She's trouble. Bitch."

"I know."

We rode the rest of the way up in silence to our room. As the door shut, I stood in front of Jaxson. "What did you find, Millie?" I asked.

She took a deep breath. "I found it three days ago. The only reason I didn't say anything until last night is because I hadn't wanted you to worry since you were coming to Mobile. I'm sorry."

"I wouldn't have slept at all. I appreciate it."

Pulling out a tape recorder, she laid it on the bed. "Dr. Michaels, the one who did your blood work, had a locker with a tape recorder regarding you being framed."

I interrupted her. "What? It clears me?"

"Yes, but one of the voices has been altered. I can't make out who it is. Even if it's male or female."

Picking up the tape recorder, I looked at it while turning the black object in my hand. "Where'd you find this?"

"Under his desk, there was a key taped behind the drawer. I have spent the last two weeks going everywhere within an hour driving distance that had a lock number 212. Three days ago, I found it at the bus station."

My head was swimming with everything. Glancing to Jaxson, he nodded. "Let's hear it."

I pressed play and the wheels spun. The recording was silent for a few seconds as I stared at the small device while nerves became more prevalent. The doctor started off the conversation while the background noise crackled. "It's been done. London McNally's blood results have been changed. It'll appear she was driving drunk with no other substance in her blood."

A strange digitally answered voice came on. "Good. She'll be put away *for a while with the evidence and what else I have planned."*

"Very well."

The digital voice answered, but harsher this time. "No one must know or I'll turn over the malpractice evidence I have. That bitch is going to get what she deserves in court after trying to take away what is mine."

"You have my word."

The line went dead. I waited for more to come, but it didn't. Only static. "Is that it?"

Millie nodded. "That's it. I know it's not much, but I thought you'd want to hear it. The original lab results were also in the locker. I want to see if we can strip away the digital voice to any semblance of someone we know."

I handed the recorder back to Millie, feeling sick remembering the hatred of the altered voice. They truly hated me to the depths of their soul.

Jaxson chimed in, "I may know someone. It might be best if we have someone away from Alabama analyze a copy of the tape."

Jaxson's hand came to my leg, breaking me away from the memory. "You're deep in thought."

I rubbed my hand over my temples. "I wish I knew why this all started. There has to be something that triggered it all."

Jaxson let out a sigh. "Hopefully seeing us happy together stops anything else after this weekend. You refused Charles repeatedly and made no attempt to speak to him this morning at breakfast. There's something not right about Rachel."

"I hope if it's Rachel, she saw I have no interest."

THE BARN CAME into view on the McCole Ranch. Ty and Levi were waiting outside. Jaxson had texted his parents as we came up the long drive. Vigorously, our son waved. "I'm glad to be home, Jaxson."

Jaxson gave me a quick kiss as he turned off the truck. "Me too, sweetheart."

As soon as the truck door opened, little feet spurred their way toward us. I knelt to embrace my son. "I missed you so much, Ty."

"Did you miss me enough for a dog?"

Jaxson scooped Ty up. "You are persistent."

"Like father, like son." I smiled as I spoke.

Jaxson gave me a wink. "Means us McCole men get what we want."

That perked Ty's ears up as we headed inside. The dog persuasion doubled in efforts. As we caught up over dinner, a fog settled over me. I wasn't sure what was wrong. An unsettling feeling loomed in the back of my mind. Thank goodness Ty kept the conversation going.

In the kitchen, I put the last of the leftovers away. Pam asked, "Are you feeling okay?"

"I . . . uh . . . I don't know. I'm tired and I feel off."

Loving, motherly arms embraced me. "Sometimes, we just need a hug."

Tears I hadn't known were being held, broke free. Between sniffles I responded, "Thank you for the hug. I needed it."

I closed my eyes and continued to sob. The grip loosened. "I'm going to go keep Ty occupied. Jaxson's here."

Jaxson watched me with worried eyes as Pam walked past him while touching his shoulder briefly. "Do you want him to stay with me tonight?" Pam asked.

Jaxson looked to me for an answer. I shook my head. "I want us all under the same roof tonight. Thanks for offering, Pam."

Jaxson enveloped me in his arms. "What's wrong, sweetheart?"

"I don't know. Your mom hugged me and I started crying. She's like a mom to me. Everything I was holding in came out."

"She loves you."

The tears continued. Jaxson held me while making promises everything would be okay.

TWENTY-SIX

TWO DAYS PASSED SINCE OUR trip to Mobile. Fall was upon us as the leaves changed colors. A few danced across the ground as I moseyed my way toward the barn.

Thinking back to the night we arrived, the emotional outburst in Pam's kitchen had been unexpected. I still wasn't sure what brought it on, but Jaxson held me through the night while I sought comfort in his arms.

Currently, Jaxson and his dad were meeting with security in the office area within the barn. There were gaps that had been noticed with the expanse of the property. Ty and Pam were baking cookies for Mallory since she'd won her dance competition. There was a new horse named Pendragon who arrived a few days ago. He'd torn his ligament and was working through a rehabilitation regimen Jaxson designed. Watching him swim for a few minutes, I smiled at Dwayne at his progress before leaving the pool area.

I stretched my arms above my head to relieve the sore muscles forming. This morning I'd danced in the workout room of the house. It relieved the stress and let me escape. I learned dancing in front of an audience wasn't something I needed. Only to dance.

My phone rang. "Hey, Dad."

"Hey, punkin'. You got a minute? I have a surprise for you."

"I love surprises."

A horse whinnied in the background. He was probably in the barn at home wearing his flannel shirt and jeans. "Well, I thought I would come visit you guys for the McCole Classic if you were up for a visit from your old man."

"Oh, Dad. I would love it. We didn't get near enough time in Mobile. Millie mentioned coming also."

"Good. I'll get with her. I need to get to the shop to finish some furniture orders. Bye, punkin'."

"Bye, Daddy."

I hung up the phone, excited to see Dad again. First, I would stop by to see Sparkles.

"Hey girl, do you want to go for a ride together later when I finish working?"

Sparkles didn't put her head out of the stall as I approached, which was odd. I glanced in her stall. Something was wrong. Froth came out of her mouth as she staggered back and forth in the corner before collapsing on her side. Her breathing was irregular.

Poison. Dad taught me the signs. A few times we'd seen it in our barn. The training kicked in. I ran to the tack room to grab the stimulant syringes, mineral oil, and tubing.

Jaxson was only a few doors down. "Jaxson! I need you!"

Quickly, I gathered the supplies and ran to Sparkles' stall as I heard Jaxson calling for me. "I'm in Sparkles' stall."

My poor horse continued to froth while jerky nervous movements consumed her muscles. "Hold on, baby. I'm going to get you better."

"What happened? Are you okay?" There wasn't time to look up at Jaxson.

I unsheathed the syringe and tapped the end a few times.

"Sparkles was poisoned. Help me get the tube and mineral oil in as I inject her with the stimulant."

Please not Sparkles. Please. Please. Please. I can't lose her.

Quickly, I injected Sparkles, who barely responded to the stab. Jaxson knelt beside me while using the tubing and mineral oil. Methodically, I checked Sparkles to see if there were any other entry points of the poison in case it were administered via the skin.

"Do you see anything, London? The mineral oil and tube is in."

Jaxson grabbed a bucket as the tube worked getting Sparkles' stomach contents out. Hopefully the oil was administered fast enough to stop the absorption before permanent damage was caused. "It doesn't appear there are any cuts. I'm checking her feed."

I went over to the bucket and saw it full of her treats along with pieces of a plant. My heart sank. I knew this plant well.

Hemlock. A poisonous plant that led to death in many cases if not caught in time.

Dread filled me. "It's Hemlock, Jaxson. Crushed in a bucket full of treats."

"Fuck."

Kneeling in front of Sparkles, I ran my hand through her soft black coat. Jaxson called the vet. "Hang in there, girl. Hang in there. Please don't die. I'm so sorry. So, so, sorry."

I had to keep it together. Hearing my distressed voice, Sparkles tried to raise her head. "Shh . . . stay right there. I'm okay."

The breathing evened out but more shallow. Sparkles relaxed as I soothingly spoke to her. I knew this was normal, but I was scared. What if she was taken from me? I tried not to let myself slip back into old habits.

Please let her be okay.

Jaxson brought me to his lap. "The vet is on her way. We're supposed to inject another stimulant shot in thirty minutes."

I nodded. "How did she get hemlock in her treats bucket, Jaxson?"

"I don't know, sweetheart. We'll look at the security feeds to see if there are any answers."

There was no doubt this was done intentionally. Jaxson knew it too. I was able to tell by the stiffness of the way he held himself.

Was there a note?

Anything?

Something that would connect the incident to Charles?

I started searching through the hay. Then everywhere. "What are you doing, London?"

"Seeing if they left a message." Then a fearful thought formed. "Can you call my dad? See if everyone is okay? I'll check on Ty."

Jaxson grabbed me and brought me to him while holding the phone to his ear, keeping me from leaving. "Hey, Mom. Is Ty with you? Okay. Sparkles' been poisoned. Yeah. Keep him in the house. Call Dad." He hung up the phone. "Hey, Ken. Jaxson. London wanted me to let you know Sparkles is sick. We have a vet coming to see her. She's hanging in there. I will."

Before I was able to ask, Jaxson sat us back down near Sparkles. "Everyone is okay."

I leaned back against Jaxson. "Do you think this was an accident?"

"No, I don't."

The tenseness in his jaw told me Jaxson was holding something back.

IT WAS THE middle of the night. The vet came and left after attending to Sparkles. It was comforting the vet believed Sparkles would pull through. The question was if there would be permanent damage. Her vitals were strong as I watched her stomach rise and fall in a steady motion. The frothing of her mouth finished hours ago.

We were nearing hour twelve after I found her. Generally death occurred within ten hours of the onset of symptoms with hemlock poisoning. With each hour that passed, the burden of my heart lessened more. I wanted to sob with relief, but kept myself calm for Sparkles' sake. Later, I would be able to fall apart.

Someone poisoned my horse. No other horses had treat buckets, but only the normal feed. After investigating further, there was no doubt it had been intentional.

No note had been discovered.

No message received.

The hemlock was freshly pulled from the ground.

What did they want?

As I stirred, Jaxson's grip tightened on me. We were on a cot outside of Sparkles' since I refused to leave. Ty was staying with Pam and Levi tonight.

"How are you doing?"

"I think not receiving any type of message is driving me mad. What happened this time? I'm married. I'm happy. I want no part of Charles. It makes no sense. Unless . . ." A new thought formed. "Unless, it's Crystal fucking with my life." I turned to face Jaxson. "Do you think Crystal had anything to do with this since we're married?"

The way Jaxson's eyes tightened told me he had similar thoughts. "I've talked to my lawyer. We've had someone keeping tabs on Crystal. They lost her a day ago." I gasped and closed my eyes. He continued. "They got an ass chewing for not telling me. I increased the security. Dad is reviewing all of the cameras from the last day. Hopefully we'll have something by morning."

Crystal wasn't done with us. I hated the thought she was so close to where Ty and I came every morning. The very thought sickened me. "When were you going to tell me?"

"When I had answers. Or you asked."

Ty's mother was crazy mad. There was no reasoning with her. For some reason, the thought of Crystal scared me more than whoever was tied to Charles. It seemed all I had to do was stay away from Charles and the person left me alone.

"London, I wasn't trying to keep it from you. I want you to know that."

"I know. Tell me next time. You wouldn't want me keeping something secret about Charles."

He kissed me. "You're right. I won't."

The grunt from my horse turned my attention back to the stall. She lifted her head as a joyful sob escaped me. Scrambling off the cot, I went to her side. Jaxson stayed near us. "Hey, girl. Take it easy. You're okay."

She lifted her head again with more noise, the tube long removed. "Are you trying to get up, Sparkles?"

My spirits lifted as she tried again and made it. Jaxson and I put comforting hands along her neck as I praised her. "Good, girl. Oh, Sparkles, you're going to be okay. You're such a strong girl."

Sparkles was unsteady on her feet as she walked toward the water bucket only three steps away; Jaxson was by my side watching her. Her coat gleamed with sweat. As soon as she was strong enough, we'd wash her off.

"She's going to be okay, sweetheart."

Eagerly, I nodded and watched. Going to the corner, Sparkles laid back down in her normal resting position. Jaxson's chest pressed against my back. I took a deep breath. "She's going to be okay."

TWENTY-SEVEN

THE DAY OF THE MCCOLE Classic drew near. Every minute of the day was busy with preparation. We hadn't told Ty yet, but we'd found a Golden Retriever puppy who would be ready to leave her mom in a week.

In a book I bought him, Ty fell in love with Golden Retrievers. His cousin, Mallory, gave him the idea of putting pictures of them in every drawer of the house to remind us of what he wanted. Needless to say, it worked.

The camera feeds confirmed Crystal was on the premises. She'd used an employee's card to get access. The employee had been scared to report it being stolen.

The camera feeds outlined Crystal's movements. After entering, she paused in front of the stalls reading the horses' nametags on the front. How had she known Sparkles was mine? There was still no connection we could find. Goose bumps ran down my arms as I remembered her in a McCole baseball cap bringing the bucket to Sparkles' stall. She'd known exactly when to come and the place was almost deserted. Perfect timing.

A warrant was issued for trespassing and a few other charges to increase the sentence regarding animal cruelty.

Of course, we were unable to find her. I wanted her out of our lives and away from our son.

I pushed the thoughts aside. Eventually, Crystal would reemerge when she needed something. Drugs drove people to do crazy things.

This afternoon, Ty and I were headed into town with Levi and Pam to get haircuts. It would be a miracle to get Jaxson away from the ranch with all he had planned.

This morning we were simply hanging out as a family. A much-welcomed rest time.

The doorbell rang.

"I'll get it," I called from the kitchen as Ty and Jaxson wrestled in the living room while I baked cookies.

Dwayne stood on the front porch with a package. "Hey, Dwayne."

"Hey, London. A couple of packages arrived at the gate for Jaxson. Levi asked me to deliver them."

"Thanks." I took the two slender, square brown boxes. "Have a good day, Dwayne. Is everything okay at the clinic?"

"Yes. We'll let you know if we need anything. I'm glad he's taking the morning off."

"Me too." We said our goodbyes and I closed the door. Leaning against the doorframe, I watched as Ty worked on besting Jaxson. His muscles strained to push his dad off. Jaxson animatedly rolled to the side, praising Ty's strength. They were two peas in a pod. A wave of dizziness came over me and I perched against the couch. I took a moment before I said anything. "Dwayne said this package arrived for you at the gate."

The lights within Jaxson's green eyes danced with excitement. "Those are a surprise for you. Leave them on the couch. No peeking."

"Me? When do I get to open it?"

He teased knowing how much I loved surprises. "We'll see."

"Jaxson!"

Ty jumped on top of Jaxson pretending to be a super hero. And the play fighting started all over again. I'd have to wait until later to persuade my husband to give me more details.

My phone rang. I answered smiling. "Hey, Millie."

"My word. Sounds like you have a crazy house this morning."

I chuckled. "Jaxson and Ty are wrestling. What are you doing?"

"Packing for the McCole Classic! And I'm bringing my *90210* seasons. We're having a girls' night chick-a-dee."

I yawned. "I can't wait."

"Girl, are you tired? It's only like nine in the morning."

I made my way back to the bedroom and yawned again. "I haven't been sleeping well. I think the stress of everything is catching up."

"Are you sure you're not preggers?" Millie said it jokingly, but my heart raced at the thought.

"Yes, I've been taking my pills regularly. I started cramping this morning. I'll start by tomorrow."

"Okay. Sorry. I know the nurse comes out in me sometimes."

Quickly, I rethought over the last few weeks and looked at my birth control packet. Every pill was taken. I was on the right day. I had the flu. *The flu. Did Jaxson give me my pills on time?* I focused on this morning when I saw spotting. That was normal for me. By tomorrow, I would have my period. Internally, I sighed with relief. We had enough going on right now. I definitely wanted children, but when the time was right.

"It's okay. I need to take the cookies out. I can't wait for you guys to get here."

"Me either. Give my love to the boys."

"I will."

Leaving the bedroom, I found Ty coloring at the table. "Where's your dad?"

"In the office."

I ruffled his hair as I went to find Jaxson. As soon as Jaxson saw me, he put a bag in the drawer. "Now, that's cruel, teasing me like that."

"I can't wait to give it to you." Jaxson approached and gave me a kiss. "You look like a woman on a mission. What's on your mind?"

Chewing on my lip, I asked, "Did you give me my birth control pills while I had the flu?"

"Yeah, I did. Millie reminded me. Never missed a day."

No antibiotics were taken. Only fever reducer. Everything was fine. I let out a breath I wasn't aware I was holding. "Okay. She just mentioned the word pregnant because of how off I've been feeling and I freaked a little. I should be over the flu by now."

Excitement danced across Jaxson's face which confused me. I thought he'd be a nervous wreck talking about babies with everything else we had going on. "You think you're pregnant?"

"No. I don't. I haven't missed a pill. You don't have to worry."

Jaxson's hand went to my stomach causing it to flip-flop. "London, I would be thrilled for you to be pregnant."

"You would?" The feelings became more confusing. Per previous discussions, we were waiting for a while to adjust to married life.

He kissed me. "Yes, sweetheart. Do you want me to get a test to make sure?"

"Would you mind?"

"Not at all."

Now, I wasn't sure what I wanted the pregnancy test to say.

JAXSON AND I leaned against the counter while we waited for the test to render its verdict. I stared at the stick wondering what fate it would yield against the black granite countertops. It was like a beacon teasing me with an unrevealed answer.

Ty went to Pam's to play with Mallory. Jaxson was calm about the entire situation—truly seeming open to the idea of having a kid.

I chanced a glance at Jaxson who watched me. "What's on your mind, London?"

"It's just that the thought of being pregnant scared me to death this morning. Now as I look at the stick, I'm not sure what I think."

Sitting me on the counter, Jaxson positioned himself between my legs. His lips grazed against my jaw. "If you're pregnant, it will be one of the happiest days of my life." The words warmed me. He nibbled my earlobe. "If you're not, we'll keep practicing until we're ready." His tongue came out and tasted me. "I have you as my wife. That's all I need."

"Jaxson—" My breathy reply was interrupted by the timer going off.

The stick was in Jaxson hand as he tilted it to me.

Not Pregnant

Those damn tears wanted to be known again and I wasn't sure why. "Now, we get to practice while we're alone. I fully accept the challenge."

As Jaxson carried me to the bedroom, the sadness abated quickly. Practicing would be fun.

PAM, LEVI, TY and I all left the hairdresser.

Not knowing where Crystal was had me on edge while we were in town. It was no wonder why I had been all over the place emotionally over the last couple of weeks, with all the additional stress she brought into our lives.

Ty helped keep my thoughts occupied as we passed by a pet store with puppies in the window. He sighed as he touched the glass. "I want a puppy so bad, Mom."

I ruffled his freshly-cut hair which had him ducking out of the way. "I know, buddy. They're a big responsibility. We'll keep talking about it. Okay?"

"Okay. But, it would be funner if we just got it."

"I know."

The storefront decorations had a fall-like feel that reminded me of pumpkins and Halloween. Last night, Ty and I convinced Jaxson to dress up with us for Halloween. As what . . . we weren't sure. Ty and I were going to brainstorm this weekend.

Swinging my arm, Ty gave me a smile. "Can we sip some lemonade on the front porch today?"

"Oh, we could do some warm apple cider since it's chilly." Ty beamed at me, still thriving on motherly attention. He would never be lacking in love from me. "You know Granddad and Aunt Millie are coming tomorrow."

He jumped, nearly taking my arm with him. "I know! I want to go fishing with Grandpa and Granddad."

"I bet that can be arranged."

Stopping in front of the pharmacy, Pam said, "Hey, London. Are you okay on time if we run in here to get Levi's prescription?"

This afternoon, the caterer was coming to the house to go over the final numbers for the event. "Yes, we have plenty of time. We'll head to the car and pick you guys up."

"Sounds perfect."

Ty and I traipsed down the sidewalk until we came to the crosswalk while talking about our afternoon plans. Fall wreaths adorned the light poles in preparation for the Fall Festival in three weeks. Something we were all looking forward to attending. I was anxious to make a homemade apple pie and other things Mom and I made every fall.

Halfway across the wide crosswalk, an engine revved distancing me from the conversation Ty and I were having about a future puppy. I stopped momentarily and looked around. Ty tugged my hand. "Did you hear me, Mom?"

The engine revved again and I zeroed in on the location kitty-cornered from us. Someone with a baseball cap stared in my direction. An uneasy feeling danced along my spine. Grabbing Ty's hand, I started walking again as the old beat-up blue car shot out from the parking space.

The engine sped.

The car was heading right at us.

Ty.

I panicked.

It took a few seconds for it to register and start moving faster. We weren't going to make it to the other side in time. The only thing slowing the car's progress was the squealing tires.

Keep Ty safe. It was all I could think of as I jerked him up and ran.

My heart sped up.

I wasn't going to make it.

There wasn't time.

Save Ty.

The car was close. Too close. In a moment of panic, I tossed Ty as far away as possible.

Screams filled the air.

He was scared. I was scared. I took off down the street away from my son. The car was closing in. I hurled myself across the next car hoping there was enough distance from Ty. Something struck my side and as I tumbled back to the ground.

Burnt rubber filled my nose before everything faded to . . . black.

TWENTY-EIGHT

B EEP.
    Whoosh.
    Beep.
Whoosh.

Beep.

Whoosh.

My body ached as the outside world permeated my distant thoughts. I felt like I was stuck in the abyss not knowing which way was up or down. A voice. A voice I loved spoke in the background.

Jaxson.

He was worried. Upset. I wasn't sure. I kept moving through the thick sludge trying to find the source of the voice. There was no sense of time.

A slight pressure on my hand helped further bring me to the surface. I was so close. Maybe if I squeezed back, he would know I was here.

"London! Ken, she squeezed my hand! London! London, sweet-heart! Call the nurse! She squeezed my hand!"

The clearly worried voice rushed me to the surface as my eyes fluttered open. "Jax—" My voice silenced not wanting to work.

Forms took shape as Jaxson leaned over me, his five o'clock shadow prominent. How long was I out? "Thank God, you're awake." His hands gently stroked my face. "Sweetheart, don't move. The doctors are on their way."

I cleared my throat, attempting to speak again. "What happened?"

"Crystal ran you over."

Choppy images of the hairdresser, then the sidewalk, then running with Ty. Tossing him. I tried to sit up. "Ty?"

Jaxson gently pressed me down against the white cotton sheets. His was wearing his red, faded, wrinkly T-shirt. How long had I been here? "Ty is okay. You saved him. He's in the cafeteria getting dinner with my parents."

I relaxed minutely. "Crystal?"

"Is in police custody. She's been arrested for attempted murder on two counts." Jaxson sat in the chair and rubbed soothing circles on my hand.

The doctor came in. The white of his coat was bright, matched with a gleaming telescope. "Good morning, London. How are you feeling?"

"Confused. Groggy. How long have I been out?"

"A little over a day." He checked a few things on the clipboard he carried. "From the impact, you had a concussion and some minor swelling. Your ribs are bruised, but the baby is fine."

"Ty. Yes, Ty is fine."

The doctor paused and looked at Jaxson. A silent message passed between them. Everything still swirled about some and was hard to process and focus fully. The doctor focused on me as he put the stethoscope up to his ears. "Let's get you checked up."

After looking me over, the doctor was pleased with what he saw. I'd be released in two days if all went well. There was a lot of stuff said that got lost in all the fuzziness.

Dad kissed my forehead. "I'm going to give you and Jaxson a few minutes while I get Ty, punkin'. He's been anxious for you to wake up."

"Okay, Daddy. I can only imagine."

Jaxson held my hand between both of his. He swallowed hard, then looked at me with happiness. "London, the baby the doctor talked about earlier wasn't Ty."

"What?"

With his hand on my stomach, Jaxson continued. "The pregnancy test was wrong. We're pregnant."

"What?"

Moving to sit on the edge of the mattress, Jaxson brought my hand to his lips. "Sweetheart, we're pregnant. It's early on and the test wasn't able to detect it. It came back in the blood work."

"A baby? We're pregnant?" My hand squeezed his as he searched my eyes. Was it true? Was the test wrong?

He knelt beside me while placing a feather kiss on the spot our child grew. "We're pregnant. Our baby is growing right here." I was speechless as I watched Jaxson place a few more kisses on my stomach before looking up. "Are you upset?"

"No. I could never be upset about having our child inside me. I'm still so tired. But, I love you, Ty, and this baby."

"Sleep, London. I won't leave you."

The darkness claimed me.

I FELT A poke on my nose. "Ty, if you touch your Mom one more time, we're going to have a timeout."

"Yes, Dad." The defeated voice had me lightly chuckling, reminding me of the bruising on my ribs. "Mom! Mom! Mom!"

My eyes opened to find Ty standing on a chair only inches from my face. "Hey, sweet boy."

"I'm going to be a big brother. You and Dad said I'd have to wait, but you were wrong." Ty puffed his chest out as he stood straight in the chair. "I'm going to show the baby how to do all sorts of cool stuff."

The hand went to my stomach as I remembered the news. "You are going to be a big brother. I'm going to need your help."

A hand came on top of mine. Jaxson's. Ty beamed. Pam and Levi sat in the corner while my dad stood at the door.

Pam gave Levi a hug and looked at me. "I cannot wait to have another grandbaby to spoil."

"If it's a boy, can we name him Bumblebee like the Transformers guy? I like that name." Nodding to himself, Ty clearly approved of the choice. I noticed he had on his Transformer T-Shirt which probably sparked the decision. Tomorrow it might be Donatello if we were playing with Ninja Turtles.

Jaxson shook his head amused. "We'll see, son."

Ty turned serious as he sat in the chair. "Grama says we won't know what the baby is for a while. But if it's a girl, will she be able to still play cars with me?"

"Of course."

As we talked, my hand stayed on my stomach as I thought about the child growing within me. Jaxson caught me several times and was unable to hide the broad answering grin.

As visiting hours came to a close, I received kisses and hugs from everyone as they left. All of the love filled me. The nurse looked expectantly at Jaxson. Sternly he spoke. "I nearly lost my pregnant wife. I'm not leaving her."

There was a standoff before the nurse rolled her eyes and walked off. I commented, "I think you may have made an enemy of the nurse."

Jaxson was back at my side rubbing my stomach. "I don't care.

I'm not leaving you or our little one. London, that bitch nearly cost me you, Ty, and an unborn child. Mom and Dad said if you hadn't tossed him . . ."

He took a deep breath and I stroked his face. "We're fine. All three of us are fine. Crystal is in police custody."

"I have my lawyers working on it so she never sees the fucking light again. She's claiming the voices told her. Bitch."

"Climb up in bed and sleep with me. It'll help."

"London, I don't think that's a good idea."

I further tempted him as I played dirty, but knew it would get me near him. "You can be near me and the baby all night."

Jaxson toed off his shoes and slid beside me careful not to touch my sore ribs. "Did I hurt Ty when I threw him? He seemed okay."

As the strong arms of my husband wrapped around me, the nightmares were chased away.

"Only a couple of scrapes. He was pretty shaken up. There was blood from your head injury. A lot of it. He's been up here with me most of the time watching you."

"I love him like my own."

"I know you do."

His hand splayed across my stomach. "I can't wait to meet this one."

"Me either."

Jaxson kissed my neck and I sunk back into him. "Rest, sweetheart."

My eyes closed and I fell into a deep comforting sleep.

TWENTY-NINE

THE CLOSING OF A DOOR awakened me. The bed was empty.

"Jaxson?" Only silence and the sterile hospital smell greeted me. "Jaxson?"

A shadow moved and I nearly screamed until the familiar voice spoke. "Hello, London."

"Caroline?"

There was a sneer to her voice which told me something was all wrong. I pushed the nurse's button to be safe. Why was she here in the middle of the night? Why was she in Colorado?

The room was mostly bathed in darkness. "Yes, it's me. Thought I would pay you a visit."

The sarcasm in her voice was off. Not like the normal Caroline I was used to and came to love. Something was wrong. "Where's Jaxson?"

"Detained. Don't worry. We won't be interrupted. If you scream, know I'll have the boy killed."

Ice chilled my veins as the answer presented itself. I felt the thump, thump, thump of my pulse. I moistened my lips. This was bad. Very very bad. "Why are you here?" My voice came out weaker than I intended.

I cleared my throat and tried again. "Why are you here?"

Caroline shook her head with an evil glint in her eye I'd never seen before. She was dressed in a nurse's outfit which would allow her to slip through the corridors unnoticed. "I'm sure you've pieced it together, London. I'm surprised you didn't before this."

Bile rose in my throat. "You were the one responsible for my drugging. You were behind it all."

"Yes, among many other things." The nurses hadn't responded. I pressed the button again. "Don't worry with the nurses' button. It's been unplugged. Plus, they're all indisposed with an emergency I arranged." A few steps toward me, then Caroline stopped. "You see, being a senator's wife requires me to get my hands . . . dirty at times, when it becomes a means to an end. My husband and I prefer for it to be handled within the family. Loose ends are dangerous."

I was a means to an end?

She held up a syringe and I shuttered. Caroline was here to hurt me. Otherwise, she wouldn't have revealed it was her behind it all. I had to think fast, thankful most of the fog from the accident had lifted with more sleep. Things were still fuzzy. I scanned the room.

My IV.

Unless she injected me directly, that would be the easiest place for her to administer whatever fatal concoction she had in that syringe. I wasn't able to chance running at this point. If she escaped, I had no doubt Ty's life would be in danger.

Naturally as possible, I folded my arms so I was able to imperceptibly remove the tape on my forearm. It was tough and stuck well. My movements had to be measured. Only tiny bits of progress were made as I stopped intermittently.

"Why did you drug me all those years ago?"

I told myself to keep her talking. Distracted.

Caroline moved closer to me and the IV pole. I pulled more tape off my skin. "I heard your conversation with Millie in the park when you were home on summer break. I happened to be walking by when I heard Charles' name and hid around the corner. I heard about your misguided thoughts with how Charles wanted to be a lawyer and not in politics. Foolish girl. Charles is destined for politics. I learned of your plans to take the job on Broadway." Disgustingly she scoffed. "His dick would have followed you. Through the years I tried many times to break you guys up. Nothing worked. I had to get you out of the picture. It was easy getting into your house and slipping you the drugs. You welcomed me as we toasted over water."

Dramatically, she sighed. "The problem was I gave you too much. I had to drive you into town and position you in the seat. Your foot fell off the gas."

"But what about Alec?"

Waving her hand as if no consequence. "Means to an end. It happens."

A woman I thought I knew was a stranger to me. The evil thoughts and plans that lurked behind in the shadows were unbelievable. Alec was no means to an end. He was a person who deserved a chance at life.

Keep her talking, London.

"Who are you? You are not the Caroline I thought of like a mom."

She leaned forward. "I'm a wolf in sheep's clothing, sweetheart. Your worst nightmare. Someone who won't be deterred because her son can't stop fucking the thing that will mess up his life. Thank goodness you never got yourself pregnant like you did with the poor unsuspecting bastard you married."

I winced. She knew I was pregnant.

"Rachel?"

A hand dismissively went through the air as she arrogantly

gloated. "All planned. She drugged Charles. Pretended she was pregnant. He fell for it. After a few months she staged a miscarriage. You nearly fucked it all up. Everything was going to plan until you got out. Something was supposed to happen in prison that never did."

"What?" I made further progress with the tape and tried not to wince as it refused to let go of my skin.

She tsked. "Let's just say you would not have been present to be having this conversation. They released you early and I wasn't notified. With you out of the picture, Charles would have been married to a family who would have ensured his way to the presidency. Do you know he's trying to back out of the engagement even though you're married?"

The tape freed and gently I pulled out the needle barely able to hide the burn. Caroline was on a roll as she walked to the end of the bed. "Even your mother got too close. Dr. Michaels, rest his soul for growing a conscience, had to force Dementia on your mother with a cocktail. I started the symptoms by poisoning her tea. She visited him and he upped the dose in a syringe with what was supposed to be allergy shots. It actually had Ativan, Xanax, Restoril, and Serax in a high dose."

I froze. "Mom doesn't have Dementia?"

What else had this woman done in my life?

Humorously, she laughed to a joke only Caroline thought funny. "She didn't. But there's no telling what those drugs have done to her system. After we dealt with Dr. Michaels, Rachel was able to get her uncle at the pharmacy to change the prescriptions. Too many deaths would have brought out suspicion."

My head swam with all the new information. The blood drained from my face. "I don't want Charles. I'm married to Jaxson. Pregnant with his child."

Caroline tilted her face. "It doesn't matter. Only your death will get him focused on the path he needs and not some misguided attempt that he still has a shot with you."

Walking back to the IV port, I knew time was up. The needle neared the line and her hand was calm and steady. I scooted the needle away in case whatever she was injecting me with could be absorbed through the skin. I shifted on the bed, moving the line to where the tip hung off.

"I'm sorry it's come to this, London. I hoped we could all live separately. Your husband's ex is a real piece of work by the way. Crystal, the little bastard's mother, helped keep the attention off of Charles. But, don't worry, your husband will pay too for that threat at the charity."

Caroline leaned in closer only inches away. "No one fucks with my son, you whore. He couldn't let you go. You were going to lead him astray from the life he was destined to have."

Standing, Caroline pushed the needle and plummeted the plunger. "It won't be long now. You'll look like you went into cardiac arrest."

Drip.

Drip.

Drip.

Water from the needle dripped on the floor. Caroline's head jerked down and she realized what happened. "You bitch. You took out your needle." Another syringe was produced. "Good thing I came prepared."

I hurled myself off the other side of the bed, letting out a scream as my ribs and head protested the sudden movement. On shaky legs, I stood. Caroline was right there with the syringe. With all my might, I held it away. The needle edged slowly to my throat.

I would not die.

My child would live.

Jaxson would not lose a wife.

I would be Ty's mother.

With a surge of adrenaline, I pushed her with all my might. Pure terror shot through me as I scrambled toward the door, stumbling and falling to my knees my head still woozy from being hit by the car.

A few feet away, the door burst open to the room. Another dark figure appeared and my eyes focused in.

Jaxson.

He had come.

Come for me.

For the baby.

We were safe.

My tired body collapsed and Jaxson was by my side in a second hoisting me up.

Caroline watched with shock on her face. Her mouth twisted in a grimace as she removed the syringe from her chest and it bounced off the floor.

Jaxson yelled while backing out of the room. Caroline took a haphazard step toward us. I clung tighter to Jaxson as he yelled. "Doctor! We need a doctor!" Jaxson yelled.

Caroline gasped for air with her arms outstretched as she kept following us into the hallway. I screamed as commotion sounded from all around us. Alarms went off.

On her last breath she said, "It was all for my son. Tell him I love him."

Her body collapsed and the truth of the situation set in.

"WE NEED A DOCTOR!" The roar of Jaxson's voice jolted me as he rushed down the hall to meet the nurse on her way. "My wife is pregnant. A woman tried to attack her. I need to know her and the baby are okay."

Quickly we followed one nurse into another room.

All the missing facts fell into place as uncontrollable tears racked my body.

It was Caroline.

Someone I thought of as a mother. I loved her.

She was responsible for Alec.

For my mother.

For me.

The stress from the day had the darkness ebbing in. I wanted to escape for just a little while. As I slipped away, I whispered. "My mom. Check my mom for drugs."

THIRTY

I AWOKE ON A JOLT remembering Caroline's face from the nightmare. It was the middle of the night. The bathroom fixture cast enough light to make out the people in my room. Jaxson sat in one chair with my dad at the end. Charles was near the door.

"Water?" My voice came out low and hoarse.

Jaxson was attuned to me, hearing even the faintest noise as he awoke. He pressed a button. "The doctor is on the way."

"The baby? Ty?"

Oh, please let the baby and Ty be okay. Please. Please. Please. Please let the baby and Ty be okay. Don't let Caroline rob me of something else.

Jaxson kissed my forehead as I prepared myself for the worst. "The baby is fine. Ty is fine. He's with my parents. Everyone is okay."

"Was it real? Was Caroline in my room?"

Solemnly, Jaxson nodded as the other two men stirred awake. I looked to Dad when all that had been revealed about Mom came to me.

"What about Mom?" Panic set in as the heart monitor raced.

Caressing my face, Jaxson tried to soothe me. "Sweetheart, you're fine. Calm down for the baby. Your mom is safe."

I took a deep breath. "I meant, did you test her for the drugs? Caroline said the dementia was induced. She's on high doses of Xanax and Serax. I can't remember the others. Mom was close to the truth. They poisoned her."

A flutter of movement happened as Dad got on the phone with Millie and the police showed up, who apparently were camped out in the waiting room. After the doctors cleared me, I retold the events of what happened.

I felt dirty after reliving it.

Betrayed. Shocked. Heartbroken.

When it all ended, I was exhausted. Charles was questioned in another room. He'd flown in with his father, who was currently being detained. Jaxson refused to leave me as he retold the events. Apparently Caroline had created a fake emergency at the clinic. She'd underestimated the new security measure that had just gone into effect. Jaxson turned around and came back to me.

Dad spent most of the morning on the phone. I was anxious to see what was happening with Mom.

The doctor checked my vitals. "Everything looks good. But you and the baby need some rest. You've been through a lot, Mrs. McCole."

I was tired, but there was only one update I needed. "Can I ask about my mom first?"

"Yes, then I'm ordering everyone to leave." The doctor stood while signing some paperwork.

"Except me. Doctor, I'm not leaving my wife." Jaxson folded his arms across his chest daring the doctor to defy his request. My husband was anxious, tired and through with being told to leave.

The doctor saw Jaxson's determined pose and nodded. "All right then."

Jaxson went into the hallway to talk to the doctor. Dad came in a moment later tired looking. "How are you feeling? How's my grandbaby?"

"We're good, Dad. What's happening with Mom?"

He sat beside me. "They've admitted her to Millie's hospital where they are going to run tests and see if it's true. I don't want our hopes to get up, London."

But, there was unspoken hope in Dad's eyes that mirrored my own. "Go to her, Dad."

"London—"

I held up my hand as Jaxson came back in the room. "Dad, please go make sure Mom is okay. Jaxson isn't leaving my side. He'll update you if anything changes."

Looking torn, Dad watched me.

"Ken, I promise I'll keep you updated." Jaxson's words were a vow.

I pleaded again. "Dad, please. It'll help ease my stress knowing you're there with her in case she's scared. Or someone else is out there."

"Okay, punkin'. I'll head that way now."

"Tell her I love her."

"I will."

Dad left and my eyes grew heavy. Jaxson whispered, "Sleep, sweetheart. I'll be here when you wake up."

STRETCHING, I AWAKENED. Jaxson greeted me. "Morning, sweetheart. How'd you sleep?"

"Good. I feel like all I've done is sleep."

He chuckled and caressed my stomach. "You're creating a life." Pausing, his face held wonder. "I've never experienced a pregnancy before."

My heart broke knowing how Ty was treated at first—a hidden pregnancy. "You'll be part of everything on this one."

A knock from the door brought our attention. Charles appeared.

"May I come in and talk for a moment?"

I nodded. Jaxson sat in the chair relaxed. I would imagine Jaxson already knew what Charles had to say. Seeing the devastation on his face caused a pain within me. So much had been robbed from him. From me. From Alec. From my mother. From so many others. I wasn't able to imagine the amount of hurt I would feel if my mother used me as a pawn—a means to an end.

Nervously running his fingers through is hair, Charles looked at me. "I know this doesn't matter. Our paths have been set and they aren't together." Jaxson cocked his head in warning. "When you went to prison, I had every intention of waiting for you. One night at a party, I woke up with Rachel in my arms. I don't remember it."

Charles took a deep breath. My stomach turned as I remembered Caroline's words of Rachel drugging him. The police informed me, with my permission, they let Charles know what his mother told me. He sighed. "After that, she said she was pregnant. Showed me a test which proved it. I had no choice but to leave you. I was too ashamed, too young to know how to tell you. So, I ended it. I thought I could be happy until I saw you at the house. Then things spun out of control. I tried to end it. Mother pretended to be ambivalent and attempted to use Rachel to bring me to heel with blackmail of taking her abortion public, which I had no clue of. I couldn't bring you into anything else and hurt you. I had no idea you were drugged. I should have been stronger."

Picking at imaginary lent, only pain emanated from Charles. "I'm so sorry, Charles. What they did to us was wrong." He nodded. "What's happening to Rachel?"

He shrugged. "Not enough. She's been detained. Questioned. I will do whatever I can to testify against her. Find whatever I can. Put her and anyone involved away."

"Thank you, Charles."

He stood with a sad look piercing his eyes. "I'm sorry, London."

He looked at Jaxson. "Take care of her. London is like no other."

"I intend to."

Charles nodded. "Let me know if you need anything."

"We will. Same to you."

He stood with his hand on the doorframe and looked back. "Know that I never stopped loving you, London."

Without a response he left as a tear fell down my face. I took a few seconds and glanced toward Jaxson, teary eyed. "I don't love him anymore. He'll always have a special place in my heart with what we shared, but it wasn't meant to be. I don't regret him leaving me, because it led me to your arms. I only hate all the harm done to everyone."

Knowing the truth soothed the wounds of the past despite all the pain it caused everyone.

Standing, Jaxson leaned over me and put his lips on mine. "London, I know you love me. You would never have married me if there was doubt."

I smiled against his lips. "I'm glad you wised up since the last time we talked about this."

He chuckled. "Me too."

Ready for my bed, I asked, "When do I get to go home? Please tell me soon."

"They said tomorrow, as long as everything looks good with the baby."

The baby.

I was going to have another child.

THIRTY-ONE

"ARE WE CLOSE?" I WAS nearly about to come out of my seat with excitement.

"Almost. Then we'll head back to my parents to give Ty his gift."

We were in Jaxson's truck heading to a surprise of some sort for me. I think it had to do with the packages he received the day of the accident. The anticipation of not knowing was thrilling. The road became bumpy and I assumed we were in a field of some sort. Jaxson's hand was laced with mine over our baby.

A baby.

I was beyond ecstatic. Pam and Mallory were already ogling over all sorts of baby items and showing me ideas for the nursery. Ty suggested Dr. Seuss after his favorite book. Jaxson and I agreed it would be the perfect theme for a girl or a boy. I wanted him involved as much as possible.

It had been a week since being released from the hospital. My ribs were still bruised, so I had to take it easy, but I felt great. Tired but great, which was normal for the first trimester of the pregnancy.

I'd only been able to see one or two events of the McCole Classic, which was disappointing. However, Jaxson insisted on as much rest as possible.

Jaxson squeezed my hand, his voice full of awe. "I can't wait to feel the baby kick."

"Me either. I'll feel better being able to feel the baby move."

Since my body had gone through so much in the last week, I was worried something was going to happen. "Sweetheart, please don't stress. We go to the doctor again tomorrow. The doctor said our baby was healthy."

I looked down at my still flat stomach. "I know. I'm trying not to stress."

Part of me was still reeling from all that had been revealed. The crazy lengths in which Caroline had gone to keep me from Charles. It was over the top. Crazy. News reports surfaced saying Caroline had been on psychiatric medicine that had a side effect of paranoia. She'd been on it for years and no one realized how far out of control she'd gotten. Charles was in a media shit storm. Charles Senior was being investigated. The engagement to Rachel had been called off, causing accusations to fly from her family. Rachel's family was now being investigated.

At least Crystal was in prison with no chance of parole. That thought brought peace that she wasn't lurking around a corner waiting to bring more chaos.

I mentally sighed. My heart hurt for Charles and all he was going through. Alone. I'd called a couple of times to check up on him. So had Millie and Dad. Jaxson was supportive and Charles never once stepped over the line with any comments. I think he was grateful for the friendship.

We needed to support each other with all that transpired. Only those affected truly knew how deep the scars ran. An innocence was robbed from all of us.

It was a double-edged sword with knowing Alec lost his life

and I had found the love of mine. It was hard to wrap my head around it all.

Jaxson was my happily ever after.

"Penny for your thoughts?" Jaxson asked while watching me with concern.

"Thinking about everything that's happened. How blessed I am." Jaxson gave me a beautiful smile I loved. I wanted a subject change. "Ty's going to be so excited for his surprise."

He chuckled. "Yes, he is."

I snapped my fingers remembering what I'd wanted to tell him when he'd first arrived from rounds at the barn. "Dad called this afternoon. Mom's making great progress. She remembered a date her and dad had at the beginning of their relationship. Doctors are pleased with her progress. They're hoping I get to see her soon."

Jaxson's warm voice filled the car. "That's excellent. I know you're anxious to see her."

"I am."

The tests came back five days ago. It was confirmed she was being poisoned with those drugs which imitate the symptoms of Dementia. For the hope of the best improvement, Mom was moved to a facility that was slowly taking her off of the medicine. Counseling was also going to be needed considering four years of her life were robbed. It was devastating to know the lengths Caroline had gone to. It was a sick and twisted game we had all been caught up in.

Per the doctors, it would be lethal to cut her off cold turkey. In a sense she was addicted and needed the drugs. The goal was to make the transition as easy as possible.

I wondered what part of Mom would still be left and what the drugs permanently took away. I prayed for the best. We wouldn't know for a while. Only Dad was allowed to visit right now. They weren't sure how long it would be until I was able to, but Mom needed as little stress as possible. I agreed, but longed for the day for

Mom to look at me and know it was me, London. Not a stranger she told about her daughter.

The truck shifted into park.

"Are we there yet?"

Lips touched my cheek. "Yes, we are."

The door opened and closed. A few seconds later, Jaxson helped me from his truck only to help me on the tailgate. A horse whinnied nearby. Jaxson hopped in the truck bed and brought me against him. One hand untied the blindfold. The dark starry night sky greeted us. "This was where we came the first night to watch the stars together."

"I remember."

Jaxson pulled out a bag. "We missed our one-month anniversary with you in the hospital. I wanted you to open your gift in the place we had our first date."

"Oh, Jaxson."

I giggled as I opened the bag revealing a certificate. This was probably what Dwayne delivered to the house. Reading the certificate there was a star named after me. Warm breath tickled my neck. "I know you no longer wish upon shooting stars, but I wanted you to have one that burns bright and reminds you I'll always be there, never fading. My wish came true that night, London. I got you and a beautiful family. I found love and happiness."

Turning in his lap, I kissed him. Hard. "I don't know what I did to deserve you. I love it. You are my bright shining star."

"There's more."

Grabbing the bag, I dug through it. Two tickets to the ballet were in it for a show in . . . I had to read it twice to verify it said London.

"We're going to London." For as many years as I could remember, I'd wanted to visit the ballet there. It was a dream of mine I once wished upon a shooting star.

"For a honeymoon. One you didn't get because you were sick. It's for next month. The doctor said it was fine for you to fly."

I clutched Jaxson to me. "Thank you! I love it. I've always wanted to see the London Ballet."

"I know. I will do everything in my power to give you all that I have. I love you more than life itself."

"I love you too with all that I am."

We held each other under the night sky as we talked about dreams of our future. Our family. Our hopes.

Jaxson's phone vibrated. "Dad says the puppy has arrived. Are we ready to give Ty his present?"

"Yes! He's going to be so excited."

We drove back to Pam and Levi's. As we pulled up, Ty ran out of our house, the front yard illuminated by the front porch lights. "Do I have a brother or sister yet?"

I rubbed my stomach. "Not yet. It's going to be after the Easter Bunny. And I'm going to get a huge stomach first."

Ty blew out a breath. "I'm going to be five hundred years old by then."

"Not quite, buddy. But, your mom and I have a surprise for you to help the wait go by faster."

"A surprise? A real surprise for me?"

We nodded as Ty bounced. Levi walked from around the house with a squirmy puppy in his hands. Ty noticed, his voice growing louder. "Is that my puppy? A puppy for me? The one that I wanted?"

Before we could answer, Ty took off and Levi sat the golden retriever puppy on the grass. In wonderment, Ty looked to us. "Is this my puppy?"

Jaxson put his arm around my waist. "She's all yours, son."

Ty hugged the puppy to himself. The puppy chewed on some grass. "Dad, she likes to eat the clovers. Can I name her Clover?"

"Of course."

We knelt down beside Ty as we all played with the puppy.

This was my life. And it was perfect.

EPILOGUE

A year later

I SAT IN THE ROCKING chair as the sun rose above the mountains, rocking Chloe while burping her after her feeding. Jaxson and Ty were sound asleep. Chloe's sweet head rested on my shoulder as I patted her back.

Finally she burped.

"That was a good one, little angel."

She nestled into my neck ready for another snooze. Chloe was almost three months old. Ty loved her unconditionally though sometimes he didn't realize she wasn't able to play catch and zoom racecars around. There'd been a few bumps and bruises along the way.

Being a mother to my two kids was unbelievable. The best experience of my life, along with finding Jaxson. A creak down the hallway brought a smile to my lips. Sometimes in the morning, Ty snuck in here and laid on the floor in front of the crib. Chloe was going through what I assumed was a growth spurt this last week and had picked up an extra feeding.

The door cracked open and Ty's head peered in and lit up. "You're up again, Mom."

"Chloe was hungry."

He made a nasty face and I giggled. One time while I was gone to visit Mom on my own, I'd pumped a bottle for Jaxson to give Chloe. The ever-curious Ty thought my milk was better than the milk he drank. He was afraid of missing out on something good. Needless to say he was cured of trying Chloe's bottles.

Walking into the room, Ty climbed up on my lap. Clover followed and laid at my feet. They were inseparable. Ty loved it. "My sister should get chocolate milk. It's much better."

"She will when she's older."

We kept rocking as I held both kids. Ty touched Chloe's purple-clad leg. *This was peace.* A month ago, the adoption for Ty officially went through for me to be his mother on paper. Crystal had been admitted to a psychiatric ward after attempting suicide in prison.

"Mom?"

"Yes, buddy."

"Do you think for Christmas this year I could get another brother or sister? I want a lot. Chloe took forever to come. I just want Santa to bring another one. You don't have to grow the baby. And then your back won't hurt."

I stroked Ty's hair as he looked at me, pleading with those puppy dog green eyes. Through the pregnancy with Chloe, my back killed me. Jaxson always rubbed it. "Ty, that's not how it works."

"Then how does it?"

It was too early in the morning to have this conversation and I scrambled how to respond. At the door Jaxson appeared smiling, his dimples prominent with his sleep-ridden hair. "What did I walk in on?"

Little legs dashed across the room. "Dad! Did you hear? I want another baby brother or sister for Christmas from Santa."

Chloe stirred but resettled as Jaxson whispered something to Ty. Then, Ty scampered out of the room wearing his Superman pajamas. With a sexy gait, Jaxson walked over to me and gave us a kiss. "Morning, sweetheart. Morning, sunshine."

Sunshine was Jaxson's term of endearment for Chloe. I kissed his lips while murmuring, "Morning."

"By the way, I'm all for making another baby with you."

I raised an eyebrow. "Jaxson McCole, I'll cut you off if you start talking about babies this soon."

Deep chuckles filled the room. "Only practicing, I promise."

"Okay to practicing."

His nose skimmed mine and the desire that always loomed below the surface came to the forefront. "Do you want to go back to bed? I know you've been up early feeding Chloe every day this week. I can take the kids for a bit. We're not heading to see your parents until midmorning."

A couple of times a month, on Saturday, we went to Mom and Dad's for brunch. They bought a house about ten miles down the road. As soon as Mom was ready, she wanted to sell the other farm and be closer to my family and me. I was shocked. But too much time had been lost. Ty loved having another grandmother.

"I may take a nap later, but I want to hold her right now. She's growing so fast."

Jaxson's big hand touched her back. "Thank you for giving me this."

A lump filled my throat at the awe in his voice. "We gave each other love and a family."

"We did. I love you, London."

"I love you, Jaxson."

He left the room and I counted all my blessings.

TWO HOURS LATER we pulled into the driveway of my parents' one-story home. Mom had been released from rehab nearly six months ago. The road had been long and hard but she was here . . . in the present. There was some nervous system damage done and she could get overwhelmed if too much happened. I hated the drugs had a lingering effect, but we were fortunate for what little remained. As the days went by it seemed to lessen, but Caroline had caused serious damage.

Millie was an immense amount of help as she worked with her doctors and the rehab facility to help Mom. Surprisingly, Millie and the cop were still dating. I think things were more serious than she let on. Currently, she was in denial. Only time would tell.

Dad stepped out on the front porch with Mom behind him. My heart warmed every time I saw her. She was healthier looking, not the frail being who had sang, "London Bridge is Falling Down" on repeat in the nursing home.

Ty raced out of the car. Jaxson called after him. "Ty, slow down."

Dad, wearing a flannel shirt, patted Ty on the head while Jaxson removed the baby carrier. "Your Grammy made fresh cookies. They're on the counter."

"You're the bestest, Grammy." He hugged my mom's leg and then raced into the house as she chuckled.

Ty never seemed to overwhelm Mom. She thrived in his presence as if her spirit was lifted. We walked up the driveway leisurely.

In her jeans and pale-pink sweater, Mom looked precious. She walked up to me and gave me a hug. "How about we sit on the front porch and drink some hot chocolate. Let the men take care of the kids for a bit?"

"I'd love that, Mom."

Jaxson gave me a kiss on the cheek while Dad helped him get all of Chloe's stuff inside. There were already two steaming cups of chocolate on the table.

Mom's movements were getting better as she leaned her cane

against the pale-yellow siding.

"I used to dream about sitting on the swing with you again someday," I commented as I took a sip of warm goodness.

"Miracles do happen. I know I'm not one hundred percent, but I treasure I got a second chance at life."

"Me too, Mom. I love you."

"I love you, too. Once we finish our chocolate, I need to give my two grandbabies some love before we eat."

The first time Mom held Chloe, Mom cried. The rehab facility allowed Dad to check her out and bring her up to the hospital. It was one of the most special moments of my life. Mom was determined to get as well as possible and see her grandkids grow up.

As the swing creaked, I nestled into my mom's side and cherished the moment. These were moments I dreamed of having again and by some miracle was fortunate enough to have back in my life. I closed my eyes and thanked my lucky stars for the second chance.

Later that evening, after the kids were in bed, I leaned against the rail of the deck looking into the night sky. The door opened and Jaxson walked out carrying the baby monitor. Chloe was fast asleep with one hand under her cheek.

Warm arms came around my waist and his chin nestled in the crook of my neck. "Are you ready for bed?"

"Mmm . . . I'm ready for you to make love to me."

"There's no place I'd rather be than with you."

As Jaxson led me into the house, I caught a shooting star above the house. We stopped and stared into the sky. "I wish everyone could know the happiness I've found."

My husband's warm eyes gazed upon me. This was the first time I had wished upon a shooting star since the accident. "I love you, London. I'll endeavor to make you happy for the rest of my life."

I leaned up on my tiptoes. "I love you, too. You're the only one for me, Jaxson."

Pressing his lips to mine, l savored him. Though my path was winding and full of ups and downs—it led me here . . . to my happily ever after.

THANK YOU

TO EVERYONE WHO was part of the process, thank you for all you did to make this possible. Mad love for each and every one of you guys.

To my editor, Nichole, thank you for putting up with all my many questions and making the story shine. I can't wait to work with you on our next project.

To my formatter, Christine, thank you for the beautiful formatting job. You always blow me away with your concepts.

To my amazing photographer April Park, it is truly an incredible experience to watch you with a camera.

To Abby, Calvin, Sylvia, and Clover, thank you for being part of the cover process. That was an amazing experience to be a part of. I'm still swooning.

To my Betas—Brandy, Kelly, Nikola, and Anna, thank you for all your honest feedback. It means the world to me.

3K's and a J—Karen, Kelly, and Jenney, you guys mean the world to me. Thank you for always being there.

To the Korner, thank you for always putting a smile on my face.

You guys are amazing and I'm lucky to have you guys in my life.

#TeamJeff, thanks for answering all my questions I had.

www.ingramcontent.com/pod-product-compliance
Lightning Source LLC
Chambersburg PA
CBHW071500170626
46811CB00007B/2645